Right Next Door

Stone Family Series
Book 3

Sophie Andrews

Right Next Door

He's a grumpy silver fox tattoo artist, and I'm the bookworm next door.

After being married for almost fifteen years, I never expected my husband to ask for an open marriage so we can "explore" and "find happiness."

I also never expected my hot older neighbor to be the one who dries my tears. He is every good girl's bad boy fantasy come to life. Well over six feet and covered in ink, he's got a gruff voice and attitude to match, but while he's been known to be a bear to other people, he's only ever a cub with me.

A summer fling with Ian Stone leads me down a path of self-discovery and kink exploration that destroys everything I thought I knew about myself, and what I want in a relationship. The deeper we tumble, the more I want him. But Ian has only ever promised me his hands and his mouth.

Not his heart.

That's not what this is, and I need to remember that before I lose myself in another unrealistic fantasy.

Content Note

As you've come to expect from a Sophie Andrews' novel, Right Next Door is a feel-good fluffy open-door romance, but it also includes emotional on-the-page discussions about grief, parental abandonment, addiction, divorce, and revenge porn. Please note, it's also a bit kinky.

Silver fox Ian Stone takes part in the BDSM lifestyle and introduces Nicole to it through a Dom/sub relationship. The following pages are by no means a how-to guide, but he—like all who enjoy it—lives by the rules of safe, sane, and consensual.

Enjoy!

To all those who need to be reminded that "No" is a complete sentence, this one's for you.

Chapter 1
Nicole

I push open the glass door of Sweet Cheeks Bakery, the happy and bright pink decor making me want to puke. The scent of freshly baked cinnamon buns, still hot from the oven, wafts through the air as I cross to the counter, intent on drowning my sorrows in a mountain of carbs and sugar, and I paste on a brittle smile for Eloise. Her eyes flicker with concern.

The bakery's owner and I have known each other for years, both of us working on the same block of Aster Street in downtown West Chester, Pennsylvania. But this morning, she doesn't offer me her typical rambling morning monologue.

I hope I don't look as bad as I feel. Though her gentle smile and tone of voice convince me otherwise. "The usual?"

I nod, throat too clogged to speak.

The usual. As if my life hasn't been turned upside down. As if my husband of over ten years didn't blindside me with a request for an open relationship.

After Eloise passes me a gigantic cinnamon roll on a plate, I sink onto a chair at a nearby table, the echo of Bryce's words in my head.

We haven't been happy for a while. You have to see that, right? Maybe we need to try something else so we can be happy together again.

I dig into the pastry, the icing thick and creamy, but the knot in my throat makes it hard to swallow, and when I try to clear it one too many times, Eloise brings a cup of water to my table as well.

"Thanks," I croak, far too close to breaking down for my liking. I dab at the corner of my eyes with a napkin, a sodden mess. Doesn't help that it's eighty degrees outside and I took a couple laps around the block to try to exercise the sadness away.

Spoiler alert: didn't work.

Eloise squeezes my shoulder before heading back behind the counter. As I gulp down the water, I hear her greet another patron, and even without her addressing him by name, I know who it is.

There are some people who have *presence*, and Ian Stone is one of those people. From his heavy and sure footsteps to the treble of his voice, he's impossible to ignore.

"How's it going today?" Eloise asks, and I glance over my shoulder, admiring the man in small bites like I usually do. Over six feet tall. Big muscles. Wavy, dark hair down to his chin. Golden skin with tattoos all over. He looks like every good girl's fantasy of a bad boy come to life.

But here he is, in the flesh, in his perfectly faded, ripped jeans and loosely laced combat boots, tugging a leather wallet from his back pocket, the seat of his pants fitting like they were specially made for him.

"Can't complain," he says. "Another day in paradise."

Eloise gestures toward the window. "This delivery situation is a pain in the ass."

He waves his hand, shrugging like he doesn't care. There is very little parking in front of the businesses on Aster Street, so all deliveries are supposed to be made to the side streets, to the back of the buildings. This is meant for better flow of traffic, but every once in a while, there's some driver who either doesn't pay attention to the signs or doesn't care. Right now, a giant truck is parked out front, effectively blocking everyone and everything from getting through.

Evidently, Ian doesn't mind.

Eloise tips her head at him. "Nothing rattles you, huh? How do you do it?"

There is an edge of sarcasm in his voice, and I imagine the way his mouth tilts to the left when he says, "Do what? Stay so young and handsome?"

She laughs. "Yeah."

"Gotta roll with the punches." He combs his fingers through his thick salt-and-pepper hair. "And I guess at some point you learn to stop giving a fuck, you know?"

I snort.

I don't mean to.

But...*when*? When does that happen? When do I stop caring so much?

At my dismissive sound, Ian glances over his shoulder, his brown eyes hitting me with a force too strong for the day I'm having.

His eyebrows furrow for a moment, but he swings back around when Eloise asks for his order. "I'll take a cinnamon roll and how about one of those new muffins you've been working on?"

"You got it. For here or to go?"

"To go."

"Gimme a minute to bring the muffins out from the back, and I'll box it all up for you."

"No problem," he says quietly, and I make sure to be totally engrossed in my cinnamon roll as he pivots toward me. I ignore the five steps he takes to my table and then wait with bated breath, simultaneously fearing and desperate to know what he might say.

"Good morning, Nicole."

Well, hell.

I wasn't prepared for my name to be rumbled that way, and I squeeze my eyes shut at the shivers racing down my spine. It could be the air conditioning.

Might be.

Probably isn't.

I keep my attention on my barely eaten bun. "Hi."

"You mind if I join you?"

"No." It's a shadow of a whisper. He's always so calm and confident, and at this moment, I can barely meet his gaze, afraid I might split into a million pieces if anyone looks at me too closely.

Which is why my head stays down.

Because I can *feel* him looking too closely.

Ian settles into the chair across from me, his large frame taking up so much room, his knees knock against mine before he adjusts, careful not to shift the table when he rests his forearms on it.

And then he waits.

And waits.

And I can't avoid him forever, so I lift my eyes to his. They crinkle in the corners when he squints, and I dare myself to hold his gaze.

"You look like you're having a rough day," he says eventually.

I shrug, playing it cool. Even toss my hair over my shoulder. Not a care in the world.

"Want to talk about it?" he asks, and I wilt. Absolutely lose it.

He hands me a napkin, but one won't cut it.

Not even three do.

He places the entire napkin holder in front of me.

I sniffle my thanks, and he bends, making himself smaller, catching my gaze after I wipe my eyes and face.

"Anyone ever tell you you're a really pretty crier?"

Despite everything, I laugh. "*What?*"

He takes the balled-up tissue from my hand to add to the pile in front of him. Then he pulls a dry one from the holder and—horrifyingly—wipes under my nose.

This hot tattooed silver fox wipes the snot from my nose!

God? It's me, Nicole. Take me now.

When he's satisfied, he crumples up that tissue then leans back in his chair, drawing my attention to his torso. To his defined pectorals under the tight beige T-shirt with a colorful depiction of a bear in a paddleboat underneath a rainbow. *Don't be a douchecanoe*, it reads.

"You're pretty when you cry," he says again, and I attempt to appear somewhat reasonable, tuck my hair behind my ears, pluck at my dress so it's not sticking to my skin.

"I don't think that's true."

"I don't lie." He doesn't blink either. And maybe *that* is true. The one man on earth who doesn't lie. Who doesn't go back on promises. Like for richer or poorer, in sickness and in health.

"Some people don't look good crying." He crosses his forearms over his chest, momentarily drawing my focus to the tattoos covering them. "June, she's an ugly crier."

"Juniper, your daughter?"

He nods solemnly. "Worse than Claire Danes."

"You're familiar with Claire Danes?"

"Baby, you forget how old I am. I was making out with my girlfriend to *My So-Called Life* before you were even a twinkle in your mother's eye."

He's teasing me, but I still feel the need to defend myself. "You're not that much older than me."

He arches his brow. "No?"

I shake my head, ignoring the unasked question. *How do you know how old I am?*

Well...

It's not like I'm keeping track or anything.

But everyone around here knows who he is, who the whole Stone family is. There are four Stone siblings—Taryn, the manager of The Nest, a lovely bed-and-breakfast not too far from here; Griffin, everyone's favorite growly fire captain; the youngest one named Roman, though I've never met him because he lives out of state; and Ian.

The man who makes my pulse jump whenever I see him.

He's the owner of Stone Ink, the tattoo shop sandwiched between Sweet Cheeks and my bookstore, Chapter and Verse. But even if we didn't work right next door to each other, I would still notice him. He's impossible to miss with his build and tattoos. Plus, everyone was invited to the party his family threw for his fiftieth birthday last year. I couldn't go because Bryce had a lecture he wanted me to attend.

I would've rather celebrated this man's birthday instead.

"I'm thirty-nine," I declare as if that's important for him to know then roll my eyes at myself.

I'm not usually so out of sorts.

Though he nods at me like he already knows my age, height, and star sign, and I feel so foolish sitting here in front of this guy who's so put together. So in control.

His gaze meanders from my face down my throat to the burnt-orange maxi dress I'm wearing. Like most things in my closet, it's nothing special, plain and shapeless but comfortable. And I am suddenly very *uncomfortable* at the way my skin pricks, almost as if he can see through the cotton material.

"So, what happened?" he asks after an eternity, during which God does, in fact, *not* take me. "Why are you here crying into a perfectly good cinnamon roll?"

"I don't think you want to hear about my sad life."

He leans forward, tapping his index finger on the table. "First of all, if I didn't want to hear about it, I wouldn't have asked. Secondly, your life isn't sad. You're only having a sad moment. It'll pass."

"I'm not sure about that." I blink my stinging eyes, trying and failing to clear my vision.

Ian catches a tear on my cheek with his thumb. "What happened?"

A few weeks ago, Ian and I headed up the crew for the annual community spring cleanup, and I think it's the fastest we've ever accomplished everything. Because of him being in charge. I am always one of the leads on the project, but I don't think very many people take me seriously—I know I'm too soft-spoken, and I'm working on it...still. Although, with him next to me? All of the volunteers hopped right to their chores.

Some people might assume he's mean from the way he looks, but he's not. At least, I've never experienced the supposed grumpy asshole side he allegedly has, according to the accounts of others. He's only ever been gentle and kind with me, and I find myself telling him everything. "My husband and I, we've been together a long time. We—"

"Since you used to come up to work with your aunt, right?"

I nod. I'm originally from Florida, and I happily accepted my aunt's invitation to live with her during the summers while

I was in college. With three brothers, I didn't much fit into the "football is life" world, and I never felt very seen or heard until Aunt Sue brought me into her home, providing a quiet book-worm a safe space to be herself. I met Bryce during one of those summers. He was on break from a graduate program, and we went on a few dates, but both of us were leaving to go back to school soon, so he said we shouldn't make any promises to each other.

I should've known then.

"We started dating once I moved here permanently, and he finished his PhD," I tell Ian to fill in the context, but it feels like I'm spilling too much information. Though he makes no sign I am.

Instead, he asks, "He's still teaching at the university?"

"Yeah, anthropology."

Ian purses his lips, motioning for me to go on.

"We started..." I bite the inside of my lip, unsure if I should tell him *this* part. Exposing our secrets feels a little too close to being unfaithful. Then again, Bryce doesn't want to be faithful to me, so... "It's not like there were sparks when we met, we were a low-and-slow kind of relationship, but that was okay with me. I never expected fireworks and..." I open and close my fist, searching for words. "Passion like that, it's only for books and fairy tales."

Ian huffs out a dubious sound but otherwise stays quiet.

I stare at the table, ashamed. "We decided to go to couples counseling. We've been going for a few months, and then all of a sudden, today he told me he wants an open marriage. He thinks if we try other things, we'll be able to figure out how to be happy with each other."

"Some*thing* else?" Ian repeats. "Or some*one* else?"

"Does it matter?" I lift my gaze to find his cheeks ruddy above his graying beard.

He breathes out a sardonic chuckle. "I guess it doesn't matter when he's a fuckwit, no."

Even after Bryce has pulled the rug out from under me, I still have the instinct to protect him. "He's not a..."

Ian arches his brow in a challenge, as if he knows I won't repeat his curse.

I set my shoulders and prove him wrong. "He's not a fuckwit. He's very intelligent. He—"

"He's a fuckwit." Ian slices his hand through the air. "The faster you accept that, the better, and I say you let him fuck around and find out."

"What's that supposed to mean?"

Ian ignores my question to ask me another one. "What did you say to him?"

"Nothing." I'm embarrassed by the way my voice cracks. I didn't give Bryce an answer, too stunned to even form coherent sentences, and we agreed we'd talk about it tonight. Although I still don't know what I'll say. "I thought he was happy. I thought *we* were happy."

Ian's dubious expression has me backtracking.

"At least, I thought we weren't unhappy." I sniffle and wipe my nose with the napkin he hands me. "I never expected... I always do the right thing. I always make the right choices, and maybe it's me. Maybe I'm the—"

"Don't," he growls. "I don't want to hear that bullshit. There is nothing wrong with you." Then he lowers his voice, each word prodding at my tender underbelly as if it's his lips soothing me, kissing each of my bruises and cuts. "Now, stop crying because you're breaking my heart."

He hands me another napkin, gently scraping his knuckles along my jaw. A silent *Keep your chin up* in his gaze.

I do, and he nods in satisfaction. I am inexplicably proud.

"I want you to do something." He leans toward me, so I

lean in too. "I want you to go home and do some research. Look up ENM."

"ENM?" I repeat quietly.

"Ethical non-monogamy and polyamory. Before you make any decisions, you need to know what you're doing."

These words are familiar to me but in a far-off way.

"Can you do that?" Ian prods, and I sit up tall. I was nothing if not a good student.

"I love homework. I'll do it."

His dark eyes glint with something I don't understand, but the way his lips curl dangerously sends shivers down my spine.

"Good girl," he says and stands to accept the box of pastries from Eloise before heading out of the bakery, leaving me staring after him.

Good girl.

I never knew how much I'd like that. How happy it would make me feel.

Because there is nothing I do better than please people, and I think I would really like pleasing Ian Stone.

Chapter 2
Ian

When I step out of Stone Ink, the sun is high in the sky, and while I don't *need* another cup of coffee in the middle of the day, I'll buy one anyway because it's a few minutes I have with my siblings every other week to catch up. As I head down the cobblestone sidewalk on Aster Street, I stuff my hands in my pockets, nodding at the familiar faces in each storefront, but it's Clara Wilkenson-Shaw who reaches for me as I pass by.

"Just who I need! Bring your strapping self over here. Come help me with this, please."

I reverse two paces and steady her as she steps up onto a small stool, holding a large vine with decorative flowers in her hands. Clara is five foot nothing, with personality to spare, and she stares up at me with her impish smile because, even on the stool, she still doesn't meet my height.

"How 'bout you just tell me where to put it, and I'll hang it?" I suggest, and she swoons.

"My hero."

I accept the tacks from her along with the flowers, moving

this way and that until I have it hung exactly right around the door to Lux & Lace, the lingerie boutique she owns with her wife, Marianne.

West Chester is a college town, not too far from Philadelphia, and while I've lived here my whole life and everyone does sort of know everyone around here, it never feels as small as when Clara corners me.

"I saw Nicole crying this morning," she says overly casually, and *of course* she did.

I don't know how this woman knows everything about everyone, but I honestly think it has something to do with all her crystals and witchy shit. Since I can already read where this conversation is going, I attempt to shrug her off. "Okay, well, I'll see you later."

She stops me from walking away with her arm like an iron bar across my torso. "She was crying when she went into Sweet Cheeks, and then she left Sweet Cheeks not crying, and I thought it was funny because I saw you go in there after her. So, two plus two and all that." She flaps her hand in the air. "I thought I'd ask the source. What happened?"

I don't especially relish being part of the town rumor mill, but I loathe the idea of anyone knowing Nicole's secrets. I shake my head. "Not sure."

Clara cocks her hip out. "You didn't see her?"

"No, I did."

"And?"

I draw my hand over my beard a few times. "And she was eating a cinnamon bun."

"You have no idea why she was crying?"

Her asshole husband was the reason she was crying. I don't think of myself as a particularly violent person, but I'd do nearly anything to have a few minutes in an empty alley with that bastard.

Telling her he wants an open relationship. Ha.

What he wants is to be able to get his dick wet without any repercussions. I've seen it happen before, these assholes thinking they know what they want, that they can handle what it actually means to be in an "open" relationship. And it's certainly not based in respect or communication.

It's selfish egotism, and Nicole doesn't deserve his bullshit.

I shake my head at Clara, but it's clear this tiny gossip-monger doesn't believe me.

"And you didn't say anything to her?"

After my brain finally cleared of my temper and my very clever imagination cleared out visions of Nicole being under my control, I told her to do some homework. To educate herself about what she was really getting herself into.

What I hadn't expected was her eagerness to please. Her readiness to accept an assignment. Like a natural submissive.

It's not the first time I've gotten half hard in her presence, but it was the first time I actually thought there was a possibility of my fantasies coming to life.

I shake my head again, earning an exasperated sigh from Clara. "You are such a liar."

I play at hurt, pressing my hand to my heart. "My mother taught me better than that."

She crosses her arms over her chest as Marianne pokes her head out the door, her natural black curls grown out on top with a perfect fade on the sides. "What's going on out here?"

I motion to Clara. "Your wife attacked me, forced me to hang up your flowers, and is now berating me for being a liar."

I've known Marianne for a long time, given that she's been my sister's best friend since grade school. She shoots her wife a pitying look. "You're making trouble again."

Clara lifts an innocent shoulder. "I'm trying to find out why Nicole was upset this morning."

Marianne laughs. "You could always ask her."

Clara's eyes go round like a hurt kitten in one of those Sarah McLachlan commercials. Innocent and pathetic. "She's so private, she'd never actually tell me."

"Because you're always in everybody's business," I say. It should be obvious.

"I am not!"

Marianne and I both stare at her blandly.

"A little bit," she amends, and when we don't give in to her, she huffs. "Fine, okay! I *may* possibly get a smidge overinvested in people's lives, but I only want everyone to be happy like me. I want them to have what Mari and I have."

Marianne wraps her arm around Clara's waist. They've been married for about five years now. Both women are originally from the area, but with more than a decade between them, they didn't know each other until Clara moved back after she graduated from a fashion school in Philly. Marianne is locally known as a whiz with numbers, an accountant by trade, but had a reputation for saving failing businesses, and the two teamed up to open their boutique. And I guess one thing led to another...

See? It's not so hard not to know every single detail about my neighbors' lives. It's actually quite easy to let them live in peace.

"Not everyone wants or needs your help," I point out to Clara, who takes no offense.

"And not everyone is such a pessimist like you."

"I'm not a pessimist."

She presses her thumb and index finger together, bobbing her head back and forth like, *yeah, a little bit.*

"I'm a realist."

"And you should *really* let me set you up on a date."

"No. Last time I did, you set me up with that boring preschool teacher."

"Gail. She is lovely!"

"As dull as a brick wall."

Clara scoffs. "Listen here, my friend. You're not exactly Timothée Chalamet, okay?"

"Who?"

"An actor." She snaps her fingers. "I need you to live in this decade."

I roll my eyes, heaving a sigh. I love the girl, but she's exhausting.

"Timothée is a triple threat."

I shrug. "Okay?"

"I need you to try a little charisma. You can be scary when you want to be."

As if I didn't know that about myself, I arch my brows and point my index finger at my chest. "Really? People are afraid of me?"

She ignores my sarcasm. "Gail is actually quite funny, but you probably frightened her, and she clammed up."

"I'm not *that* big of an asshole."

At that, Marianne squints in thought. "You're probably ranked lowest on the Stone asshole chart, but that's still relatively higher than the general population."

I toss my hands out at my sides. "Well, sorry I don't have patience for dicks who don't say please and thank you to servers like your friend Gail."

It gets under my skin when people don't use manners or have general decency for others, especially to servers. They're waiting on us and splitting tips. It doesn't cost us anything to be fucking nice to them.

"Or maybe you're being a little too picky," Clara says, her

head slanted to the side in curiosity. "Because you have someone else you'd rather be on a date with."

I don't like that knowing smile on her face, and I step back, shaking my head. "There is no one else I want to be on a date with, and I definitely don't want to be set up again, but thanks for the offer."

"Seems like I hit a nerve."

I wave her off, taking a few steps backward. "Gotta meet Taryn and Griffin for coffee."

"Oh, great! I'll take an iced latte."

"Not happening."

Marianne laughs with a wave. "See you later."

I hold up my hand in a goodbye then pivot toward Cuppa Jo.

Marianne Wilkenson has been in my life so long, she's practically another sister, making Clara like another sister as well. And I could never actually be mad at her. At any of them. While I find each of my siblings—biological or chosen—annoying, I'd never have it any other way. After all the shit I've been through, I want to keep my family close, and if I have to take a little ballbusting in exchange for having them in my life, so be it.

I walk into the coffee house to find Taryn and Griffin already seated at our usual table by the window, drinks in hand. I accept my coffee from my sister when she holds it out. "Thanks." I sit next to her and across from Griffin. "Cap."

He adjusts his baseball cap with his firehouse number and emblem on it then nods. "You're late."

I'm usually the first one here, so I'm the one who orders our drinks and saves our seats. But not today. "Clara cornered me."

Taryn sips her drink. "She's not happy unless she's up somebody's ass."

"That's what I said."

"What did she want now?" Griffin asks, spine straight, arms folded over his chest. He's a doll stuck on a factory setting who can't ever relax. You can take the man out of the military, but you can't take the military out of the man, I guess. Even for twenty minutes with his siblings.

But then again, he wouldn't be Captain America if he weren't always such a soldier. Serves him well since he's the fire captain now. A father of twins. He raised them on his own their whole lives after their mother died, but he's got Andi now. The former nanny turned girlfriend.

And ironically, it was all set up by Clara.

"She wanted to know why Nicole was crying." I keep my attention on a small divot in the table, so I don't see my siblings' reaction, but I can imagine. The slow blinks and wrenched necks.

Because why would *I* know anything about Nicole?

It's Taryn who asks the question. "Do you know?"

I comb my fingers through my beard. "Nope."

"I don't believe you," Griffin says, and I lift my focus as my sister shakes her head in agreement.

"You're both as bad as she is."

Taryn snorts. "That's offensive."

My sister was the latest one to star in Clara's games, and now she's a few months into a relationship with Dante, the contractor who renovated her bed-and-breakfast. But I'm happy for her. She's been through a lot of shit with her ex-husband, and she deserves someone who worships her, takes care of her two kids. It's about time she has someone to lean on.

Which makes me think of our younger brother. Moving on from the subject of Clara, I ask, "Either of you heard from Roman lately?"

"Not really." Taryn leans her elbow on the table. "I texted him on his birthday but never heard back."

Griffin shrugs. "No. Why?"

I scrub a hand through my hair, wishing I had a hair tie to put it up. "He's being distant again. I thought we were making progress. He was talking to all of us more, and now it's like he's disappeared again."

Taryn has softened toward Roman in the last few months, probably because being with Dante has taken a lot of the stress from her shoulders, so she has more room to empathize. But still, she's not completely thawed. "You can't force him to do anything he doesn't want to. If he doesn't want to be involved with our family, that's his decision."

"I know, but..." I worry about him. He might be almost forty years old, but it's still hard not to think of him as my baby brother. Taryn and Griffin are less than a year apart, and they've always been tight, and while Roman is closer in age to them, it was me he was with all the time. We have twelve years between us, and I always sort of saw him as *my* baby.

After our father left for the second time and for good, I took on a lot of responsibility. My mother, the best woman to ever exist, worked herself to the bone to provide for the four of us, and I couldn't stand by and let her shoulder it all herself, especially when I was old enough to make money. So I got a job painting houses, and whenever I wasn't in school or working, I was babysitting Roman. He followed me around everywhere. Everything I did, he did. Even down to fixing up my car. That kid was changing oil before he was potty-trained.

And, for as close as we were, I haven't seen him in years.

He's had a rough go of it. I mean, we all have, with our dad walking out on us and our mother dying so young and suddenly. But he was still in college when we had to bury her. He had a full ride on a football scholarship with a future in the NFL ahead of him. Then Mom passed, and everything went downhill for him. He tore his quadriceps muscle clean off the bone and needed surgery to repair it. Unfortunately, that addict gene got its claws into him, and he never graduated, too wrapped up in pills, drinking, and grief to recover.

I paid for therapy and rehab, but none of it worked or stuck. Roman is my biggest worry, even more than my own children, and the most painful thorn in the side.

And I'd love to have him home again.

Have us all back together.

"Anyway." I sigh, suddenly tired. "How's everybody been?"

As Taryn and Griffin fill me in on summer plans with their kids, I pretend I'm paying attention, nodding and humming in all the right spots, but the more my siblings tell me about how great everything is going with their significant others, the more my mind drifts back to Nicole.

Wondering if she'll do that research I told her to, and if she'll have the courage to talk to me about it again.

I hope so.

After all, she said it herself, she loves homework.

And I love a girl who can follow orders.

Chapter 3
Ian

I an and Roman text thread:

> Hey, kid. Just checking in.

> Again.

> Saw that Corvette you posted the other day. Looks sweet.

> The owners must be happy with the job you did.

> I'm proud of you.

> Give me a call sometime or something. We need to catch up.

ROMAN

Hey, brother.

ROMAN

Sorry I'm not responding.

Right Next Door

Chapter 4
Nicole

’m good with directions, and I like having guardrails. It's the unknown that worries me, which is why I liked the assignment from Ian. It gave me something to focus on and taught me more than I ever expected.

In the past six hours, I've spent more time reading about the differences between polyamory, open relationships, and swinging than actually working. We're not super busy today, so I should have been catching up on reports and looking forward to planning events in the coming months, but instead, I learned about the different types of relationship hierarchies and what the best practices of ethical non-monogamy are: communication, established boundaries, and discussion of long-term goals.

I took a bunch of notes about that.

Because if I'm going to make a decision about this open relationship, I need some guidance and understanding.

I have no idea what Bryce is thinking, and that's the worst part. Not knowing.

Is this because he's not attracted to me?

Does he want this because he truly thinks it'll help?

And did he talk about this with our therapist Bonnie but not me?

I need answers.

But more immediately, I'd like another opinion. From the man who apparently knows more than he lets on.

From my perch in the corner of my store, I watch Ian outside on the sidewalk, pretending like I'm rearranging one of the display tables, when really, I'm leering like a pervert. At the way he stands with his hands in his pockets, listening intently to whatever the other man is saying, gesturing to his arm, wrapped up in clear plastic. Ian has his hair pulled back into a tiny low ponytail, which is how I know this man must have been his client because Ian always makes sure his hair stays out of his face when he's tattooing since it has a tendency to wave and curl.

But it's not as if I watch him *that* much.

Only enough to learn the basics...like work and eating habits. He has a sweet tooth yet usually only eats pastries for breakfast. He lives in an apartment above his shop, and sometimes when I open the bookstore, he's on his way out for "a little something" from Sweet Cheeks. Always offering to buy me whatever I want. I've never taken him up on the offer, afraid of how that would look. Letting him buy me things.

People around here talk, and that's the last thing I want— gossip being spread about me.

I had enough of that when I was younger. I don't need it here as an adult.

Especially with whatever is going on between my husband and me.

After Ian clasps hands with his client, he moves to turn back to his shop, and I leap up from where I've been hiding to race outside.

"Wait!" I say a little too loudly, but Ian—cool as ever—slowly turns, as if he expected me to be here.

"Hi, Nic."

"Hi. Hey." I clear my throat. "Hello."

"Hi," he says again, lips twitching at my nervous stammer. "You all right?"

I nod. "Fine."

"Good."

God. Why does he have to be so gorgeous? Intimidatingly so. And nice. If his personality matched his outward gruffness, it would be so much easier to ignore him. But in all the years we've worked next to each other, I have yet to figure out how to block him out.

"I, um, I was..." I motion back toward my store. "Reading."

He assesses me from my head to my toes and back as if to make sure I'm not going to pass out. Who knows. I've never talked about this kind of thing with anyone, and my blood is pumping so hard, it is not out of the realm of possibility that my legs will simply give out.

Especially as he waits patiently for me to go on.

"About what you told me earlier."

His eyebrows tick up in interest. "Oh yeah?"

"I told you. I'm a good student."

"Seems so," he says, voice laced with quiet approval, and he shortens the distance between us from a few feet to a few inches.

He leans against the brick of his shop while I twist my fingers into a knot behind my back, mentally reminding myself to stop fidgeting. "I was hoping I could ask you some questions, because I figured..." I swallow the lump in my throat. "I assumed you knew about it since you told me..."

He nods. "I can't promise I have all of the answers, but I might have some."

I've lived almost four decades, and yet standing here with Ian, I feel as if I know nothing. Like I'm a young girl, inexperienced and shy. Which...I guess is true. Even though I'm a grown woman, I've only ever been with Bryce. He's been my one and only relationship and sexual partner.

And now, I'm suddenly faced with making this decision about what I want, and I'm overwhelmed. So hearing what this obviously knowledgeable man has to say might be helpful.

I think.

But right now, all I feel is self-consciousness.

And sweat.

"So, uh..." I swing my arms out to the sides in an attempt to air myself out. "Do you do...poly relationships?"

He shakes his head.

"Oh, you're not into it?"

His dark eyes shift over my shoulder for a moment in thought before meeting mine again, and being the sole recipient of his attention is *a lot*. Because when Ian Stone listens, he *listens*. When he speaks, it's with thought and purpose. He never does anything because he has to. He does it because he wants to. Having him stand here and tutor me, for all intents and purposes, is... Well, it's staggering.

I know he's not doing it out of a sense of obligation. He's here with me, talking in soft tones that send goose bumps over my skin, because he wants to be. Doing *exactly* this.

"As a concept, I'm fine with it," he says, and it feels like an incomplete statement, so I roll my fingers in the air.

"But...?"

"But," he starts with a breath that puffs up his chest, "if it were you, and it were up to me, I'd be a one-woman man."

So, like... If he and I were together...he wouldn't want to share me...?

My answering laugh sounds manic to my ears. Because that

theoretical scenario would never happen. Not because of me, but because of him. I've heard the gossip.

The gorgeous grump of a man whose ex-wife up and left him one day after a weird spiritual journey. She supposedly opened up some expensive retreat which offers "medical" treatments that aren't all above board. At least, according to Clara.

Since then, he's been focused on his family and his business, only going on the occasional date. I've never seen him with anyone around town. Not that I've been *very* interested.

Only as a neighbor might be interested in learning the bare minimum.

"Why are you laughing?" he asks, closer than he was a few seconds ago, and I have to tilt my head back to hold his gaze. I'm average height for a woman, but he makes me feel positively diminutive.

"Because you'd..." I lick my suddenly dry lips, his eyes following the movement. "A guy like you would never ask a girl like me out."

"Guy like me?"

I nod, at a loss for words.

"What's that supposed to mean?" He doesn't sound upset, merely curious.

"You're..." I wave my hand up and down the length of him. "You're handsome and well-known in the community. You have your own business. You could have anyone you want."

He squints, head angled to the side. "And a girl like you, what's that mean?"

"Married."

That sets him back on his heels, and he lets out a rueful sound of amusement, hand rubbing his jaw through his beard. "That's for fucking sure." His eyes make another circuit of my body. "But you're beautiful and well-known in the community.

You have your own business. If you weren't married, you could have anyone you want."

I'm not so sure about that. I am by no means beautiful. I'm plain, and I don't say that as a way to fish for compliments. It's the truth. There is nothing exceptional about me, besides my eyes. Maybe. They're blue and are a bit too wide for my face. Everything else I'm made of came from the ingredient list of white bread.

And I am well-known in the community for all the volunteering I do. Not necessarily for being a delight at the parties or some charming pageant queen. I own a bookstore and have the reputation of being the "nice girl." The one who will always stay late to help put away the chairs and will happily dog-sit while you're on vacation.

Nothing that screams risk-taker or the object of Ian Stone's affection.

Except, with the way he's standing so close to me—like maybe I'm not so plain to him—I can see the striations in his dark brown irises, the outline of his pupils, expanding by the second, and the words are out of my mouth before I've really thought them through. "You would never ask me out."

He grunts but doesn't disagree. Only shifts toward me ever so slightly so his mouth nearly touches my ear, his voice dropping to a rasp, sandpaper scratching across my skin. "Don't let this affect you. What's going on in your marriage, it has nothing to do with you."

"I don't... I'm not sure..."

He nods as if he can see every tornado of thought as it swirls in my mind. "You are. You're taking his request on yourself, but it has nothing to do with you or who you are. You're still the same person you've always been."

I bite into my lip as I consider his words. "But if I haven't changed, then why? Why does he suddenly want this?"

"You have to ask him that." Ian steps back, taking his heat and scent of cloves with him, and when I don't reply, he juts his chin out at me. "You afraid to?"

"No." I force a laugh, a flip of my hand.

"Kinda," he says, because he apparently knows me better than I know myself, and I give in with a nod.

"Yeah, kinda."

"Don't be afraid." He uses the tip of his index finger, barely a touch, to direct my chin up. "Make your decision, whatever it is, and stick to it. If you want to give this experiment a shot, it's up to you, but never be afraid to ask for what you want. Hear me?"

It's a question, but it sounds more like a demand. To hear him.

"Yes."

"Good girl," he says and moves to back away, but I can't let him go. Not yet.

"What if other people start thinking bad about me?"

"First of all, it's no one's business but your own, and stop giving a fuck about what other people think or expect of you. Do what makes you happy."

Is that even possible?

I've spent so much of my life caring. Trying to please others, to be the perfect daughter, the perfect wife. But what have I gotten in return? A family I'm not very close to and a husband who wants to sleep with other people.

I want it to be possible, to ignore all the noise.

And when I look up at Ian, meeting his gaze, it quiets. "You really think I should...do what makes me happy?"

"Life's too short to waste it stuck in a place where you're unhappy. And don't you dare second-guess yourself." He drags his fingers over my forearm, lifting it up between us to skim his index finger along the gold links of my bracelet. "Looks pretty and delicate." He slips his finger under it, along the thin skin over my pulse, and toys with the metal, tugging on it slightly. "But it's actually quite strong. Don't forget that."

Then he's gone with a wink and cluck of his tongue.

And I'm left staring at the spot he'd stood, letting his parting words sink in.

Looks pretty and delicate, but it's actually quite strong. Don't forget that.

I am strong. I can't forget that.

Chapter 5
Nicole

I walk inside the home I've shared with Bryce for the last fifteen or so years, though the familiar scents and sights don't feel like home anymore. It's more like a set for a play. Like the books are for show and the walls are merely a facade. I make my way into the living room to find my husband.

Hunched over his laptop, Bryce has his elbow up on the arm of the couch, hand set against his head, his dark blond hair disheveled. I'm sure he's filling out grant paperwork. This is how he always looks when he's doing that, perturbed.

I watch him for a few moments in his usual button-up, sleeves rolled to his elbows, and slacks that have seen better days. He's handsome, in that approachable, nerdy way that once charmed me, but now, I'm not sure I see anyone but a stranger.

Yet I know everything about him.

How he hates tomatoes on sandwiches because he thinks they make them soggy and that he has read every *Game of Thrones* book but hated the show. He uses CBD to help him sleep, though once he does finally fall asleep, he almost always wakes me up with his snoring. Most of all, this man has never once hinted at wanting an open relationship. We've supported each other through life's ups and downs, including when his father died a few years ago, and I've been there for all the times our relationship has taken a back seat to his work.

Besides the hurt, I think that's what is bothering me the most. I have always been at his side, even when I didn't want to be. I've gone to the conferences and applauded him. I've attended the boring parties and fundraisers. Whether it's a question about what's for dinner or where to go on vacation, I've always compromised for what he wanted. But now I'm seeing it all in a different light. Our entire relationship has always been about what he's wanted. I didn't compromise; I gave in.

Like usual.

I was pleasing him.

Because that's what I do. I don't make waves. I don't ask for more than I think I deserve. I say yes and smile and keep others happy. But what about me?

What do I want?

Finally, Bryce notices me. "Hey."

"Hi." I toss my purse down and step out of my ballet flats. "How was work?"

He shrugs. "Summer."

Bryce is tenured at the university and well respected in what he does, but I don't believe he actually enjoys teaching. He does it because he has to. He needs to keep teaching for access to research and fieldwork. Over the summer, he works with graduate students and usually spends a few weeks away doing fieldwork.

Which has me questioning if that's one of the reasons he's suddenly interested in an open marriage.

Maybe he wants to be free to do what he wants while he's

away, without repercussions. Then again, he could have done that at any time, and I wouldn't have known. It's not like I check up on him. I've always trusted him, and I never expected him to want to be with anyone else.

At least, until now.

Until everything I've known has been flipped upside down.

I sit in one of the chairs across from him, and I get right down to it. There is no point in beating around the bush. Right?

WWISD?

What would Ian Stone do?

That's my new life motto, and he wouldn't waste time hemming and hawing. He'd face the problem head on.

So will I.

"We need to talk."

Bryce nods and sets his laptop aside, elbows on his knees, hands clasped together between them, staring at me in his usual friendly manner as if we're about to discuss buying a new rug and not the future of our marriage.

"I did some research today," I tell him, pulling up the notes app on my cell phone, where I wrote down my questions. "And I want to know what exactly you're picturing when you say open relationship."

His mouth slants to the side in thought, and I'm not sure I've ever had a weirder conversation in my life. Waiting to hear if he still wants me after all of our time together, because as much as Google told me that's not what this is supposed to be about, that's what it feels like—he simply wants someone else.

Finally, he shrugs and says, "It means we see other people. Explore. Have some freedom."

Bryce thinks all day long. It's his job. To study what makes humans human, but when his eyes meet mine, I'm not sure he's ever been less human or more dismissive.

It's clear he hasn't really considered what he's asking for. He's put less thought into it than I have, and I've only had two conversations and a few hours down a Reddit rabbit hole.

"And what about rules?" I press. "Boundaries?"

He holds up his hands, as if he's never heard those words before. "Why do we need rules? Isn't the point of this to break free from all that?"

"Clearly, that's what you want." I think back to discussions we've had with Bonnie about being open with each other, and my husband sure is open to being open. But I'm not sure I'm okay with that. "So, do you want to sleep with whomever, whenever, without any consideration for me?"

He drops his chin for a minute before telling me, "That's not what I'm saying. I love you, Nicole. I do. But I need...more."

"More," I echo, the word tasting bitter on my tongue. I study him, this man I've spent nearly two decades of my life with. He seems so different from the Bryce I knew when we were younger. The one who would stay up late discussing philosophy and literature, who would laugh at my Jane Austen references.

What changed?

Him or me?

"Do you even still want to be with me, Bryce?"

His expression softens, and with the way he jerks his head back, it's like he's surprised I'd ask him that. Even consider it. "Yes, of course I want to be with you."

I want to believe him. But there's a nagging doubt in the back of my mind. "And what about me? Do you care what I do when I'm not with you?"

He hesitates, then shrugs again. "I trust you. You're not the type to...you know."

I suppose my anger has been building all day. More than

the pain of hearing him basically tell me he's bored of our relationship, is the rage.

It sends fire up my spine, red filling my vision. "Trust me to what?" I snap. "To not sleep around? To not have a life outside of you?"

If I weren't so pissed, maybe I would laugh at his look of utter astonishment. That I would speak to him like this. But he's unleashed something in me, whether he's meant to or not. He set something in motion this morning that he can't take back.

And I like it.

I'm tired of always doing what's expected of me. Because fuck them. Right? That's what Ian Stone would do.

Stop giving a fuck about what other people think or expect of you, and do what makes you happy.

I turn to my husband, my resolve hardening. "Fine. You want an open relationship? Let's have an open relationship."

He blinks, surprised. "Really?"

"Yes," I say, my voice astonishingly steady. "But I'm not going to sit at home and wait for you, Bryce. I'm going to live my life. I'm going to find out what makes me happy."

He opens his mouth, then closes it again, seemingly at a loss for words, so I keep going. "My rules are that I don't want to know what you're doing. I don't want to hear about dates or other women, but I expect you to use condoms and birth control, and I want you to be honest with me when this is all over, which is the end of the summer. We have until then to figure out if this marriage is still something we want."

He easily agrees. "Okay."

I feel like we should shake on it to make it official, but even that is a little too weird for me, so I take my shoes and purse, and head upstairs to the bedroom. I have no idea what I'm doing, but I know one thing for sure—I'm not going to be the good girl everyone expects anymore.

I'm going to find out who Nicole Kelly really is. And maybe, just maybe, I'll find out what it is I truly want.

Chapter 6
Ian

In the days since I sat with Nicole while she cried over her cinnamon roll, I've thought of little else. Of the way her enormous blue eyes shone with tears and how those wispy strands of walnut-colored hair floated around her temples. It's not as if I hadn't noticed her before; I always had. I couldn't *not* when she worked right next door to my shop, stretching those lithe limbs of hers to hang decorations in the window of her bookstore. But now, I can't fucking stop noticing her.

How she always starts the day with her hair up in some kind of twist or ponytail, but by the time she walks out the door, it's down. Or how she takes a break every afternoon to pick up a tea from Cuppa Jo. Not to mention how she writes cute little quotes on the sandwich board sign she sets out every morning and takes in every evening whenever she closes up. Although at this point, she's at Chapter and Verse more often than she's not.

Nicole took over ownership of the store after her aunt moved to Maine. It was no secret that was always going to happen, but I recall a time when Nicole was nervous about the handoff. Thinking she wouldn't be able to handle it. I always knew it would be fine. She would be great.

It's also no secret her husband is a fucking punk. At least, not a secret to me. Anybody who takes a smart and beautiful woman for granted doesn't deserve her in the first place.

Having finished my latest tattoo appointment, I fill my aluminum water bottle from the dispenser in the corner as I coast my attention around the shop.

My home.

My kids.

They're all in their early twenties—and my greatest accomplishments by far. My eldest, Jasper, works on a piece at his station in the corner, while Jaybird, my middle son, and his best friend, Cash—my adopted third son, for all intents and purposes—watches something on an iPad, while my daughter, Juniper, and her best friend, Riley, whisper at the reception desk. Sloane, the lone female tattoo artist here, busies herself by cleaning up her work area. It's a little after four, a rare downtime between appointments. Most of our clients are booked out months in advance, but we also take some walk-ins for smaller art. Lately, there's been a rise in small, cartoonish pieces. Something college kids will come in and pick out of a book or the kinds of matching tattoos best friends or married couples get.

The mere thought of a married couple slingshots me back to Nicole in my mind, and I lean against the reclaimed wood counter, rapping my knuckles to Gwen Stefani singing "Just a Girl." It's Riley's turn to be in charge of the soundtrack today.

As I sip my water, I observe a few passersby on the sidewalk, which will become more crowded once people clock out of their nine-to-fives. That's when we hit our busiest time of day, evenings and weekends. But for now, I enjoy the quiet.

And the sight of Nicole strolling down the street with a to-go cup in her hand. Right on time.

Today, she's in a gray T-shirt dress that's wide and hangs down to her knees, almost as if she's trying to hide everything underneath. Drives a guy wild imagining it. Especially because everything that is showing is so pretty. All that creamy golden skin and toned legs capped off in sandals that display a thin ankle bracelet that makes my brain sputter to a stop whenever she wears it.

Everything about her is so dainty. She's fine spun silk, from her slightly upturned pixie nose to her smile that seems so fragile. Yet there are so many more layers to her that I'd love the opportunity to peel back.

I know she grew up in Gainesville, Florida, the youngest in a family of all boys, and from being Juniper's parent, I understand how tough that can be for a girl. I also know she's kindhearted and quiet but is always the first to volunteer for community events, heading charity drives. The first one to arrive to set up tables for festivals. She genuinely loves living here and cares for all her neighbors.

So I don't know what the hell she sees in Bryce, who crawls out of whatever hole he lives in once or twice a year to pretend he's above it all. I have a feeling he doesn't appreciate how well-loved she is.

A jealous motherfucker.

Then again, I would be jealous if she were mine.

Jealous *with* her.

Not *of* her.

I watch Nicole as she tucks a few strands of hair behind her ear. She stands on the sidewalk, unmoving. I can't be sure, but I think she's staring at my shop.

Curious, I smile to myself, waiting to see what she'll do. No Doubt ends, and "Dreams" by The Cranberries picks up—Riley really does have the best musical tastes out of all the kids

—as Nicole straightens her shoulders and crosses the street, heading straight for Stone Ink.

I force myself to stay still, relaxed against the counter, when she opens the door. Her eyes widen when she sees me, as if she didn't expect anyone to be waiting for her.

"Hey, Nicole."

She steps inside so the door can close behind her. "Hi."

"How're you doing?"

She nods, her attention behind me, checking out the black-painted walls adorned with framed photos, showcasing a diverse range of our tattoos and piercings. I like the way she studies everything carefully, her gaze sweeping over each detail with an almost scholarly interest.

She does everything carefully. It's evident in the way she moves and speaks, slowly and precisely, choosing each word and action with care. The way she navigates her world, following the rules and doing what's expected of her, I can't help but wonder what it would take for her to let go, to let herself be free, even just for a moment. I bet she'd be captivating.

I want to captivate her.

I want to *be* captivated.

Behind me, Riley and June perk up. Even though the bookstore is right next door to us, I can count on one hand the number of times Nicole has been in here, and I would still have a few fingers to spare.

"Oh my gosh, hi!" June makes her way around the desk to greet our visitor. My daughter, the social butterfly. "You're finally here for a visit!"

Nicole lets Juniper push her farther into the shop while Riley leans her elbows on the counter. "Or are you here to finally get something done?"

Riley's our admin, social media guru, and does all of our

piercings while she's finishing her marketing degree. She and June both attend the university.

"I'm actually here to talk to Ian," Nicole says a bit too timidly for my liking, and my daughter shoots me a look of surprise. I'm not a monk, far from it, but I keep my exploits well away from the shop and Aster Street. Gossip spreads fast around here.

"Go make yourselves busy," I suggest, and the two young girls barely conceal their curious gazes as they head to the break room, leaving Nicole and me alone.

"So, how are you, really?" I start when she doesn't, probably second-guessing her decision to come in here.

Her throat bobs on a swallow, and it's too tempting to stare at the freckle on the right side of her throat, under her jaw. Instead, I set down my water bottle and lean back against the counter, crossing my arms and ankles.

"I'm okay. I, uh... I just wanted to tell you... I agreed."

I freeze. "You agreed?"

She keeps her focus on her cup, her thumb repeatedly rubbing over the edge, her nails painted a light purple. A matching set of rings still on the fourth finger of her left hand. She clears her throat, flicks her eyes up to mine. "To the open marriage."

I attempt to keep my expression neutral, even as my blood rushes in my ears and not unexpectedly to my cock. Not that anything is going to happen between us. But, shit. Nicole is beautiful and available now.

At least, in theory.

Fearing she might pass out for how her knees are knocking together, I guide her to sit in one of the leather chairs in front of the window.

"And?" I motion for more information.

"And..." Her gaze darts all over the place, anywhere except

me. "I don't know why I did it. I... I think not agreeing would have been worse, but now I don't know what to do."

"You don't have to do anything you don't want to do. No is a complete sentence."

She nods, but I can read the uncertainty in her eyes. "I know. It's just... I've never really done anything like this before. I don't know where to start."

If she's expecting me to be her Mr. Miyagi, she'll be doing more than waxing on and off, that's for goddamn sure. But I try to offer her the support she needs anyway. "There's no time like the present to start exploring."

Her cheeks turn a pretty shade of red, and she covers her face with her hand. "Oh my god. Pretend I never said anything. This is so humiliating."

"You have nothing to be embarrassed about." I tug on her arm, lowering her hand from her face, and I duck down to meet her gaze. "You could wade into this. You don't have to think about your marriage or sex or anything."

Although, now *I'm* thinking about sex.

And from the way she stares at my mouth, maybe she is too.

"Start with something easy," I tell her. "What's something you've always wanted to do, but never have? Travel somewhere or learn a new hobby, make a purchase...?"

"I've never really thought about it."

I nudge her elbow. "Come on, there has to be something."

She bites her lip, and I have to fight the urge to reach out and run the pad of my thumb over the soft skin there. "There's something, isn't there? Too afraid to admit it? You can tell me."

She answers after a few seconds, both of us leaning into each other's space. "I've always wanted to get a tattoo."

"Yeah?" My imagination takes flight, and I immediately picture her naked, all her virgin skin on display for me to tattoo and do as I'd like. My newest fantasy, apparently.

"But the idea of being stuck with a needle over and over again is not something I'm really interested in."

"I'm not going to lie, it'll hurt, but it's not too bad, depending where you get it."

I can see her mind chewing on that information. Then she winces. "I've also been..." She closes her eyes and shakes her head, obviously uneasy about whatever it is. Eventually, she lifts her chin, her eyes shining with amusement. "I've been afraid to ask you about it. You're kind of intimidating."

"You're intimidated by me?" Not gonna lie. Kinda turns me on to hear it.

She waves her hand up and down my body. "You're covered in tattoos, and you look like you've fought a crocodile with your bare hands."

A loud chuckle bursts out of me, one that startles even my kids. They all whip their attention to me. Probably because I'm not usually a big laugher. There are very few instances when I'll let my guard down, and it's only with my family.

And, apparently, Nicole Kelly.

"I really appreciate that," I tell her in response to the crocodile-wrestler comment. "Thank you."

Her answering smile is my new obsession. "You're welcome."

"If you want to get a tattoo, I happen to know a guy who can help you out with that. On the house."

She thinks it over, her lip trapped between her teeth again. "You'd do that for me?"

"Of course. I'd do anything for you."

I don't know where those words came from, but they feel truer than anything that's come out of my mouth in the last few years.

Her breath hitches, and I can see desire ignite in her eyes. Before either of us can say anything more, the sound of the door opening steals our attention, and Riley makes her way up to the front. "Hi. Welcome to Stone Ink. How can I help you today?"

I press my hand to Nicole's lower back, escorting her outside. "I think you should come back tonight before you lose your nerve."

"What time?"

"Come over after you close up. Then we can have the place to ourselves."

Her smile is slow to grow, a little nervous but hella fucking cute. "Okay. I'll see you tonight."

Chapter 7
Nicole

After my conversation with Ian, I can't stop thinking about my tattoo. The idea of getting one always seemed cool and sexy and not for me. No one had ever teased me outright, but as the youngest sister of three very popular and athletic brothers, I'd learned early on that I didn't fit in, and my ugly duckling phase lasted much longer than I would've liked. By the time I was old enough for a tattoo, being a Plain Jane was so deeply ingrained in me, I never thought change was possible.

Not that a tattoo is a big change.

But at this moment in time, this small choice feels *huge*.

After closing up Chapter and Verse, I end up outside of Stone Ink at five after eight. Peering through the window, I spy Ian and Jasper chatting in the front corner, both of them holding their cell phones, while Sloane finishes up with a client. When Jasper heads toward the back, Ian raises his attention to the window, almost as if he senses I'm here. He tips his head back, a gesture for me to enter, so I take a deep breath, set my shoulders, and walk inside the tattoo shop for the second time today.

Sloane does a double take but makes no other indication that she's surprised. Sloane and her kids are frequent patrons at the bookstore, so I've gotten to know her a little bit, and she's great at hiding any and every emotion. Something I've never mastered. Aunt Sue always said I was an open book, everything I thought played on my face.

Ian approaches me with an easy stride, and I hope he can't tell how nervous I am. Although, after he sweeps his gaze over me, he gently curls his hand around my elbow as if I might run away, so he, too, can probably read me just fine.

"You all right? Want a drink or snack or anything?"

I shake my head. "I'm okay."

He guides me over to his workstation, where, besides a big chair I assume is for customers, he has a stool, portable desk, and a small drawer cart, along with some floating shelves on the wall. Each artist has a station with similar tools and products, but it's easy to tell where each of them works. Sloane has pictures and coloring pages from her kids, next to Cash's space with a few plants on his shelves. A skateboard is hanging on the wall in Jaybird's space, while Jasper's station is mostly bare, save a book. Ian has a few stickers and framed photos, a snapshot of who he is as a person: a dad, a friend, a man with ties to the community, and a deep sense of loyalty.

I perch on the edge of the chair that he points to and says, "Get comfortable. You're gonna be here a while."

So I move back, attempting to relax, though my palms are already clammy.

He sits on his stool, facing me, his knees spread wide, his feet on either side of the chair. "Have you got any ideas about what you want?"

"I was thinking about a quote from Jane Austen."

"Yeah?" He crosses his left arm over his torso and rests his right elbow on it, running his hand over his beard. It's thick but trimmed short, the hair over his chin completely silver, while the rest is salt-and-pepper.

A totally inappropriate notion to tunnel my fingers into it enters my mind, but I immediately toss that idea out.

"You're a big fan, right? Named the cat after a book or something?" he asks, his thick fingers doing exactly what I'd been thinking.

"Yeah." Darcy is our store cat, a beautiful ragdoll who adores the attention from patrons and spends most of his days sunning himself in the front windows.

"From *Pride and Prejudice?*" he guesses, and I nod. "What do you like about Jane Austen?"

It's a question I've been asked multiple times, and my answer never changes. "I like how she wrote about strong, intelligent women who were ahead of their time. They knew what they wanted and weren't afraid to go after it, even if it went against societal norms." I pause, my gaze drifting to the wall of tattoo designs. "I guess I've always admired that about her characters. They were brave in a way I never felt I could be."

"You're being brave right now. Doing something you've been afraid to do."

We both turn toward each other, and our gazes don't just meet. They collide.

My breath catches in my throat, and I go warm all over but not from nerves. This... *This* is different.

Ian squints, eyes smoldering, nostrils flaring slightly, and this is exactly what I was talking about with him the other day.

Sparks.

He's got this simmering tension below the surface. What's so intimidating is how he seems as if he might erupt at any moment. I'm positive I wouldn't withstand the heat.

"What quote are you thinking about?" he asks, and I nibble on my lip, telling myself to be as brave as he thinks I am.

"I will be mistress of myself."

He likes my answer, his smile pure sex.

And I like him staring at me like this, even if I might liquefy into a puddle on the floor.

"Do you know what font you'd like or if you want any other details?"

"Flowers, maybe?"

"Don't say it like that," he orders with mock solemnity. "You're the mistress of yourself. If you want flowers, tell me you want the fucking flowers."

I nod a few times, my pulse hammering in my neck. "I want flowers. Wild flowers."

"Good girl," he murmurs, and I need to cross my legs to keep from lifting my dress, fanning my damp panties. "How about location?"

That part, I haven't thought of yet. "Somewhere it's not going to hurt a lot."

Before he can reply, Sloane stalks over, looping a bag across her body. "I'm outta here."

"You in tomorrow?" Ian asks over his shoulder.

She shakes her head. "I have an appointment with Micah."

"Then I'll see you later. Let me know if you need anything."

"I will." She offers him a ghost of a smile. Though I'm not best friends with the employees of Stone Ink, I know them well enough to recognize Ian is a father to them all, whether they're related by blood or not.

Sloane glances at me. "See ya later, Nicole."

"See you."

Once she's gone, leaving us alone, Ian brings his gaze back to me, and something in the air shifts. A tension. A charge.

I lick my lips, and his eyes follow the movement as he rolls his stool even closer. We're practically breathing the same air.

"So," he starts again, "you want it somewhere it's going to hurt the least?"

I surreptitiously wipe my palms on my dress. "Is there such a place?"

He places his hand on my bare knee, his fingers stretching up under the cotton over my thighs. "Everyone has different pain tolerances, but the best places are usually the fleshiest ones. If you're tattooing over bone, that's where you're going to feel it the most." He drags his fingertips back down over my kneecap, and goose bumps rise all over my skin. He must feel it but doesn't acknowledge it. Instead, he wraps his fingers around the underside of my knee. "For your first tattoo, I'd avoid your feet, ribs, or neck. But once I've got you hooked, I'll brand you wherever you want."

My mouth literally goes dry.

And he winks. He knows *exactly* what he's doing.

I clear my throat. "How about my forearm?"

He takes both of my wrists in his hands and extends my arms out to him, slowly rotating them side to side, inspecting them. "You thinking inside or outside?"

"Inside."

Again, he drags his index finger over my flesh, from my left elbow all the way down to my wrist, then back up to midway. "I think it'll look really good horizontal. Do some long-stemmed flowers this way and then have the quote up here. What do you think?"

I nod, unable to form words.

With a squeeze to my hand, he stands to walk over to the counter, where he finds a thin binder and hands it to me when he returns. "You can look through here for examples of fonts. You might—"

I don't need the binder. I point to the framed phrase on the wall, elegant cursive written with thick strokes. *Write your troubles in the sand and carve your blessings in stone.*

"I want that font."

When he sees where I'm pointing, he grunts a quiet, pleased sound.

"Can you do that?" I ask, and he nods slowly. I frown, confused. "What...? Why are you...?"

He turns to face me. "That's my tattoo."

I don't understand. "What?"

"That's my tattoo," he repeats and lifts the hem of his shirt to reveal the thick slab of muscle that makes up his torso, along with the hair and colorful art lining his chest that narrows to his waist. So sexy.

But that's not what he's showing me, and I refocus on the inked words covering his upper right rib cage. That's his tattoo. The exact thing he has stuck on his wall is carved into his skin.

Without thinking, I reach out and skate my fingers over it. This time, it's his skin with goose bumps.

"I'm sorry," I say immediately, but he shakes his head, slow to place his shirt back down.

"Don't be." Then he sits and gets to work, sketching something out in a notebook. "Do you want color?"

"I don't think so."

He nods absently, hand moving over paper. He pauses to reference another binder, flipping through until he finds pages of flowers and draws a few of them, delicate stems and vines, thin leaves, and different-sized petals. When he's done, he shows it to me. "What do you want changed?"

"Nothing."

He sets the notebook in my lap. "What do you want changed, Nicole?"

"Nothing." I laugh. "I swear. I love it. It's perfect."

He lifts his brow, a stern dip to his chin. "Are you sure?"

"Yes."

"Okay." He takes the notebook back, knocking it lightly against my shoulder as he stands. "I'm going to make the stencil, and then we can get started. If you need to use the bathroom, it's down the hall on the left. Help yourself to water in the front or the bowl of candy on the desk. If you want something else, let me know."

While he works, I use the restroom, pop a hard candy in my mouth, then fill up a cup of water, anticipation making my fingers tremble. By the time I've finished the water and have made my way back to Ian's station, he's wearing black rubber gloves, has his hair pulled back, and silver wire-rimmed glasses are perched on his nose.

God? It's me again. Don't take me just yet.

"All right?" he asks, and I nod jerkily, slipping onto the chair, wrapping my fingers around the arms in a white-knuckled grip. He notices and squeezes both of my wrists between his index fingers and thumbs, trying to loosen my hold. "I'll take care of you. I promise. I'll be gentle."

I swallow the watermelon in my throat and release my hand so he can turn my left forearm up on the portable desk. He has a towel set down and double-checks the position is comfortable for me then cleans and shaves the length of my inner arm, describing every step along the way. "I'm going to put the stencil down." He holds it over me, waiting for my direction. "You want it as centered as possible, I'm guessing?"

"Yes, please."

He presses it on then strips the paper back to reveal the outline of the design. "Everything look good to you? You can check it out in the mirror if you want."

I don't need to. "It looks great."

"Okay. I'm going to do the flowers first and then the words

because that'll take a little longer with the shading." He tosses the paper away and spins on his stool for the gun. That's when I close my eyes. "What music do you like?"

"Hozier, Sam Smith, Allison Russell," I mumble, listing them off to forget about the needles soon to be piercing my skin.

A few seconds later, Hozier's folksy music fills the space, and the hum of the tattoo gun starts. Ian places his hand near my wrist. "Try to stay relaxed and tell me if you need a break. The first touch will be a shock. Don't hold your breath."

I don't move, every muscle and cord in my body still and tight.

"*Nicole.*"

I open my eyes to find him staring at me. "Don't hold your breath," he directs again, and I didn't realize I was. "Nice deep breaths, okay?"

I inhale deeply, blowing it out through my mouth.

"Good girl. Keep it up."

I drop my head back against the rest, and then the needle is in my arm. I spasm in response, but with the way Ian's holding me, I can't move.

"It's all downhill from here," he murmurs, and I chance a glance at my arm. With his head bent over me, I don't see much besides his hand moving, but I definitely feel the burning sensation as he inks me with his art.

A minute in, he asks, "Would it help to talk?"

I squeeze my eyes shut. It's like a hot knife cutting into my skin. "I don't... I'm not sure I can form words at the moment."

"Okay. Just keep breathing."

Seconds lapse into minutes, and although I know it's not true, it feels like I've been here for hours. I focus on inhaling, exhaling, and releasing the tight fist my fingers have made in my lap, but it's difficult. Every single part of me is tense.

As if he knows what I'm thinking, he says, "You're doing so well. The outlining is the hardest part. I know."

I let out a groan, and for a moment, he lifts the gun, but I don't dare open my eyes.

"I'm sweating," I mumble, and a few moments later, a fan turns on.

"Totally normal. It's your body's stress response."

That makes me laugh, and I force my eyes open to watch him work—or what I can see of him working. Mainly the back of his head.

"You have a lot of sweaty women in your chair?"

"None I like as much as you."

I work on unclenching my fingers, shaking them out. Without looking up, he asks, "Do you need a break?"

"No, I'm okay."

He agrees with a hum. "Doing so good. I'm done with the flowers. Halfway there, baby."

"You smell good," I blurt, obviously delirious from pain.

"Thank you." I hear a trace of amusement in his voice.

"Like paper," I go on, feverish and babbling. "When we get a box of new releases, they smell good, fresh, but I like worn paperbacks the best. How soft the paper is to touch, the spine cracked so many times some of the color is faded and chipped. It smells a little bit like freshly chopped wood and a little bit sweet like vanilla."

He glances at me with a teasing glower. "Are you comparing me to old books?"

"No. You smell better."

"Well then, I guess I don't mind being compared to old books. Especially if they're your favorite." He shuts off the gun and swipes a damp paper towel over my forearm before spinning his stool away from me.

I peek at the work so far. My skin is red, but most of the

tattoo is there. The flowers are whimsical, and the lettering is almost finished. It's amazing, and it's not even done.

When he turns back to me, he says, "I'm going to do some shading of the letters and a little bit in the flowers to give them depth, okay?"

"Okay."

"You need a break?"

"No. I'm good."

He holds my gaze, his dark eyes blazing behind his glasses. He doesn't verbalize it, but I know he's somehow pleased I'm not asking for a break. A buzz of satisfaction zings through me, and he starts up the gun again. This time, I'm expecting the first bite of the needle and hold still.

He rumbles his appreciation. "Good girl."

The pain becomes more of a manageable sting as opposed to the sharp slicing sensation from before, but I think that's only because of the lingering effects of Ian's praise.

Even as I'm still sweating, my nipples pebble and tighten with each of his honeyed words. "You're doing so good, baby. Just a little longer."

I close my eyes and focus my mind on the feel of Ian's hands instead of the press of the needle, and after only a few more minutes, he finishes, shutting off the gun. He drags his fingertip over my knuckles. "Take a look."

I tip my chin down, viewing the beautiful new addition to my body.

"What do you think?"

I smile. "I love it."

He cleans off my arm then sticks a clear adhesive over it, instructing me to leave it on for three days. He removes his gloves before plucking a small tube of Aquaphor from one of his drawers. "Use this, and try to keep it out of the sun while it's healing."

I check the time. It only took an hour. "That's it?"

He holds his palm out to me, helping me to stand. "Do you want it to be?"

I know it's innuendo. He's offering up more than this tattoo.

And yet, I hesitate.

Ian sets his glasses down, keeping his eyes on me the whole time, patient and understanding. I'm not sure if it's adrenaline or him, but yes, I want more.

I recall sitting with him at Sweet Cheeks and what he said about Bryce. "Fuck around and find out, right?"

His lips slant deliciously as his hands find my waist as if he's done it thousands of times before. "Fuck right."

And then his lips are on mine.

Chapter 8
Ian

Nicole stills at first, clearly taken aback, but after a few seconds, she loosens and melts into me. Her hands slide around my shoulders and up into my hair as I pull her into me, leading her down the hall, away from any prying eyes on Aster Street who might see us through the front windows.

Because as much as I'd like to think I have self-control, I clearly have none when it comes to this woman. All it took for me to fall to my baser instincts were a few conversations about her asshole husband and a flirtatious smile.

I know this is a bad idea, but I can't make myself stop. There is no calling the animal back now that he's been released. And he wants her.

Nicole is lean but soft, her breasts pressing against my chest, her ass round under my palms. I grab it, lifting her slightly, earning a squeak that I take advantage of, gliding my tongue along her lips until they part. She tastes faintly of the candies we keep in a bowl for clients who need a boost in sugar.

I would not suffer if it was the only thing I'd ever be able to taste again.

Sticky-sweet citrus from her tongue.

When I groan into her mouth, she whimpers, her hands fisting in my shirt, and it's not enough. I need more. I need all of her.

I back her up against the wall, my hands on either side of her head, my hips searching for hers. She's so small and delicate compared to me, and I want to protect her yet can't wait to feel and see this magnificent creature unleashed.

I break the kiss and trail my lips down her neck, nipping and sucking at her sensitive skin. She gasps and tilts her head back, giving me better access. The fast beat of her pulse against my lips is an echo of my own.

She's desperate and clawing at me. As much as I am for her. My cock is hard behind the zipper of my denim, and when she lifts her leg, wrapping her thigh around my hip, I become steel.

"God, baby," I murmur, pulling away only long enough to admire the rapid rise and fall of her chest when she breathes. "You were waiting for this, weren't you?"

She nods and yanks me back to her, my mouth to her neck. I don't care about leaving marks. In fact—fuck it—I want to leave a mark. Let that piece of shit see what he's missing. I suck hard on the slope of her shoulder, only releasing her when she gasps.

I slide my hand up her thigh, under the soft material of her dress, and it moves easily, pooling at her hip. "I'm going to touch you," I inform her to make sure this is what she wants. "Find out how long you've been waiting for this. How wet you are for me."

She nods, her lips brushing mine. "Yes, please, *please.*"

Her panties are thin and damp, and I push them aside, slipping my index and middle fingers over her pussy, trailing along the length of it, from the patch of hair at the top to where I feel soft and wet skin. I part her open, earning the sweetest trembling breath from her before sinking my fingers inside.

The amount of her desire has my own skyrocketing. Not that it wasn't off the charts before.

"Fuck, baby," I rasp, finding her clit easily, her body reflexively jerking at the touch. What I wouldn't give to restrain her. Find each and every way she'd respond to my fingers.

My mouth.

My cock.

"You liked me marking your skin, huh? Got you all slippery here." I rub soft, quick circles, making her hips buck away from me. A little too much for my liking, so I tighten my hold on her thigh with my hand, keeping her leg up and open, allowing me room to move my hand, thrust my fingers in and out of her.

Find the spot that *really* makes her squirm.

"I got you," I tell her, licking into her mouth when I'd actually like to be licking her pussy. "Feel this?" I shift my wrist slightly, making it easier for me to stroke her. Those tight walls clenching around my fingers. "I feel it."

She groans, her kisses turning frenzied and nipping. "How... Why are you doing this?"

"Why, what? Why am I making you come?" I back away a few inches, admiring the flush of her skin, the sheen of sweat on her temples and across her collarbone. This woman needs more orgasms in her life. "Because you want it, and I want to be the one to give it to you."

I'd make her come as many times as she'd allow me to.

Especially with her fuck-hot whimpers and barely audible *please, Ian*s. As if I'd ever not give her anything she asked for. Let alone *pleaded* for.

"I want to make you come so hard, you see stars. I want to give you the whole goddamn galaxy."

"Yes, yes," she moans, and I can feel her growing close in the way her fingernails dig into my shoulders and neck. With a few swipes of my thumb over her clit, her inner muscles tighten and flutter around my fingers as she comes with a cry.

I continue to stroke her, press the heel of my hand against where she's most sensitive, slowly bringing her back to earth, waiting until her shaking and trembling subsides before I release my grip on her thigh. She's pink and panting and so pretty it hurts.

Once she catches her breath, I place a kiss at the corner of her mouth and then one more on the other side. I don't have to ask, but I do anyway. Because every guy needs his ego stroked once in a while. "Did you see stars?"

She licks her lips. I do too. And then she smiles, lazy and a little loopy. "The whole Milky Way."

I hum my satisfaction and slide my fingers out of her. They're coated in her orgasm, and I keep my eyes on hers as I bring my fingers to my mouth, tasting her. She watches me with her pupils blown wide, and I can see the fire in them. I would love to give her more, but I don't want to push her too far, too fast.

So instead of doing what I really want to, which is get down on my knees and lick her until she comes on my tongue, I press my forehead against hers. "You're so brave."

But it's as if my words flip a switch, her body going rigid.

Nicole pulls away from me, eyes wide and wild, breath coming in quick, shallow pants out of her parted lips, still red and swollen from my treatment of them. I instinctively tighten my grip on her waist. "Are you okay?"

She shakes her head, wriggling out of my hold. "I... I have to go. I need to go."

I reach for her, following her out of the darkened hallway. "Nic, wait. Talk to me. Tell me what's wrong."

She dodges my touch, her words tumbling out in a hurried jumble. "I just... I need to think. This is all so fast, and I... I have to go."

"Baby, please, hold on a minute. Take a breath." I step toward her, but she retreats further, walking backward, stumbling into Jasper's chair.

"I'm sorry."

"You don't have to apologize," I say as she darts to the door. If anything, I should be the one apologizing for freaking her out. Clearly, I went too far.

"I'm so sorry, Ian." She reaches the door, but I place my hand against the glass so she can't open it.

"Don't run away."

She shakes her head, eyes downcast, and the sight of her caged and frightened makes my stomach churn. I never want her to feel trapped, especially not by me. So I step away.

"I wish you'd stay. At least catch your breath."

"No, I can't. I've got to go."

"I'll walk you out to your car," I say, opening the door, which only gives her an out, and she rushes away from me.

"No, that's okay. Thanks for the tattoo and...you know. I'll, um, see you around. Okay? Okay."

I watch from the sidewalk as she literally runs away, footsteps fading when she rounds the corner to where she usually parks her car. My heart hammers in my chest, a sickening mix of adrenaline and fear, and I scrub a hand over my face, the scent of her still lingering on my fingers. *Fuck.*

Inside the shop, I lock up and pace the length of the floor in an attempt to calm my racing thoughts. What the hell just happened? One minute, she's coming apart in my arms, and the next, she's bolting like a frightened deer. I replay the scene in my mind, trying to pinpoint where I fucked up.

Was I too intense? Too pushy? I assumed she was right

there with me, her body responding to every touch, every word. But maybe I read her wrong. Maybe I read the whole damn situation wrong.

I stop in front of my workstation, bracing my hands on the back of the chair she sat in an hour ago, as she stayed as still as possible while I tattooed her. She was brave—is brave—for putting herself out there. For going against the grain I know is so difficult for her to do. To come to me for help...and maybe comfort.

Or that's probably wishful thinking. That she'd ever actually want me for anything more than what I gave her tonight. Some art and a nice finger-fuck.

But goddamn, it felt...different. Being around her is a balm to my soul. My life has not been easy, but Nicole is... She is a quiet afternoon. She is a night under the stars. Warmth and sunshine, peace and calm.

I may have worked hard not to let things overwhelm me, but that's only because I've had to face so much. I can't allow every little thing to have space in my life. Otherwise, I might not ever get out of bed in the morning. But the woman with the soft voice and gentle smile is a reminder that life can be easy. Moments can be rejuvenating.

And the trust she placed in me tonight felt monumental. To give her a permanent marker as well as touching her in ways that I know were earth-shattering. For her *and* for me.

I should go after her. Make sure she's okay. But something tells me that would only make things worse. She said she needed to think, and I have to respect that, no matter how much every instinct in me screams to chase her down and make this right.

Instead, I pull out my phone, my thumbs hovering over the screen. I have her number from when we coordinated the cleanup, but we only exchanged a few texts, which included messages from her like **Meet you at 8? At the corner of Lindley and Franklin.** and **Can you please pick up the pallets of water from Debra at the community center?** and **Thanks for all your help today!**

My replies were thumbs-up emojis like a fucking tool.

So, now what? I suddenly text her like I have a brain? And say what? **Sorry I made you come so hard you had a panic attack.**

I shove the phone back into my pocket and clean up my space, putting everything away, trying not to remember the sounds she made and the way her sweet little pussy clenched around my fingers.

From her reaction, I doubt I'll ever experience that again, so I might as well imprint it in my memories. But the thought of never having her again makes my chest ache. The idea of hurting her is even worse, and I rub at the spot above my heart, as if that could ease the discomfort.

I've never felt this torn up over a woman before. Not since Heather, but even that was different. This feels bigger, more consuming. Like Nicole has the power to wreck me in a way no one else ever has.

And that scares the shit out of me.

Yet underneath the fear, there's something else. A fierce protectiveness. A deep, primal need to make this right, to make her feel safe and cherished. To show her that she deserves to be worshipped, to be loved.

But all I can do is let her figure out what she wants. This is about her. Not about what I want or need.

So, I guess I wait. And hope.

Chapter 9
Nicole

Dizzy with fear, confusion, and straight-up panic, I plant myself on the floor after closing and locking the door to my house, back against it, legs splayed out in front of me as if I sprinted home.

I may as well have for the embarrassing display of awkward limbs as I ran away from Ian and Stone Ink. I don't even remember how I got home.

Only pure hysteria.

Which is funny because if this were 1885, I would have been prescribed an orgasm and bed rest. But it's an orgasm that sent me into a tailspin.

Never in my entire life have I ever experienced pleasure and all-consuming urgency like I had tonight. With a man whom I did not promise to love for the rest of my life.

And I am completely overwhelmed.

I let my head drop back, staring up at the ceiling in the dark entryway until I hear footsteps upstairs and Bryce's voice calling down. "Nicole?"

"Yeah."

His head pops around the banister. "What are you doing?"

"Just...resting."

"You've been working too many hours," he says congenially, and *what?*

What am I supposed to say to that?

How am I supposed to act like all of this is perfectly normal?

That our marriage has never been better and this is simply another night of me coming home late when I was shot to the moon on a rocket ship named Ian Stone?

None of this is normal for me. I don't know how to act or feel other than a nauseating mix of exhilaration and betrayal. I didn't know someone could be trapped and free all at once. Like a bird let out of its cage, only to be stopped by a window.

"Are you coming to bed?" Bryce asks, and there is nothing I want to do less than lie next to my husband right now.

But I force myself to stand and use my hand along the wall to steady myself as I begin to slowly climb the stairs like a drunk sailor. By the time I make it to my bedroom, Bryce is in bed, watching something on his iPad, having no idea what I did tonight, and guilt makes my skin crawl.

Yes, I agreed to this open relationship, but I've never cheated on anyone. Although, I suppose, I'm not cheating. I'm allowed to do whatever I want. We're a living embodiment of that *Friends* episode. We're essentially on a break, and anything we do this summer can't be held against us.

Intellectually, I understand romantic relationships come in all shapes and sizes, and I know monogamy and marriage are not one-size-fits-all. Yet, I've only ever known couples in a monogamous relationship between two people. At least, that I know of. Who knows what my friends and family do behind closed doors?

I watch my husband for a moment, wondering what he's

done behind closed doors, what he plans to do. If he thinks about his actions like I'm thinking about mine and what it means for us as a couple, for himself as a single person.

What I did with Ian, kissing him, learning the feel of his lips, begging him to make me come, riding his thick fingers like some wanton creature... What does that make me?

Images that I should probably forget but never could assault my memory, and I flinch reflexively. That's what makes Bryce glance up, and he offers me a bland smile. He has no idea.

About what happened in a darkly lit hall of Stone Ink.

I smile back at him. Like a puppet. Doing all the things I'm supposed to. I start to get ready for bed, and he reminds me that we need more toothpaste. Because I'm the one in charge of grocery shopping.

I nod, although toothpaste is the last thing I care about.

In the bathroom, I strip down, taking stock of my body, searching for evidence, a mark in the size and shape of Ian's hand on me somewhere. There isn't, but I almost wish there were. Proof that I saw a different world. Ian Stone promised to show me not only the stars, but the whole goddamn galaxy. And he did.

I touched the moon, skipped among the stars, and floated in the darkest depths, guided to the light by Ian himself. And what scared me the most was how I immediately wanted it again. Wanted more.

But then I crashed back into earth, brought low by gravity and the reality currently sniffling and coughing ten feet away from me now. I roll my eyes at Bryce's incessant throat clearing. It's his allergies, and I'm not sure if he's extra annoying now because of my too-few-short hours with Ian or because he probably never took his Allegra.

With a sigh, I change into my pajamas and toss my dress

and underwear into the laundry basket, briefly wondering if I should bring it down to the washer now. Get rid of the evidence. I don't and instead remove my jewelry, taking time to admire my new tattoo. I flush hot at the reminder of Ian's hands all over me, a heavy pulse still beating between my legs, still needy for more.

After shaking out my hands, I focus on washing my face, lotioning my skin, and brushing my teeth. One task at a time, one foot after the other, I can pretend like nothing has changed, and yet when I open the bathroom door, I have to confront the truth.

"You feel okay?" Bryce asks. "You were making weird sounds in there."

I cross the room to the air filter and remove the top to fill it with water. "Fine. A bit of a headache."

He doesn't say anything until I turn around, and I'm halfway back to the bathroom to deposit the little jug I keep there to make sure Bryce gets his stupid purified air. "What's that? On your arm."

I lift it, playing dumb. "Oh, this? A tattoo."

He sets down his iPad and shifts to get a better view, but I don't move. I make him come to me. He lifts my arm, twisting it this way and that. "You've never mentioned wanting a tattoo before."

I bristle at his tone, at the implication that I'm somehow not the kind of person who would have a tattoo. I don't even know what that kind of person is, but maybe I'm just overemotional now. Easily triggered. Irritated at anything and everything he does and says.

"I guess there's a lot you don't know about me," I say with as much attitude as I can muster then snatch my arm away from him to put the jug back in the bathroom and shut off the light.

Bryce doesn't move from his position by the side of the bed, blocking my half of the mattress. "Like what?" His laugh is pure condescension. "I think I know you pretty well."

"Do you?" I slant my head, my nearly *never* present temper overtaking me. "Because I thought I knew everything about you and never expected you would want an open marriage. Yet here we are."

He runs one hand through his hair. "Is that what it is? You're mad at me, so you went out and got a tattoo?"

"I got the tattoo for *me*." I huff. "As much as this—" I gesture to the space between us "—is because of you, I can do things for myself every once in a while."

He flops his hands down to his sides. "So you are. You're pissed."

I let the truth come screaming out of me. "Yes! Yes, I'm pissed, Bryce. I was completely blindsided by you, and I don't know what to think about anything anymore."

"Then why did you agree?"

I turn around in a tight circle.

Why did I agree? Because a man with dark eyes and a growly voice told me I have to stop giving a fuck about what other people think, and even though I'm hurt by Bryce and this experiment of an open marriage, I think... I think maybe I deserve more than what I've settled for. If I'm honest, our marriage stopped feeling like a marriage a while ago. We're more like roommates than lovers. We almost never go out anymore, and when we do, it's usually for some event for his work. And we don't have much to say to each other. We've argued more in the last year than in the first decade we were married, and I think, deep down, he's mad at me because we never had children.

We had agreed not to have any, enjoying our freedom and the ability to do what we liked, but we stopped traveling together years ago, and he stopped holding my hand around the time his brother had a baby—years after I had my tubes tied.

If I were brave enough, I'd confront him about that. Ask him if this is some revenge plan or a way to get back at me. Or a plain old midlife crisis. I don't know.

But either way, I fear it would lead to something I'm not necessarily ready to face. That I want this chance to fly. See, explore, and, yes, experiment.

I face my husband once again and tell him the one thing I am absolutely sure of. "There is more to me than being the mousy bookstore girl who smiles and nods to keep everybody happy. I am a woman with her own goals and desires."

"I know," he says, a little too understanding. Like my confession lends allowance to whatever it is his desires are. "I want you to be happy."

I nod and swipe my hand over my hair. "It's...fucking weird."

He sputters out a laugh. "Did you just say 'fuck'?"

I shrug. "I curse now too."

He chuckles and nods as if happy he's finally corrupted me after all these years. "Nice."

But that has nothing to do with him, and everything to do with Ian.

The man I ran out on. Who I'm not sure I can ever face again after that embarrassing display of cowardice.

"Let's go to bed," Bryce says, and I don't fight him on it, turning off the lights before slipping under the covers, keeping myself as far away from him as possible. I roll to my side, at the very edge of the mattress, but my mind is in no mood to sleep, so I scroll through my phone. First, to my social media. I don't post often, once or twice a year, but I find the photos from our wedding, our smiling faces, and the big ugly necklace I wore because my mom wanted me to use hers as my "something borrowed." But it's gaudy and straight out of the 1970s. I find a photo of Aunt Sue and me standing in front of Chapter and Verse on the day I officially took over as owner. Aunt Sue is my rock, and it took me a long time before I felt confident enough to run it on my own, especially when the independent bookstore business is a rocky one. It's impossible to compete with the monopolies, but the local community comes through to help me eke it out every year. Though, a few years ago, we were hit with a bad storm, and a burst pipe not only took out half the ceiling, but almost our entire inventory. Bryce and I took out a loan to help keep the store afloat, and I'm still working on paying it back, slow and steady.

I tap out of my own profile and find Stone Ink's. The page is full of colorful photos of their work and the occasional picture of the artists. One in particular is of Ian, glaring at the camera, caught in the middle of drawing something in a notebook. Ian is an amazing artist, known for his photorealistic tattoos. There are dozens and dozens of posts showing off his art: the portraits of animals, including a gorilla, snake, and cat. There's one of a guy's chest that appears as if his skin is ripping open to reveal the Superman logo. Another man has a tattoo of Zach Galifianakis and the baby from *The Hangover*. It could be a still shot from the movie. It's no wonder there is a multiple-months-long waiting list for an appointment at Stone Ink, and yet Ian put me in his chair without a blink and gave me my tattoo as a gift.

I lightly skate my fingertips over the wrap still covering the ink before curling them into a fist at Bryce's snore. Then I grab my pillow and head downstairs to sleep on the couch.

Chapter 10
Ian

"Help! I need help!" Eloise bursts into Stone Ink like her ass is on fire and plows straight toward me. "My walk-in died. I need to move everything out and find a place to store it until I can get it fixed," she nearly shouts in one big gust of air.

I grab her by the shoulders. "All right. All right. Take a breath. We'll figure it out."

I push her into my empty tattoo chair and jut my chin toward Jasper, who retrieves Eloise a cup of water and some candy, which she gratefully accepts with shaking hands. Once she seems calm, I ask, "Did you call somebody to repair it?"

"Yes, but they can't come until tomorrow. Everything will spoil by then."

It's June, and the humidity has been killer lately. "All right. We'll fit as much as we can into our fridge in the kitchen, and then I can take some upstairs to my place." I wave at June for her attention then point upstairs. "Why don't you go see what you can move around? Make some room."

Eloise starts listing everything off on her fingers. "I have bowls of icing, butter, milk—oh god! My sourdough starter."

"Not the sourdough starter," Jay says from his position next to a girl getting inked on her side.

"Shut up," I grumble at him, but he balks.

"I'm not joking. It's serious business to lose the sourdough starter."

Eloise flings her hand out, eyes wide, like my middle son gets it. Then she crumples. "Oh my god!"

"It'll be fine. If I need to, I'll call Taryn to see if she can take any at The Nest, but for now, why don't you see if anyone has any room to spare in their kitchenettes on the next block? Jas and I will start moving things over here. Okay?"

With everyone's instructions, we break up, Eloise to the left to find refrigerators we can borrow, and Jasper and me to the right to start carrying all the items the workers at Sweet Cheeks are packing up tightly.

We're about fifteen minutes into the job when Nicole shows up, startling when she sees me. "Oh. Hi. I'm, uh, here to help."

Ever since our...session the other night, the woman has ducked and dodged me at every turn, but now she and her bleeding heart have nowhere else to run. I hand her two bowls of some fruit compote. "The kitchenette next door is full, so these are going upstairs to my apartment."

She nods. "I told Eloise I have a small fridge in the back of the store, but it wouldn't be able to fit much more than a gallon or two of milk."

"It'll have to do." I follow her out the back door of the bakery to the back entrance of Stone Ink. A lot of the downtown buildings were erected during the turn of the twentieth century and designed for mixed-use, with businesses on the bottom and apartments on top. Depending on the ownership, some of the buildings have been completely gutted and reno-vated, while others still have the apartments intact. I live right on top of my business because I'd been able to buy the indi-vidual property, but I know there is an office on top of Sweet Cheeks, and Sue used to live in the apartment above Chapter and Verse. Now it's shared by a pair of recent college grads who I think are solely keeping Eloise in business.

The back door of Stone Ink opens up to a landing, which can take you into the shop or upstairs to my place. I direct Nicole up, and it feels a little weird that the first time she enters my apartment is to pack the refrigerator with pie fillings. I don't miss the way her gaze coasts around, briefly pausing to study the framed photo on the wall of my mother or the furniture in the living room, but with a tap of my elbow to hers, she follows me and we put everything away, in time for Jasper to hand over a half-made cake.

Twenty minutes and another couple of trips later, we have the walk-in almost clear, helped by Taryn coming by to accept whatever was left over. I double-check the shelves inside to make sure we have everything when Nicole steps in behind me, a tremulous smile on her face when she realizes what I'm doing. "We had the same idea."

I pivot to face her, and after the last few days of being treated as if I have cooties, I'm torn between annoyance and desire. Because as much as I want to hold on to the thin thread of frustration at the situation, it's nowhere near the power of my craving for her. I lean into her space, intent on apologizing, when all of a sudden, the door closes, shutting us inside.

Nicole whips around. "Hey, wait. We're still in here!"

Someone outside responds, "Oops, sorry!" Yet the door doesn't open. I hear something moving, some scratching, and then, "The handle is jammed. I can't open it."

Nicole turns to me with terror in her eyes, but I hold my

hand up. "These are made with safety precautions. Don't worry." I call out to whoever is on the other side, "Where's the release in here?"

"It's on the left side. Look down."

"Found it." I push it, but nothing happens. I press it again. And again. And again. "What the fuck?"

Nicole wheezes, fingers tunneling into her hair. "Oh my god. This is how I die."

"You're not going to die. It's just stuck." I prop my hands on my hips as I raise my voice to speak to the person outside. "Hey, where's Eloise?"

"I'll get her. Hang on."

A few seconds later, what I assume is a hand slaps on the fridge. "Ian? Nicole?"

"Eloise!" Nicole thumps the side of her hand on the door. "You have to get us out of here! I'm claustrophobic!"

I roll my eyes up to the ceiling, muttering a curse before I move close to the door. "Eloise, did you know the release was broken inside here?"

The hesitation before she answers already tells me all I need to know. "Maybe."

"Jesus fucking Christ, Eloise!"

"Don't yell at me," she says as Nicole slants her attention to me.

"Don't yell at her."

"I'm not yelling," I grit out. "We're stuck in a refrigerator, and you just said you're claustrophobic."

"Yes, but aren't you supposed to be the coolheaded one?"

"I see you have an attitude when enclosed in tight spaces."

She fans her face, turning in a circle. "Don't remind me. Oh god. Oh god..."

"Eloise," I try again after a deep breath, "is my sister still here? Tell her to have Dante come over. Maybe he's got some way he can get us out. We can't be the first people to be stuck in a fucking refrigerator."

"Yeah, hold on!" Eloise bangs on the outside of the door a few times. "We'll have you out in no time! Promise!"

But in the meantime, I'm stuck in a 6x6 box with a girl who is starting to sweat, either from her fear of being locked in here or me. Either way, if she passes out, it's all my fault.

I turn a crate over and tug on her arm for her to sit. I inhale and exhale loudly, directing her to do the same. "You need to breathe."

She does for a minute before placing her elbows on her bent knees and squeezing her eyes shut. "When I was eight, my brothers locked me in a steamer trunk. Told me they were going to show me a magic trick. But they just shoved me in and locked it. Made me disappear for hours."

"Jesus fuck. What kind of demons are you related to?"

That earns a shaky laugh. "The worst kind."

I watch her as she rolls her neck side to side, breathing slowly in through her nose and out through her mouth, her fingers curling into fists as her lips move, forming silent words that I think are "You're okay. You're okay. You're okay."

I slide down to the floor, back against the metal door, hands folded in my lap, legs crossed out in front of me, making sure I appear as relaxed as possible to keep her calm, even as I have the urge to shout and kick at the door.

I'm genuinely worried about her having a panic attack, so I attempt to take her mind off our current situation. "How's the tattoo doing? Healing okay?"

She flutters her eyes open, those big blue irises red-rimmed. "Yeah." She runs her fingertips over it. "It's good. Thank you." She bites into her bottom lip as if steeling herself. "I love it."

"And about what happened after... I'm sorry. I don't want you to feel uncomfortable, and I clearly crossed a line—"

"No, you didn't. I wanted you to. I asked for it. Please don't apologize." She blinks a few times as if she might cry then focuses her gaze on the floor. "If you apologize, it'll mean you did something wrong, and you didn't."

With her brows angled down and shoulders rounded over, she seems at war with herself, clearly upset, and I have to take some responsibility for it. "Even if I didn't do anything wrong, I still shouldn't have touched you. You have a lot going on, and I have not made it any easier on you, so for that, I'm sorry."

She shakes her head, her voice barely above a whisper. "You haven't made it easier, but only because you showed me what I've been missing."

"What you've been missing...in your marriage?"

She nods, and hell if that doesn't make me want to puff up my chest. Also want to sock that nerdy fucking mop of a man in the mouth.

After a minute, she collects herself and swipes her hand over her forehead, then meets my gaze straight on. *Brave.* This girl is brave. "I've been avoiding you because you made me feel things I never have, and it freaked me out. Because..." She licks her lips, coughs out a sad little laugh. "I don't know what I'm doing, but I know I want more of *that.*"

I swallow the lump in my throat and replay those words in my head, making sure I understood them right. She wants more. "With me?"

She lifts a shoulder. "If you want to."

I wipe my hand over my mouth and beard, biting back a sardonic chuckle. If I want to? That's all I've thought about for the last three days. "Yeah, Nic, I want to."

Her eyebrows arch like she can't believe that, and when I

hear people gathering outside, I move closer to her. "Don't give me that bullshit about a guy like me and a girl like you."

"It is kind of hard to believe, though," she says a second before I hear Dante on the other side of the door.

"Yo! Ian, Nicole! I'll have you out in a few minutes."

A drill starts up, and I take one of Nicole's clammy hands in mine. "Don't put yourself down. You are mistress of yourself, remember? You ask for what you want."

She smiles shyly, tucking her chin toward her chest. "I guess so."

I give her hand a squeeze, and she squeezes back. "If I'm mistress of myself, what does that make you?"

She really does have some attitude hidden behind that good girl, doesn't she?

I cluck my tongue, seeing how far I can push her. "Master."

She smiles. "What exactly does that mean?"

"Nothing." I flick my hand up, clearing the air since she thought I was joking. Might as well run with that. "I was kidding."

"No, you weren't." Her amusement melts. Those soft blue eyes of hers study me, seeing so much more than I want her to. She slowly lifts her fingers to my face, combing them over my beard, dragging her thumb along my lower lip. "You meant *something*. I can tell."

She doesn't need to tie me to a chair. Use a lie detector. Extract all my secrets with torture. All she has to do is blink those stunners at me and run her fingers over my beard. I'll tell her anything she wants.

"How?"

She tilts her head. "How what?"

"How can you tell?" How can she read me so well?

Maybe the same way I read her?

How I can decipher the shy curve of her mouth when she's

hesitant to say what's on her mind. Or the way she bites her lip when she's nervous. Or blinks rapidly when she's trying to hide something.

"I'm not sure," she says, almost as if she's afraid to admit it. "A feeling, maybe. It's funny..." She trails her hands from my face to my throat and down my chest to my sides, where she holds on to my T-shirt. "I was always so intimidated by you, but now it feels..." She tips her head, nibbling on her lip. "Like I know you." She blushes scarlet and covers her face. "It's stupid. That's stupid. Pretend I didn't say that."

When she shifts away from me, I don't let her, hooking my finger into the collar of her dress, twisting the material in my grip. She's not going anywhere.

"I'm not going to pretend you didn't say it, because you're right." I tug her toward me, ghosting my lips across hers. "It feels like I know you too."

When she doesn't move, I chance a kiss, one that starts as a press of my mouth on hers and leads to long caresses of her tongue, pulls of her lip between mine.

By the time we're done, she's slow to open her eyes, swaying into me, and I can't help but chuckle.

She's so goddamn cute.

"Are you going to tell me?" She scratches her fingernails over my pecs.

"Tell you what?"

"Your secret. Whatever it is you're hiding."

I heave a sigh like she's a pain in my ass. When really, I'm just not sure what her reaction will be. I made her come with my fingers the other night, and there's nothing I want more than to make her come again and again and *again*.

But she's married.

Fucking *married*.

Sure, she and her asshat of a husband are doing this experimenting or whatever the fuck they want to call it, but it doesn't change the fact that she still wears her wedding ring.

I may have tried a lot of shit in my life, but I've never slept with a married woman. And I never plan to.

Although the temptation to do more with *this* married woman is already too hard to ignore.

"What are we doing here?" I ask, for possibly the first time ever in my life.

She blinks once then twice, a third time. "I don't... I'm not sure, but I know I don't want to stop."

I'd been so cavalier when she first told me. *Fuck around and find out.*

Well, now *I* fucked around and found out.

I can't go backward. I can't simply erase what happened between us. I won't be able to forget and go back to the way things were before, acknowledging each other as if we're acquaintances at neighboring businesses and nothing else. These last few days of her hiding away from me made me feel like shit, and it'll be even worse when she decides she's done with me.

But then again, I can't pass up what she's offering me. Whatever it is. I want it.

I need it.

For better or for worse, I'm in this now.

I bury my hands in her hair, holding her head so she can't look anywhere but right at me. "I'm a Dominant."

Her brows narrow. "A what?"

"A Dominant."

Her pupils dilate, lips part, and it's a few seconds before she responds. "Like BDSM?"

I nod.

"With, like, whips and paddles and...*Fifty Shades of Grey?*"

I shake my head. "I never read it, but no. I don't do whips

and paddles. At least, not unless my partner wants me to, but it's not what I like."

She licks her lips, evidently interested. "What do you like?"

"I like control."

Her jaw bobs. She stays silent, though she breathes faster.

"I do it with pleasure instead of pain. I control my partners with orgasms. When and where they have them or how many."

She blows out a breath that fans over my face.

"I don't—"

"I want to try it," she interrupts, and I search her eyes for the truth. If she really wants it or is simply confused.

She's gone through a lot lately, and this isn't something to jump into.

She has to trust me. To really want this.

But she's biting her lip, blinking, *and* fidgeting with her hair. None of that's making me feel particularly comfortable with her interest in the lifestyle. A lot of people think they want to do it but don't take it seriously—like her fuckwit husband and his idea for an "open relationship"—and when that happens, people get hurt. At best, emotionally. At worst, physically.

Yet, I am nothing if not a fucking shithead like the rest of the male human species because the idea of her submitting to me makes my dick throb and my mouth literally water.

"You want to try it?"

Her sass breaks through the nerves. "Do I have to say, like, *yes, sir* and *no, sir?*"

There is no other person who can make me smile and laugh like she does. "No, but I would ask you to do things."

"Like what?"

"Things to make me happy."

"For example...?"

"Insistent little thing." I tweak her nose. "I might tell you to wear certain clothing or run different errands. To not touch yourself or *to* touch yourself." I let my hands drift from the back of her head down her spine, scrunching up her dress. I could easily tie her up with it. Blindfold her. "Whatever I want. Whenever I want it."

"That sounds..." Color rises high in her cheeks. "...intense."

Something hammers outside, but in here with Nicole, I feel nothing but peace and calm. I stroke the side of her head, sifting the sleek strands of her hair between my fingers. "Of course, there are rules. Certain lines won't be crossed, which would be discussed beforehand."

"It's ironic, isn't it? How all of this is supposed to set us free, but it's full of rules?"

"Rules keep you safe." *Keep me safe.*

Already, I fear I'm too far gone over this girl. Any more, and I'll lose that last piece of my heart that isn't broken. And maybe I should think that over for myself.

I stand and turn away from her to shake out my limbs, tension filling my muscles, my heart beating faster, but I feel Nicole behind me. Her hand on my back. Her cheek near my shoulder. And it takes everything in me not to pull her into my arms, wrap her up, and keep her there.

"I know you're trying things, figuring out what you want, but—" I gesture between us "—I'm not sure this is a good idea."

She sweeps her fingers over my ribs, the tattoo she admired with the writing that matches her own, as she comes to stand in front of me, fisting my T-shirt. "Please, Ian. I want to know what it's like. I want to feel it again, how you made me feel in your shop."

When I don't immediately answer, she tugs at her hair, features screwed up like she's in pain. "I'm constantly thinking —overthinking—and worrying, and I don't want to be like that anymore. I walked into Stone Ink on Tuesday and..." She holds her arm up to show off her tattoo, the wrinkles on her face smoothing, blue eyes glowing. "I made this decision, and it felt so good to follow my gut. And you, you... God, I don't know if I've ever..." She drops her arm, and her throat bobs on a swallow. The truth wrapped around each of her words and the glassiness of her eyes is a punch in the solar plexus. "You made me feel better than I ever have, and I didn't have to think about it. I didn't have to make any decisions. I wasn't worrying. I was in the moment with you."

When she lifts her shoulder in an embarrassed shrug, it breaks my heart. I won't say no to her. I can't. Not when I can recall the taste of her on my tongue, feel the phantom wetness on my fingers. Let alone knowing how she feels right now is how I feel. How I always want her to feel. Confident and free.

"Listen," I start, dragging my hands over my head and neck before taking a deep breath to steady myself. "If you really, truly want to do this, you need to be completely honest with me and with yourself. If you want to fuck around and get back at your husband..." The thought makes my jaw clench, and it takes me a bit to continue. "That's whatever, but if you want to be an actual submissive with me, it's different. We need to have different kinds of conversations, and you have to be sure."

"I'm sure," she says almost immediately.

"Really?" Because I sure as hell am not.

I don't know how the fuck I'll make it out of whatever this arrangement is without losing my goddamn mind over her.

To say nothing of how my heart beats more erratically the longer we're trapped together.

"I'm sure," she says and stands on her toes to kiss me.

Right as the refrigerator door swings open to reveal Dante with safety goggles, drill in hand, and a red bandanna tied across his forehead like the fucking Karate Kid. Nicole leaps away from me, and Eloise throws herself at us. "I am so, *so* sorry! I knew the lock was busted, but I never thought I'd have lots of people coming and going in it. I'm due for an inspection soon, and I was going to get it fixed before then, but I guess I'm getting a whole new walk-in. Good lord, the money I don't have." She elbows Nicole. "Small business problems, am I right?" Then she hugs me. "You're my hero."

I stiffly pat her back. "I didn't do anything."

Dante waves his hand. "Yeah, he didn't do anything. I did."

Eloise jumps at Dante, hugging him while my sister watches all this with a smug smirk. I point my index finger at Taryn, ready to get the hell out of here. "I owe you and your boyfriend a dinner."

"Thanks, man," Dante says, tossing me a thumbs-up as he tries to wiggle out of Eloise's grip.

"Let's go, Nicole. Get some fresh air." I motion for her to exit ahead of me, and we burst out onto the sidewalk on Aster Street.

She tilts her head back, breathing deeply for a minute before turning her attention to me. "I'm glad it was you I was stuck with. I'm not sure I would have made it with anyone else."

I shake my head, stuffing my hands in my pockets so I don't touch her. "You're stronger than you think you are."

She considers that for a bit then crosses her arms, toying with her necklace. "Strong enough to..." She darts her gaze around, making sure no one can hear when she says, "Be your submissive?"

"As long as you're honest with yourself and trust me completely, then yeah." The problem is, I'm not sure she can do that. Nicole is sweet and soft-spoken, a people pleaser. As a submissive, she would be pleasing me but only because *she* wants that, and I don't think she has any idea what she wants right now.

With a sigh, I check the time. I hate to leave this conversation, but I have an appointment coming up, and she needs to really think about her decision. "Text me your final answer tomorrow. Yes or no."

She backs up toward Chapter and Verse, a playful curl to her mouth that lands a direct hit on my heart. "Yes, sir."

And I know I'm in for it with this girl.

Chapter 11
Nicole

It took hours to come down from the panic and exhilaration of being trapped in a walk-in refrigerator with Ian. At first, I couldn't feel anything but straight-up fear. I couldn't stop the flashbacks of being locked in that steamer trunk as a child, that cramped, tiny space. My fingers had started tingling, my legs like jelly, but then Ian took my hands and sat me down, quickly and efficiently pulling me out of the spiral of panic until all I could see and think about was him.

He calmed me. Comforted me. Told me he is a Dominant.

And suddenly, my world expanded to three times its size. No wonder why he was able to talk to me about ENM and was so open about...everything. The man is *experienced*.

More than I ever could have imagined.

After I got home last night and had an awkward conversation with Bryce about our day—because, no, it's still not "normal"—I opened my laptop to do more research about what exactly a Dom/sub relationship entailed. Of course, I had the stereotype in my head, and there was almost too much information out there for me to input, but still... I want to try it.

I want to learn anything and everything I can about Ian. *Do* anything and everything that might bring me to that same place he took me to in his shop, where he gave me a whole universe of pleasure.

After a night's sleep, I *know* I want it all.

While Bryce finishes packing up for his annual summer trip, I type out a text to Ian. It takes me multiple tries to get the wording exactly right. I don't want to come off immature or flippant, so I settle on something casual and to the point. I hope.

> I've thought about it, and my answer is still yes.

Plucking up every ounce of courage I have in my entire body, I lay it all out there.

> I want you.

"What are you doing?"

I jolt, nearly flinging my cell phone across the room at my husband's voice, his backpack looped over his shoulders and his suitcase at his side. I press my hand to my chest. "You scared me."

He leans his elbows on the kitchen table next to where I'm drinking my coffee, trying to see my cell phone screen. "Who are you talking to?"

"A friend."

When he tries to snatch my phone out of my hand, I hold it against my chest. "What are you doing?"

He shrugs. "You're so engrossed. Got me curious."

Curious? Yeah, right. We agreed we didn't need to tell each

other anything about what we were doing. "You weren't ever interested in who I texted before. You can't start now."

It doesn't take a PhD in human behavior to see he's jealous, but that's too damn bad. He asked for this.

"Nicole, come on. Don't be like that."

Previously, I would have left this alone, let the ripples settle, but not anymore. I scoot away from the table and dump the dregs of my coffee down the drain before putting the cup in the dishwasher and turning to him. "I'm not the one upset. You are. Because you suddenly want to see who I'm texting. I'm not asking you who you're texting or what you're doing, and it seems to be the only thing that has changed is the definition of our relationship. When it was closed, you didn't care who I talked to, but now it's open and you suddenly want to know. Why? This is what you asked for. It's what you wanted."

"Yeah, but..." He huffs and combs his fingers through his hair. "I'm about to leave, and I guess I'm... I don't know. I'm going to miss you, but you're acting like you aren't going to miss me. So, yeah, I guess I am a little jealous."

I fold my arms over my chest, not sure if I believe him. "You're going to miss me?"

"Of course." He curves his hands over my shoulders, thumbs stroking over the slope of my neck. "I always miss you."

I close my eyes, shaking my head, unable to understand what he wants. For a long time, I thought I knew him, but I don't anymore. I don't get him. I don't get what he wants. "You confuse me."

"What's so confusing?"

I duck out of his hold. "Everything. If you miss me, then how can you say you want to experiment and allow other people into our relationship?"

"Because what I feel for you hasn't changed."

That's funny, because in the last few weeks, I feel like

everything has changed, especially what I feel for him. It's amazing how much you can pull away from a person in such a short amount of time.

He must read it on my face because he plants his hand on the counter like he suddenly can't hold himself up. "Have your feelings for me changed?"

I lift my shoulder and tell him the truth. "Yes, Bryce, and that's what I don't understand. How you can say you're interested in seeing other women but still feel the same about me, because I'm not able to separate physical and emotional relationships like that."

"You don't love me?" he asks with these huge puppy-dog eyes, and I almost laugh. Like he is the victim in all of this. He is the one who asked for exactly what he's getting, and yet he can somehow still make me feel guilty. Like it's all my fault.

I swipe my hand over my face. "I don't know, Bryce. I love you as a person. I don't want to hurt you. I want what's best for you, but I have to be honest that it hurt to hear I'm not fulfilling what you need. It made a pretty big dent in my self-esteem."

"I'm sorry," he says, but he's only trying to smooth the waters. There is no real conviction behind the sentiment.

And quite frankly, I am ready for him to leave. I motion toward the time on the microwave. "You've got to go, or you'll be late."

He checks his own watch then brings his eyes back to mine. "I guess...I'll see you later?" When I nod, he leans forward to place a kiss on my cheek. "I'll text you when I land."

"Have a safe flight."

"Thanks," he mumbles, tossing one more glance toward my cell phone. Then he's off, out the door, gone for a month. To do who knows what.

By the time I have a handle on my frustration and clean out the coffeepot, I receive a response to my texts.

IAN

Then it seems we have to have some
conversations. When are you available?

Tonight after I close up. Or tomorrow
morning. Whenever is good for you.

IAN

First things first, there will be times when
what we do will be good for me and what I
want, but if I ask you, I want an answer. Not
deference back to me.

I smile to myself at the irony. A man who is supposed to be dominant, *my* Dominant, is telling me that I need to speak up for myself. I need to take charge. What a revelation.

I would prefer tonight. I'm feeling a bit
anxious about everything, and I think the
sooner, the better.

IAN

Okay. Tonight.

But it can't be around here. I don't want
people to know or see us together.

IAN

We can go somewhere private.

Not your place and not mine either.

IAN

I like that you're setting boundaries. Good
for you.

Warmth infuses me.

Thank you.

IAN

I'll drop you a pin later. Meet me at 9?

Sophie Andrews

Sounds good.

To say the day was a slog would be an understatement. I was so busy, fielding calls from a publishing house about working with a debut author—fantastic—and the university about putting up a table at their volunteer fair—great but more work for me—and listening to one of the high school workers have a breakdown over a fight with her boyfriend, I almost forgot about my meeting with Ian.

Almost.

Around six, I received a text with a pin to a bar about thirty minutes away, off Route 3, and from that point on, I had trouble concentrating on anything other than him and our forthcoming conversation. I barely ate half of the turkey sandwich I'd packed for myself as I ordered more stock then tried to take my mind off everything by reorganizing some shelves, making room for my July Fourth display, where I plan to highlight nonfiction about the American Revolution and the battle of Gettysburg.

My workers always tease me about finding a hobby so I don't work so much, but my hobby is reading. My passion is books. This shop has been my home for the better part of my life, and I don't mind ten- and twelve-hour days. In fact, I think I prefer them, especially now. In the last few years since I'd taken over from my aunt, I'd started staying from open to close. Bryce never complained about it or asked me to come home early, which, looking back, might have been a sign that maybe we were a little too comfortable with the status quo. Now that he's gone for a month and I have time to discover what I want for myself and my life, what is the point of being at home?

So, I stay until closing and flip the sign, lock up, then check myself out in the bathroom. I tie my hair up in a ponytail because the wet-noodle look that's going on from the humidity isn't cutting it, and I swipe on some lip gloss. I don't generally

88

wear a lot of makeup because I never had much interest, but also, the older I get, the less I care. Yet, here I am, caring about what I look like.

I pinch my cheeks to bring some color to them and attempt to pull out a wayward eyebrow hair before smoothing my shirt. I chose a loose skirt and top this morning, but they're both creased from all the sitting I did today, and I can only hope Ian doesn't notice.

Then I roll my eyes at myself because he isn't the type to care about wrinkled clothes. The guy wears jeans and T-shirts every single day. But my nerves have gotten the better of me— my imagination and worry spinning out of control—and I shake my hands out as I exit the back, reminding myself to relax. Stay calm.

I'm simply meeting my friend.

My friend Ian, whom I've agreed to enter into a kink relationship with.

Who is the other man in my marriage.

Oh my god.

What am I doing?

I pull up to the roadside biker bar and contemplate turning right around, too far out of my element with all of this, but before I can, someone knocks on my window. I spin my focus to find Ian bent down, face close to my window when he waves. And suddenly, nothing else matters.

Not when he tips his head for me to step out of my car or when I put my hand in his waiting one, and especially not when he wraps his thick arms around me, hugging me tightly as if he knows I need it. His breath ghosts over my ear when he speaks in a hushed tone. "Just because you said you want to do this doesn't mean you can't back out at any time. Remember, no is a complete sentence. We only do this because you say so, okay?"

When I nod, he leans back and places the knuckle of his index finger below my chin, tilting my head up to meet his gaze under the neon light of the bar sign. "Say you understand."

"I understand."

"Your consent can be revoked at any time without any repercussions or hard feelings."

"My consent can be revoked at any time without any repercussions or hard feelings."

"Good girl." He places a single kiss on my forehead then takes my hand to lead me into the bar.

It's dark, smoke-filled, and everything I'd assume a biker bar to be, with big, beefy guys seated on stools, wearing leather cuts and hair past their shoulders. A few play pool while women look on. A television in the corner plays some baseball game, while an Ozzy Osbourne tune fills in the background. No one bats an eye at Ian and me. They don't recognize us, nor I them.

"I assume you've been here before," I guess when I sit next to Ian at the bar.

"Once or twice."

The bartender sidles up to us as I place my forearms on the bar, only to immediately remove them from the sticky top. I don't drink beer, and seeing as that's all they have, I look to Ian, who orders us each a Miller. Once they're set down in front of us, I hesitate. "You don't have to drink it," Ian tells me. "I ordered so we don't waste his time while we're here talking."

I nod but try a sip anyway. I don't hate it, but I don't like it either. Ian notices and places his hand on my thigh, an inch above my knee, and squeezes. "I'll get you a water."

He orders me a water and scoops a bucket of peanuts from a container in the corner, and I have to laugh as he shucks them, tossing them into his mouth. He fits in with this crowd, while I stick out like a sore thumb in my white peasant top and purple skirt.

"I feel kind of silly being here, dressed the way I am," I confess, and Ian shrugs.

"You look cute."

I bite back a smile, and he wraps his foot around the leg of my stool, yanking it closer to his. I let out a yip of surprise, clinging to his bicep, but he merely grunts a barely audible, "That's better." Then he offers me a peanut he's freed from a shell. "So, now that no one can overhear us, you're welcome to tell me why you're afraid of people seeing us together."

I swallow the peanut and accept another from him, pressing it between my thumb and index finger. "Oh, um... I...I have a hard time being the center of attention. I don't like it."

"Yeah, but no one would know what you're doing or what *we're* doing."

"Just in case. I don't want anyone to get the wrong impression of us if they see us together."

"You know we've been together in public before, right? We've talked to each other and sat next to each other. Ran that cleanup together. Been stuck in a refrigerator together."

That pulls a laugh out of me. "Yeah, but that was different. We weren't *together*."

He hums a sound I can't interpret as his eyes take a slow journey over my face, studying every part of me like the Cliffs of Moher or Victoria Falls. Like I'm something really special to look at and he's trying to remember every moment.

Eventually, he offers me another peanut. "I'm glad you said that, because while we do this, there is no one else. I know that you've agreed to an open relationship with—" He stops himself, angling his face away from me as he cracks a shell. "You might be in an open marriage, but this..." He turns to me once again, voicing a warning. "Is not open. I don't share. If that's not what you want, I won't be offended, but we won't go any further. That is my hard limit."

I easily agree. I don't like the idea of him being with anyone outside of me either. "Yes, okay."

"What are your limits? Besides not being seen together."

"Bryce and I—"

Ian's eyes squint, his shoulders hiking up as if his body is prepared to take a hit, and I briefly wonder why he would be anxious. Insecure, almost. He's never anything but confident.

Except for this one fleeting moment that is already gone by the time I finish my sentence.

"Agreed that we'd take the summer to figure out what we want. So this," I say, vaguely motioning between Ian and me, "would only be until he returns from his work trip."

Ian slants his head toward me. "He's away?"

I swallow the sudden lump in my throat. "For a month."

"A month," he repeats. The shell of a peanut crunches between his fingers, disintegrating into dust, and I'm not sure whether it's a good or bad thing we only have a few weeks together.

"So, besides the whole...keeping it secret thing, there is also a time limit."

He doesn't answer for a long time as he shucks three more peanuts, and I watch as the tension slowly drains from his spine, his shoulders lower, and his chest expands on a deep breath. "Okay. If those are your terms, I accept."

I smile and lean my elbow on the table, immediately remembering why I didn't have it there in the first place and brush it off. His mouth ticks up at my squeamishness. Then he hits me with a question I assumed he'd ask. "Now that we have that out of the way. What do you want to do? What would you like to try with me?"

I let my attention drift around the bar as I contemplate my answer. "I'm not really sure. I was, well, I did some research last night and—"

"I like that about you," he cuts in, and my previously kicked-around ego inflates so much I feel like I might float away if not for his hand on my thigh.

"You are so naturally curious about everything. I really like that." He holds a peanut out to me, and with my renewed sense of self, I attempt a bold move and incline my head, taking the nut from between his fingers with my teeth. His eyes spark, nostrils flare, gaze zeroing in on my mouth as I chew, swallow, and lick my lips. He arches a brow, pleased.

"I was doing research, but I got overwhelmed by all the information. I feel like I don't actually know what I want. Not until it comes up, you know?"

He offers me another peanut that I take from him with my mouth, this time closing my lips around his fingers. While I chew, he brings his fingers to his mouth, licking them, and if the lights were on in this place, my skin would be the color of a tomato.

"Let's start off simple, then," he suggests. "We'll ease into it, so you'll know if and when you're ready for more."

I lick my lips, salt lingering on my tongue. "What's starting off simple?"

"Letting me lead you in ways that have nothing to do with sex."

"Like what?"

"Like you drinking that entire glass of water before we leave."

I immediately pick it up to take a few sips.

He pushes the basket of shelled peanuts out of the way and places his arm along the back of my stool as he takes a gulp of his beer. "Tell me about your day."

I fill him in on all that I did, and he shows sincere interest, asking questions about events I have coming up, and how I decide on what stock to order. The whole time, he watches as I drink my water like some people watch the stock market. As if my drinking this water is of great value. So I ask him about it. "Why do you care about me drinking this water?"

"I know how hard you work." He plucks at the drawstring of my top, releasing the bow I had tied, allowing the cotton to gape open, displaying the shadow of my cleavage. "I also know you don't take very many breaks. You work from open to close most days and probably don't drink as much water as you should. I'd even bet some days you work through lunch."

When I don't argue, he invades my space, his eyes practically black in the dim light. "No more, Nicole. You need to take care of yourself, and I will require proof. Every day. You need to text me pictures to show me you're drinking water and eating."

"Okay." My voice cracks at his stern tone, so I try again. "I will."

"And if you can do that, then maybe we'll move on to the fun. But if you don't, we won't play."

"Yes, sir."

He smiles beneath his beard, his big and tattooed hand hiding it, but I catch it before he wipes it away, and I vow to call him sir as often as it takes to make him smile full-out.

Which is three more times in the hour we sit, talking about nothing in particular: how Aunt Sue is doing in Maine and why Juniper is driving him up a wall lately with her boyfriend and constantly arguing about how she needs to move out of Ian's apartment.

When we finally leave, Ian guides me through the dimly lit parking lot to my car. The night air is cool and refreshing after being in the smoky bar, and the neon sign casts a faint glow on his face, highlighting the wave in his hair, the strands a mix of black and gray, tucked behind his ears. I knot my fingers together. "So, what now?"

"Now," he says, caging me in with his hands on either side of my shoulders, "we take this one step at a time."

For a minute, all we do is stare at each other, and I use the time to study him closely, the individual bristles in his beard, the wrinkles around his eyes, the slight bump on his nose, the uneven way he's breathing. It's not until I feel him tremble as he rests his forehead against mine that I appreciate he might feel as out of his element as I do. Which is strange because he is the one who's done this before.

He curls his fingers around my neck, keeping me in place, as if he's afraid I might leave.

Even if I could, I wouldn't.

His breath is warm on my face, and underneath that addictive scent of cloves that always follows him around, I catch a faint smell of beer and peanuts. It's strangely comforting.

"You're in control here, Nicole."

And I realize I've misunderstood the idea of a Dom/sub relationship this whole time. He might be the one in charge, but only because I've given him that power. Nothing happens without my say-so. His power can only remain in balance if we both understand that is exactly what it is—a balance.

For possibly the first time in my life, I have the ability to shift it all. It is as empowering as it is scary. To know this man, whom I've always thought of as formidable, can be halted with one single word from me.

One of his hands moves up to the back of my head while the other dips down, banding around my waist. He brushes his lips over mine once, twice before finally settling against them. His tongue sweeps out, seeking entrance, and I grant it willingly as I wrap my arms around his neck. There is not one inch of space between us, my chest and stomach against his, all his hard-packed muscle like a wall against my breasts. Each of my breaths is torture, my nipples tightening, blood thickening as it pools between my legs. When he presses me against my car, I can feel the hard length of him along my hip, sending waves of heat through my body.

But as quickly as the kiss started, it ends. Ian pulls away, his breath coming in ragged pants as he regains control. Me? I'm still somewhere in the atmosphere and murmur a drunken, "Wow."

He chuckles, low and deliciously rumbly, brushing his thumb against my cheek. "Yeah. Wow." He clears his throat then steps away from me. "Now, get in your car and drive safely home. Text me when you arrive."

"I will."

He leans down to drop a quick kiss to my head, opening the door for me. I sit behind the wheel as he shuts it, waiting while I start it up and pull out of the parking space. In the rearview mirror, I see him watching me until I'm out of sight.

The drive home is a blur, my mind consumed with thoughts of Ian, but as soon as I park, I text him, wanting to please him. Do as he asks.

I'm home.

His response is almost immediate.

IAN

Good. Now get some sleep. Sweet dreams, Nicole.

I'm not so sure they'll be sweet, but I'm sure I'll dream.

Chapter 12
Ian

My shotgun apartment is narrow but deep, with almost no exterior light, save for the big loft-style windows in the combination of a living room and dining room that overlooks Aster Street in the front, and the two windows in the kitchen and my bedroom that face the back parking lot and alley. The bathroom and June's bedroom unfortunately don't have any natural light, a complaint I hear on a near-daily basis from her.

We've been living here for the last few years, since I sold my house to buy the property of Stone Ink and the top apartment outright. Before that, I was renting, struggling to afford my house's mortgage and the lease on the building, but with some good luck and a hell of a lot of work, I've turned a pretty lucrative corner. I even have a nice little retirement fund going, though I don't plan on quitting anytime soon.

Especially because I'm at the top of my game, professionally and personally. At least, that's what it's felt like for the past week.

Every morning, I wake up, and I'm met with a text from

Nicole. Usually a short greeting or smiling-face emoji. I return the message immediately because there is nothing I enjoy more than making her happy. And she clearly enjoys making *me* happy since she easily and continually follows my directions. Whether it's to have a good breakfast or take a five-minute rest during her workday, she does, proving it with either a photo or deliberately walking by Stone Ink's window, catching my attention to show me her takeout sushi for lunch or snack from Eloise.

My girl *loves* to earn my praise in return, and it is no different this morning.

After I texted her to drink a glass of water, she responded with a video of her drinking it while standing at her kitchen sink in the hottest little pajama set I've ever seen, and it's not even showing anything much. It's just that it looks soft, and she obviously doesn't have a bra on underneath. It's Nicole at her most comfortable, which is when she's at her sexiest. Messy bun and no makeup. Hair sleep-mussed and polka dots all over her pajamas.

Adorable.

Utterly fuckable.

Which makes me even more impatient to get my hands on her.

She's been so good all week that I have to reward her.

> You think you feel ready to take the next step?

NICOLE

> With you? Yes.

NICOLE

> Yes, please.

> Since you asked so nicely...

Right Next Door

Her response is almost immediate, and I can practically hear her voice in my head.

I love that little bit of sass. Keeps me on my toes.

I also love that she is trusting me to help her explore her desires. I am well aware that this is not some insignificant fling for her. This is an opportunity for her to reclaim her power and figure out who she is and what she wants.

This also isn't some random hookup for me either. If I wanted that, it wouldn't be hard to find, but unfortunately for me, my heart is set on the bookshop girl next door. I guess, if I'm honest, it has been for a long time, but I haven't been able to act on it.

Until now.

While it might not be everything, it's as close as I can get, and I know better than to throw away a good thing when I have it.

Hours later, I meet Nicole at the back door of her bookstore and motion for her to follow me. No one is around to see us, but still, I'm careful before I clasp her hand, leading her upstairs to my apartment.

"June's out for the day," I tell Nicole, and as soon as the door is closed, I push her up against the wall, my mouth on hers, unable to wait any longer. I can be a very patient man, but it's been too long since I've been able to touch her like I've wanted to. My hand on her leg, fingers tangled in her hair, her bottom lip trapped between my teeth.

I do it all, give in to what I've fantasized about all week. A reminder of how sweet she is, how good she feels under my hands, how pliant her mouth is under mine. She whimpers into the kiss, pressing closer, her hands in my hair, and I groan in satisfaction, loving how eager she is. With a few more nips to her lips and a quick taste of her throat, I step back, my gaze trailing over her.

Her dress is long with flowers all over, showing more skin than she usually does with thin straps and a lower neckline, displaying the top curve of her breasts and the valley of her cleavage. She is beautiful.

"This is different from what you usually wear," I say, my voice lower than I mean it to sound, fingers curling into the soft material at her hips.

"You notice what I usually wear?" She tries not to appear too delighted. It doesn't work.

I'm glad of it.

"You walk past our window every day. I'd have to be dead not to notice you."

Her cheeks flush a fetching pink. "I wanted to look pretty for you."

I brush my thumb over her cheekbone and jaw. "You always look pretty."

"I look plain," she argues, as if she really believes it.

And doesn't she know?

Doesn't she know that her mouth is so expressive, anyone can tell how she's feeling by simply watching her smile. It's always there, but if a person looked close enough, they would be able to tell if it's forced by the rise of her top lip. When she's naturally laughing or smiling, it's high and shows off all her teeth, even some of her gums. Her fake smile is one where her top lip is straight across.

It doesn't matter what she wears or how she does her hair. One glance at me, one mere hint of her real smile, and I'm done for.

I'd do anything to make her happy. *Keep* her happy.

To say nothing of making sure she never cries. A true tragedy is watching those baby blues fill up with water, clumping her lashes together.

That morning in Sweet Cheeks will stick with me forever.

The way her chin trembled and the tip of her nose pinked.

Being able to comfort her that day will remain one of the greatest privileges of my lifetime.

I drag the pad of my thumb over her lower lip, tugging the corner out from her teeth, rubbing back and forth across it. "I don't want you to change anything about yourself, unless you're doing it for you. Don't do it for any other reason besides it's what you want. Don't think about what I want or what...he wants." I practically spit those two words out, hating the thought of her husband. "You do what you want, got it?"

When she nods, I do too, squeezing her chin between my fingers. "Good girl. Now, we're going to ease into this, all right? Start off easy with a little bit of play. If you don't like it, let me know, and we won't do it. You can call it off at any time."

I take her hand and lead her through my apartment, too quick for her to study the living room or kitchen. I guide her into the bathroom and hit the light, illuminating the mostly nondescript room, save for all the bottles of makeup June leaves littered around. "Lift up your dress and put your hands on the counter."

She obeys, hiking the thin material up to settle over her hips and leaning forward with her hands on the counter, staring at the mirror in front of her. Next to her, I unplug a small egg-shaped vibrator that I had lying on the towel after I washed and charged it.

"This was one of my errands this morning." I place my hand on the back of her upper thigh, slowly gliding it up and down. "It's a remote-controlled vibrator."

She doesn't move an inch. I'm not even sure she breathes, so I remind her to and then ask, "Did you ever use one before?" When she shakes her head, I slide my hand up over the globe of her ass, gripping it tightly, discovering that I actually do like her answer, if the tightening in my chest is any indication. I like that she hasn't experienced this, so I can be the first to do it with her. Slipping my fingers beneath her underwear, I find her slit, swallowing the triumphant growl building in my throat. "So wet for me already." She inhales sharply when I trace the shape of her with my fingertips, barely touching, merely re-familiarizing myself with her. "Have you been thinking about what we did downstairs? How I made you come? You want to do that again?"

She nods, her breath coming in short gasps.

"Words, Nicole. You need to learn to use them. You won't get what you want without them. Understand?"

"Yes," she says, the single syllable shaky.

"Yes what?"

"Yes, sir," she says quietly, her eyes meeting mine in the mirror, not such a brat anymore.

I push my fingers into her, flicking them in a way that draws a long sigh out of her, making my dick hard. I'm turned on by all of her, but especially her sounds. Her breathy sighs and needy pants. I look forward to each one I can draw out of her.

With a click, the vibrator comes to life, and I press it against her collarbone so she becomes accustomed to the feel of it. "There are fifteen settings, and I can control it from my phone."

I skate it over the slope of her chest, leaving it on one of her nipples for a few seconds before moving it to the other until they're both hard, pointing through the fabric of her dress.

"Please," she breathes, her eyes locked on mine in the mirror.

"Please, what?"

"Please touch me with it."

I oblige, sinking it below her underwear and holding it to her clit as my other hand works her, my fingers still stroking her inside, steady and insistent. Her skin prickles, and she reflexively widens her stance, swiveling her hips. She moans and arches her back, but I pull away from her, not wanting to give in just yet.

When she lets out a low whine, I shake my head. "You're going to have to learn you only get to orgasm when I allow it."

I push the pulsing vibrator inside her, and she gasps. I keep it on a low setting, a constant thrum, but not enough to put her over the edge. Then I shift behind her, making sure her underwear is in place, with the small loop to retrieve the toy tucked away. I straighten her up and lower the skirt of her dress.

"You're going to go back to work, and so will I, but I'm going to control when and how often the vibrator turns on."

She whimpers, and it makes my dick hard. Loving how much she wants this.

"But," I start, meeting her eyes in the reflection in the mirror as I leave an openmouthed kiss on the side of her neck that has her going limp in my arms, "you cannot come until I tell you to." I straighten her up once again and set my hands on either side of her waist, squeezing so I have her full attention. "Do you understand? You cannot orgasm."

She nods, though I'm not sure she really heard me with her eyes unfocused.

"And no touching yourself," I add for good measure.

"H-how..." She clears her throat and seems to recognize the seriousness of the situation. "How will you know if I do or don't?"

I answer with a warning nip of her earlobe. "I'll know if you do."

Then I turn off the vibrator and physically circle her, pushing her to go with a tap to her ass. "Back to work, beautiful."

I watch as she walks away, a slight stagger to her step, and I can't help but smile.

Chapter 13
Nicole

As torturously slow as the morning was, the afternoon is worse.

So, so much worse.

As soon as I get back to Chapter and Verse, I sit behind the counter waiting for Ian to power on the vibrator, convinced it will start soon. Five minutes pass. Ten, twenty, and then half an hour melts into a whole hour that I lose to anticipation.

It's killing me. All the waiting and wanting and desperation.

So with a deep breath, I try my best to ignore the egg inside me and work.

The first buzz hits while I'm checking out a little old couple here for their monthly read from the mystery book club. I very nearly crumple to the floor, and when I yelp in surprise, the only excuse I can come up with is a bug. I swat around my head like a maniac until they skedaddle with their bag, leaving me to fall into the counter as I writhe in the pleasure being given to me by two inches of silicone and a man on the other side of the brick wall.

I feel like a flame has been lit inside me, and I'm teeming with so much heat and energy, I think I could dig through that wall if I tried hard enough. Only so I could beg him to relieve me.

Please.

Make me come.

Just as I start to sweat and sigh, it shuts off, and as welcome as the reprieve is, the empty feeling of being so close to the edge only to be yanked back unexpectedly isn't very nice.

But that's how it goes.

On and off.

For hours.

While I stock books.

While I'm in the middle of a phone conversation with a customer.

And, most mortifyingly, while I'm receiving a delivery. The moan I inadvertently release makes the guy's gaze drift over me in a gross way, although I can't find it in me to care at the moment. Not when I have to grab hold of the wall to keep myself steady. As soon as I have the boxes piled up and the back door locked once again, I hightail it to the bathroom.

Completely and utterly unable to take it anymore.

Everything tingles. My skin burns. Even my scalp feels like it's on fire.

I've never felt anything like this clawing need before. It even makes it hard to breathe.

I'm panting, practically heaving as I hike up my dress, fumbling with the material, everything made more difficult with my trembling fingers. I don't bother pushing my underwear down, only stuff my hand inside, slipping my fingers over my slit.

I'm soaked, and everything feels swollen and heavy. I lean my other forearm on the wall, resting my forehead on it as I circle my clit with my fingertips. I bite back a groan as the vibrator goes up another notch, and all it takes is two more swipes of my fingers to come.

Shaking from head to toe, I can't hold back my moans anymore, riding high, flying over the edge Ian kept pulling me back from all day. It's both immensely satisfying and still not enough.

Not with the vibrator hitting a higher speed yet again.

It's like he knows.

I groan, my hand slipping off the tiled wall, and I drop my skirt as I stumble to the door.

That's it. I have to call it.

This game is too much.

Intent on running next door to Ian, I open the door to find him in front of me.

Here.

In my shop.

His cell phone in his hand and his eyebrows narrowed over his dark brown eyes.

"Hello, baby," he murmurs low and slow, almost like he expected to find me here. Like he planned this all along.

"H-hi." I swallow thickly, my forehead sweaty, the cotton of my dress sticking between my legs. I don't know if I've ever been more uncomfortable in my life.

He ticks his head to the side, his voice giving nothing away. "You okay?"

I nod. "Yep. Yes. Mm-hmm."

He steps closer to me, so close I can feel his breath on my cheek and count the individual strands of gray in his beard. He studies me for a long time while the egg still vibrates inside me like a godforsaken torture device, and he merely stands there as if reading a menu, deciding what to eat. He drags his thumb and forefinger over his mustache and down to his beard like he has all the time in the world. Again and again, he brushes over his facial hair as I slowly melt into a human puddle at his feet.

Finally, after three centuries, he presses something on his phone, and everything in my body quiets.

Except for my blood.

And the tension.

Or the still-rising heat.

But other than that, I'm *totally* calm.

"C-can I help you with anything today?" I aim for a smile, but it feels sideways. *I* feel sideways. "Find a book you might like?"

His eyes light with something I can't quite comprehend as he backs me into the bathroom, pivoting me so I'm trapped between him and the door as he locks it. "I specifically told you not to come, didn't I?" When I nod, he shakes his head, voice stern. "Words, Nicole."

I clear my throat and answer, "Yes, you did tell me that."

"And I told you not to touch yourself, right?"

"Right."

My pulse hammers in my throat as he lowers his hand from beside my shoulder to graze the side of my breast. He wraps his fingers around my wrist.

I think I might die.

"But you did, didn't you? You touched yourself. You orgasmed when I specifically said you couldn't."

I start to shake my head, but he cocks an eyebrow in a challenge, and I sag. He glowers at me, tsking a few times like I'm bad.

I'm *never* bad.

I'm always good.

I always make the right decisions.

But this, doing what I'm not supposed to, feels good. More

than this moment, it feels right to make the decisions I want as opposed to what I think I'm supposed to do.

The only expectations I want to meet anymore are the ones Ian sets for me.

The ones that I know will bring the most delicious form of sin when I don't.

He's so stern, my nipples harden to painful peaks. The tiny hairs on the back of my neck stand on end. And I think I finally understand what people mean when they say they're scared of him. *This* is the growly bear version of Ian Stone.

And I think I like it even more than the one I've known.

Especially when he lifts my hand up between us and quietly chides, "My naughty girl."

His naughty girl.

I'll be anything as long as I'm his.

"Did you come?" he asks, and I tell him the truth.

"Yes."

"Did you touch yourself?"

"Yes."

"Which fingers?"

Confused, I don't answer, so he glances down at my hand between us.

"Which ones did you use?"

When I press my index and middle fingers together, he draws them into his mouth, sucking firmly while holding my gaze. I nearly come again from the intensity of it. From the suction on my skin and the echo on my throbbing clit. I imagine his mouth there, and I instinctively know it would be good.

Better than anything I've ever experienced before.

I exhale a noisy breath, squeezing my thighs together, and as if he recognizes I'm almost there again, he pulls my fingers out of his mouth and settles my hand at my side. "You know what this means?" he asks, twirling a lock of my hair around his finger. "Next time we play, I'm going to make you suffer."

He grips my hair in his hand, holding my head in place to kiss me, his tongue invading my mouth, taking no prisoners. It's greedy and a touch rough, with his fingers tugging on my hair at the root. He yanks up my dress, but when I wrap my leg around his hip, he knocks it down and nips at my jaw. "No, baby," he says against my throat, "you don't get what you want right now."

He slips his hand into my underwear and removes the vibrator by the thin loop, all without touching me. I'm achy and need him to soothe it.

Curling my fingers into his T-shirt, I do what I originally intended and beg. "Please."

He merely kisses me again, this one softer and infinitely sweeter. "No."

"Ian," I whine. "I need you."

"I know." He steps away from me to wash the vibrator in the sink before drying it and slipping it into his pocket. Then he curls his arm around my waist, all but lifting me up. He holds me against his side, combing his fingers through my hair, pressing my face into his throat, where I smell the now-familiar scent of cloves from what I learned is his beard oil, making it soft enough to nuzzle.

I nuzzle against him like a cat, and he strokes the back of my head a few times. "This is your punishment," he murmurs, his chest rumbling under my palm. "You come when, where, and however many times I want. But *only* when *I* want. I'll give you more than you think you can handle and then give you more, but it's not up to you. It's up to me." He nudges my face up with his hand at my cheek. "So, next time I tell you to come or *not* to come, I expect you to do as you're told."

"Yes, sir," I say, unable to keep the smile from my face.

He whacks my butt. "Brat."

A moment later, he has the door unlocked and is leading the way out to the floor, where two of my younger workers have arrived for the evening shift. They both smile and wave, obviously having no idea that I was locked in the bathroom with Ian for the last ten minutes. While I head behind the register, he peruses the bookshelves leisurely, as if he didn't just edge me as punishment until I begged.

Mr. Darcy hops down from his perch and tentatively approaches Ian, who bends down, holding out his hand. After a few seconds, the long-haired ragdoll cat arches into Ian's palm. I catch myself smiling as Ian speaks to Darcy—what he says, I don't know, but whatever it is, Darcy seems to like it.

And I can't help but compare Bryce to Ian, who is so self-assured yet good-humored enough to have a full-on conversation with a cat. While Bryce never has the time or desire to come to the store, let alone pay attention to Darcy, who definitely feels some kind of way about him.

Bryce doesn't like cats, so Mr. Darcy has had to stay at the store overnight. He doesn't mind, but I do. I'd like Darcy to live at home with me, but it's a battle I gave up long ago since Bryce threw down the "you'd sacrifice my health" card with his allergies. So, Darcy stays here while I dutifully refill air purifiers at home for my cat-phobic husband.

The two men could not be more different. If not in personality, then certainly in physicality. Bryce has the look of an academic. Like he hasn't seen the sun in twelve years and dresses as if he's Indiana Jones—the classroom version. And Ian... Well, Ian looks like he could actually get himself out of the Temple of Doom.

"While you're here," I start, turning to retrieve a book from our special-order shelf and hold it out to him. "Jasper's book came in."

Ian accepts *The Glass Castle*. "Kid never stops reading."

Jasper was in last week, asking for recommendations on memoirs. It's rare Ian's eldest child and I speak, but if we do, it's always about books. "One thing we have in common."

"Give me something to read," Ian says, and I'm taken aback.

"You want a book?"

"Yeah. I want to read something you like." He gestures to my tattoo. "That book. I want to read that one."

"Really?"

"Of course." He straightens himself from where he was leaning against the counter. "I want to know what you love."

I bite into my lip to keep from grinning too broadly and head to our classics section to find it. When he has it in his hand, he examines the small hardback, part of the series I ordered with cute and colorful covers. The kinds of books that would look great on a shelf or coffee table, even if they remained unread. A tragedy, for sure, but still cute. This Austen is pale blue with rows of magenta flowers on the cover.

"*Sense and Sensibility*," he says with a nod, reaching for his wallet. "I'll take it."

He tries to pay for it, but I remind him that he gifted me my tattoo. So this is my repayment. He shakes his head, eyes narrowed, a silent message that *I* will pay for *this* one way or another as I slip his and Jasper's book into a small paper bag along with the little square ads I print myself, listing the upcoming events, including poetry night and Drag Queen Story Hour. When Ian points that one out, I wince. "Yeah, I got some complaints about that event. They want me to cancel."

"Are you going to?" he asks, brows drawn.

"No, but I'm nervous for the safety of the performers and our store."

"You're worried someone's going to fuck with the store?"

I shrug. I don't want to make a big deal out of it. *Don't feed the trolls*, as Aunt Sue always said. "A few comments have been left on the Facebook event. Overall, our customers love the idea. They're excited, but I'm worried about people who are not our customers, who aren't even involved...getting involved."

He makes a noise I can't interpret as he stares down at the little sheet like he's trying to incinerate it before meeting my gaze again. "Anything you need help with, I'm here."

Ian has constantly extended his hand when a person needed it, but for the first time, I'm not afraid to ask for it. I suppose I should finally give up the ghost on attempting to do everything myself and accept the help when it's offered.

"Thank you," I say, and he nods, looking toward the door.

"I've got to go. I have an appointment."

I always thought people winking were cheesy, but when Ian does it, it feels like a secret. Because he never winks with a smile. It's more like a promise.

And when he winks at me now, my panties are in danger of being incinerated. I'm left staring after him like a lovestruck Regency lady ready to swoon at any moment.

I almost do when he texts me a few hours later while I'm in bed with the latest Kristin Hannah. It's a photo of himself, angled so his naked lower torso and upper legs are in frame. He's wearing black boxer briefs with the book strategically placed in the middle, but even without seeing what I know is an impressive length, there's already too much to take in.

The thick muscle of his thighs, sprinkled with hair and tattoos, including a cobra coiling around his right leg. His stomach is bulky with muscle yet defined by lines. He's naturally tanned, as if he spends time outside without a shirt. Of course, there are more tattoos, including what appears to be a bust of one of those old-school pinup girls with a naval hat, and the words *Hello, Sailor* in script on ribbon bracketing her above and below. It's really cute and kind of on-brand for him.

But as a whole, he's hot. The muscles, the tattoos, the perfect amount of hair, he's quite literally mouthwatering.

And he's reading my book.

I hope you love it.

IAN

I'm sure I will.

IAN

But you know what I would love even more?

I think I already know yet ask anyway.

What?

IAN

A photo.

IAN

Show me what you're doing right now.

The same thing you are.

IAN

Show me.

I attempt to take a good picture, one that rivals his for sexiness, but with my plain cotton pajamas, I don't have much to work with. Even with my knee propped up and my shirt artfully rumpled to expose some skin of my stomach.

He responds to my photo immediately.

IAN

You know what I would be doing if I were there?

What?

IAN

Not letting you read.

IAN

That's for damn sure.

I think of how Bryce and I have slept next to each other in this bed every night, but I've never been as excited lying here as I am now. Because of a text. Although, I don't like the idea of Bryce in this space, even if it's virtual, so I shove him out of my mind and text Ian back.

What else?

IAN

You want to know what I would do if I were there with you right now? Put your hand in your shorts to touch yourself, and maybe I'll tell you. Send me another picture to show me you can follow directions.

I toss my book aside and do as he instructs, snapping a photo to send.

IAN

Tell me what your pussy feels like.

I've never sexted before, but I have no time to be self-conscious about it when I need to respond to him.

Wet.

IAN

Are you still sensitive from this afternoon?

Very.

IAN

Pet your pussy for me. Pretend it's my
fingers.

IAN

Circle your clit nice and easy.

IAN

Bet you're making those sweet little sounds
of yours, aren't you, baby?

I am, yeah. I can't help it. I need to come. But of course, he
knows.

IAN

Now stop.

IAN

Hand out of your shorts and take a picture to
show me.

So I do. Whimpering to an empty room.

IAN

You're such a good girl.

IAN

And good girls get rewarded.

IAN

Now, read your book, and you can tell me
about it tomorrow morning. I want a full book
report.

I bite into my lower lip, already making plans to follow his
orders to the letter. He wants a book report? I'll type one up
and deliver it to his mailbox.

Yes, sir.

Chapter 14
Ian

That little minx wrote an actual goddamn book report. Put a header in the left corner with the date and everything. Got my dick hard just reading it.

Never in my life have I been turned on from words written on a page, yet knowing exactly how much Nicole wants to please me makes my blood pump hard and fast.

It arrived in a plain white envelope with the mail, my name written in her pretty cursive. Not knowing what it was, I immediately took it to the back to read, finding a typed summary and response to her book, and it took everything in me not to cancel my appointment and go to her instead.

Especially when this peacock tattoo is going to take me hours, until well after she closes her bookshop. Stone Ink has general hours that it's open, but I'm pretty loose with the schedule. If any of the kids have appointments that they want to come in early for or stay late, I don't care. As long as they lock up properly, it's okay with me. And today is one of those days that I've got a long one in the books. An elaborate colored piece all along the side of this woman.

So, in lieu of seeing Nicole in person, I text her.

> I received your book report. I am impressed.

> You are a very good student.

In my mind's eye, I can see her light up, hands twisting behind her back, cheeks flushing at the praise.

NICOLE

Thank you.

> I wanted to see you tonight, but I'll be here late.

NICOLE

That's okay.

> It's not. Because you deserve your reward.

NICOLE

I can wait.

> I know you can. But you've waited long enough.

> I want you to go home tonight and get yourself off.

> And film it so you can send it to me.

NICOLE

You want a video?

> Yes.

NICOLE

Of me?

> Yes.

NICOLE

Touching myself?

> Yes, Nicole. I want a video of you touching yourself. I want to watch you get yourself off.

She doesn't respond for a while, and I'm half tempted to go next door to check on her. See what she's doing.

> Is that a problem?

She still doesn't answer, and I don't like it.

> What's wrong?

NICOLE

> All the pictures and videos I've sent you before have been innocuous. I've been covered up.

Besides the fact that she used the word innocuous in a sentence and I fucking love her brain, I need to know why she has a problem with this task. So I can understand if this is a boundary for her, but also because I want to know what has made her anxious. Even over text, I can tell she's nervous about something.

She normally answers me immediately.

But she's holding back. There has to be a reason.

> We need to talk. On the phone or in person, out back. Up to you. Decide in the next minute or I will. I have an appointment coming in, but I'm not working until I find out what's going on.

A few seconds later, my cell phone buzzes in my hand, her picture flashing on my screen. No one would know it's her. It's a cropped photo of her shoulder and hair from a selfie she'd sent me the other day after she ate lunch. I answer with a terse,

"Nicole."

"Hi," she says quietly, and I step out back, kicking at pebbles on the ground.

"What's wrong? Why are you suddenly anxious?"

The background noise on her end quiets, and I assume she stepped into the back room. "It's...stupid."

"It's not stupid. Nothing that worries you is stupid. But I need to know what it is." So I can destroy whatever it is. For my own sanity.

If it hurts Nicole, it will meet its demise.

Person, animal, fucking inanimate object, I don't care.

But she doesn't answer, and I eye the back door to the bookstore, picturing her only a few feet away from me. I check to see if it's locked—it is, and I rattle it. "I need you to talk to me, baby. This doesn't work if you don't communicate with me."

"It's..." She sighs, a sad little sound that tempts me to break down this fucking locked door to get to her.

"What? You're killing me here."

"I know. It's just hard for me to say out loud. I don't talk about it. I haven't talked about it in a long time. Not even to Bryce."

I fist my free hand and tilt my head up to the sky. I hate hearing his name in our conversations, a reminder that whatever this thing is between Nicole and me isn't real. Her marriage to that motherfucker is. I'm merely an escape.

An escape that's currently crawling out of his skin because something is bothering his girl.

I stalk away from the building, crossing to the other side of the street, where a small warehouse takes up most of the block. I lean against the cement wall, glaring at the back door of Chapter and Verse. "If it's that hard for you to talk about, I'm picturing the worst, so I won't force you to talk about it, but I'd appreciate it if you did."

"It's not..." She clears her throat. "It's nothing physical. I wasn't hurt like that."

"Okay." I blow out a breath, fingers tangling in my hair. She wasn't hurt...like that. Still, she was hurt in another way.

"It happened while I was in college, so it was a long time ago. I was embarrassed and didn't tell anyone. Except for Aunt Sue. It's why I started coming up here during summers."

"If there is one thing you should know by now, it is that I will never betray your trust."

"I know." Her laugh is pitiful. "You are one of the best people I know, and I want to tell you. It's just that it happened so long ago, I feel like I shouldn't still be bothered by it."

"Time has nothing to do with how your hurts heal." I know that from personal experience, and whoever said time heals all wounds was a fucking liar. "You can feel however you want about anything. It doesn't matter how long ago it happened."

A moment passes before she begins explaining it. "I wasn't very different in college than I am now, except maybe a little more naive. I was used to growing up with brothers and athletes, but I never really fit in, so I truly didn't realize it when one of the baseball players was paying attention to me at school. We had a freshman gen ed class together, English Comp, and we were paired up as critique partners. And the whole time, I thought we were just friends. What did I know about flirting?" She lets out a wry laugh. "Nothing."

I remind myself that she said she wasn't physically hurt, and it's the only thing keeping me cool and in the moment.

"One day, we were both walking to the cafeteria, and he cornered me. Told me how he really liked me, he thought I was cute, and said he'd really like to take me out. And I was shocked and...flattered. I told him yes, and he kissed me." Nicole exhales a long breath. "His girlfriend saw the whole thing. Slapped him and then slapped me."

"Jesus Christ," I grumble, and she lets out a soft, sad sound like a wounded bird.

"Yeah. It was really embarrassing, but...I probably could have gotten over that, if not for him saying I threw myself at him. He told her I'd been after him for weeks, flirting and begging for his attention. The girlfriend, of course, was fuming and had a huge tantrum right there in the entryway of the cafeteria. Everybody heard and saw, and even that—maybe the humiliation would have passed eventually, but..."

I rub my hand over my forehead, completely unable to guess where this story is going. "But...?"

"She—well, I always assumed it was her, but I couldn't ever be sure—made some video. It was a poor Photoshop edit, but suddenly everyone on campus knew my face from it having been put on top of some woman in a porn video."

I squeeze my eyes shut and bend over, hand on my knee like I got kicked. "Oh, baby, I'm so sorry."

"Everywhere I went, I was *that* girl. Even if everyone knew it very clearly wasn't me in the video, it still marked me, you know?"

"What happened? Did anyone ever face any consequences?"

"No. I suppose it could be defined as revenge porn, but this was well before any laws about that were passed. I was so mortified by everything, I didn't even want to go to the administration, but my roommate convinced me to, although they couldn't do anything. Couldn't prove anything. I didn't tell my parents, but they also wouldn't let me transfer schools either, so I basically lived in my room. I went to class and right back to the dorm. I'm not sure if anyone ever found anything new to gossip about, because I stopped talking to people. Only my roommate and one or two other girls. I had them, my books, and Aunt Sue."

By the time Nicole finishes the story, I'm sunk down to my haunches, gutted on her behalf. "If something like that had ever happened to Juniper, I would have lit the world on fire. I want to for you now. What can I do?"

"Nothing."

And then the back door of her bookstore opens, her head poking out so those big rainstorm eyes find mine, and I'm up and jogging to her before I can think better of it, because all I can do right now is hold her. She lets me, and I shove my cell phone into my pocket to curl my arms around her, one hand planted on her opposite hip, the other on the back of her head. She tucks her head against my shoulder, her fingers gripping my back like I'm her lifeline.

Nothing has felt as important as this moment in a long time, and I will hold Nicole as long as she needs. As long as it takes to prove that she's safe with me.

She eventually turns, her nose tickling the skin of my throat before leaning away to meet my gaze. "I told you it was a long time ago, and it feels silly to still be hanging on to it."

"It's not silly. Are you kidding? I want to go down to Florida right now and light some people up. I don't care if it was a month, a year, or three decades ago. That shit sticks with you, and it never should have happened."

She nods, casting her eyes down toward my chest, where she places her hands, the nail of her index finger scratching the B on my *Be Fucking Nice* shirt. "Thank you for listening."

"It's literally the very least I could do. The very most would be to build a time machine so I could go back and punch that kid in the face then make out with you myself, but..." That earns me a soft laugh, and I allow myself a caress of her cheek. "Thank you for telling me, and don't worry about the video. I—"

"No." She presses up onto her toes, bringing us closer

together by another inch. "I want to do it. I think..." She swallows, licking her lips, before tipping her chin up with pride. "It'll help me to leave all that in the past. I'm not worried about what you will do with the video. I know it's only for you."

I cup my hands around hers. "I would never do anything to hurt you, and I will never be careless with anything you've sent me. If you'd like, you can check that I've already deleted everything from my phone."

Except for my home screen photo.

"No." She smiles. "I trust you." Then she glances around to make sure no one can see before placing a quick kiss on my lips. "I will make you that video tonight."

She slips out of my hold as a sweet blush colors her cheeks, and I know before the door of her store closes shut that I've gone and fallen for this woman.

This unattainable woman.

I think about her for the next eight hours as I complete my work, and it's almost midnight by the time I close up shop. My cell phone has been burning a hole in my pocket. At around ten, it buzzed with a text. I knew exactly what it was, and I think I sweated more than my client did, knowing what was waiting for me.

June's in the living room when I get upstairs, and I offer her a wave and a few words. She's in the middle of painting her nails and watching some K-drama, so I head back to my room, where I immediately play the video.

The screen fills with Nicole's face as she sets up her cell phone on what I assume is a nightstand next to her bed, and I'm permitted the first glimpse of where she sleeps. In a room with taupe walls, cream-colored sheets, and framed grayscale artwork of leaves. She bats at the air with her hands as she speaks to me. "I'm not sure if I should, like, introduce what I'm about to do or... I don't know. I'm..." She presses her hands to her cheeks and giggles nervously, shaking her head. "I guess I just get started."

She shrieks quietly, shaking out her hands, and I cough a laugh at how fucking cute she is. Wearing one of her matching pajama sets, this one mint green, she scoots backward to the middle of the bed on her knees, then strips off her shirt, while keeping eye contact with the camera.

Fuck, it's hot.

I'm already hard, my cock straining against my jeans, and I unbutton my fly, pushing my jeans and boxers down enough to free myself. I grip my shaft, stroking slowly as I watch Nicole strip off her shorts so she's naked, and I see her fully for the first time.

She's thin but soft, her stomach swelling beneath her belly button, her hips and thighs wider than her shoulders. I don't have long to admire the teardrop shape of her breasts and how they're tipped with peach-colored nipples or the patch of trimmed hair between her legs because she lies down, spreading out horizontal to her phone.

She cups her tits, her thumbs brushing over her nipples, and I echo the movement by swiping my thumb over the head of my cock, already beading with moisture. The longer she plays with her nipples, the more tense my thighs become, and I grit my teeth.

I'm good at edging myself and others, but I don't want to tonight. I want to give in. Come hard with her. Finally let go of all I've been holding in.

When she finally skates her hands down to her thighs, I swallow a groan and watch as she spreads her legs. I can't see her pussy from this angle, but I can imagine. And it's more than enough to be a voyeur as her back arches when she dips her right hand down, touching herself.

From how her arm is moving, I guess she's found her clit,

circling it, and I stroke myself faster, matching her rhythm. But I stutter when she licks the fingers of her left hand, using them to roll and play with her nipple. I let out a rough exhale at how beautiful she is, free like this, letting me in while she pleasures herself.

It is more than I deserve—more than any man deserves—but I will repay her one thousand times over.

On the screen, she moans, the hand between her legs speeding up, and I'm right there with her. The pressure in my balls intensifies, the telltale tingle at the bottom of my spine building until my hips are bucking up to meet my hand.

And a moment later, I come, watching as Nicole does too, her body going utterly still, even as she flushes red all over. It's the most gorgeous thing I've ever seen.

I slow my strokes, milking every last drop of pleasure from my body as the work of art on-screen relaxes. I wipe my hand off on my T-shirt like I'm suddenly thirteen again and yank it over my head to toss into my laundry bin. Nicole turns her head to her phone—to me—and smiles. Beatific.

Then she removes her hand from between her legs and rolls over to offer me a better view of her fingers. They're glistening wet, and I know exactly what they taste like. My mouth waters, my cock twitching, ready for more, as if I'm not fifty-one years old.

She reaches for her phone to bring it closer, her face filling the screen once again. Her cheeks are rosy, eyes glazed over with satisfaction. "I hope you liked that," she whispers, a small smile playing on her lips. "G'night, Ian."

The video cuts out, and I'm in deep shit here. Falling so hard and fast for this woman, even as I know this arrangement is only for the summer.

I press my hand to my head. It was about this age a stroke took my mom, and while I memorized the signs of a stroke because of that, I can't remember any of them right now. I can't even recall if you feel a stroke in your chest and head.

I pull up my pants and do a quick search to learn that, no, I am not having a stroke.

But I may be in love.

Fuck.

Chapter 15
Ian

Ian and Roman text thread:

> Griffin's having a big shindig for the 4th. You should come down.

> I haven't seen you in so long, I think I forgot what you look like.

> Everybody misses you. We'd love to see you.

> Hope everything is going good for you. Love you, kid.

Chapter 16
Nicole

"Costco?"

Ian gestures for me to follow him through the parking lot to the big box discount store. "Yeah." He throws his hands up in innocence. "I'm following your rules. So, instead of taking you out somewhere around the neighborhood, I'm taking you here."

I snort a laugh. "You're kidding."

He tosses me an offended look. "Have you never had Costco pizza before?"

"I've never even been to a Costco."

"Oh, baby. What have you been doing with your life?" He reaches for my hand but stops himself and snaps his fingers instead. A surprising wash of disappointment settles over me that we can't hold hands like he wants to. Like I want to.

I reposition my purse from my shoulder to across my body, purposefully nudging him with my elbow. When he slants his gaze to me, I smile, hoping he can understand that if this were another time and place, I would love to hold his hand. But there are still too many eyes.

He nods his understanding and lowers his voice. "Prepare to have your life changed."

"Should I be doing stretches or something? Exercises to warm up?"

He tips his head in mock gravity. "This is a marathon, not a sprint. The key is to take your time and stick to the plan because it's easy to be pulled off course. We need paper supplies, drinks, and a few miscellaneous items." He arches his eyebrows in my direction. "Do not get distracted by the fun pool floaties. Because you'll see that blow-up unicorn and think you need it for only ten bucks, and then you're left with a fucking blow-up unicorn in the middle of your living room."

"So I can assume you bought the blow-up unicorn pool floatie."

"I thought one of my nieces would want it." He shrugs. "They didn't."

"Do Taryn or Griffin even have a pool?"

"No, but that's what I'm saying. It's easy to lose track of yourself in here. Stay close to my side, all right?"

"Yes, sir." I laugh at his serious tone. That big bad Ian Stone loves to shop at Costco. *Precious.*

When the automatic doors open, Ian flashes the attendant his member card before turning to me with a glint in his eyes that I have never seen before. Part excitement, part determination. He cracks his knuckles like we're about to race then shoots a toothy, almost feral grin my way. "Are you ready to fucking rage?"

And, oh my god, he is magnificent.

With his hair loose, muscles on display in the fitted, retro D.A.R.E. T-shirt, and big, tattooed hands rubbing together, I think I've found a new kink: Ian Stone at a Costco.

He takes an oversized cart in hand and leads the way into the store, giving me a quick rundown of the layout that includes electronics and home goods. This place literally has everything. Who knew?

We head over to the bakery, past the meats and frozen fish. The size of this place distracts me, let alone the sheer number of salmon patties sold together.

"What do you like?" Ian asks, dragging me back to his side from where I wandered off toward the giant blocks of cheese.

"What do I like?"

He points to all the baked goods, the big cakes and pies, and trays of little cupcakes and cookies decorated with red, white, and blue sprinkles. I point to them. "They're cute."

He puts the cookies in the cart along with a coconut cake then continues on toward the refrigerated section. We pass all the outdoor items, and I stop to check out the lawn chairs. "I told you," he says, so close to my ear that I startle. "Before you know it, you'll have a unicorn."

"I can't believe they have all this. And for so cheap!"

He clucks his tongue. "Sounds like we need to get you a membership."

"Or I could borrow yours." I bump my shoulder into his side, aiming for playful flirtation, but with the way his dark eyes hold mine, it doesn't feel playful or flirtatious. And for a moment, everything and everyone in the store fades.

Weeks ago, I assumed a man like Ian could never be attracted to a woman like me. But here we are, the back of his hand skimming mine, sending an electrical current up my arm, sparking something deep in my chest. A shock to my system. He is attracted to me. Enough that he licks his bottom lip as if thirsty. As if only I can quench his thirst.

It would be so easy to close the few inches of space between us. I am tempted. Too tempted.

Until a baby cries somewhere, bursting our bubble, and I step back.

Ian juts his chin in the direction he wants me to go. He instructs me to grab a big pack of hot dogs and hamburgers and "anything else you want."

"Why do you keep asking me? I don't need any groceries."

"No, but you're coming to the picnic."

I wrench back into a woman pushing a cart with her baby inside. "Oh, I'm so sorry about that." I hop out of her way, right into Ian's space, up against his chest. "What picnic?"

"My brother's. Griffin always hosts for July 4th. He's got the biggest house for everybody. Plus, you know, in case one of the kids sets themselves on fire with a sparkler, Cap can take care of it."

I blink, confused. "What are you talking about?"

He leans down, his eyes level with mine. "You are coming to Griffin's house for a picnic tomorrow." When I shake my head, he cocks his head to the side, a silent reprimand. His voice is so low I have to shift closer to hear him. "Are you disobeying me?"

Yes.

And no.

But also... I think I might want to?

"I can't go to your brother's house?"

"Why not? Your store is closed. Do you have other plans?"

"Well...no, but—"

"So, you're going to come." He takes off, pushing the cart down another aisle, and I have to quicken my pace to keep up.

"I've never been there before. Won't it be weird that I'm randomly showing up?"

"No." He studies the popsicles before choosing the twenty-four-count "real" frozen fruit bars.

"But—"

"But nothing, Nic. I don't know why you're questioning me, first of all, but since you need an explanation... No, it won't be weird. Lots of people are coming. Eloise, Morgan, Clara, Marianne. Even Ned might stop by."

Ned, the semi-agoraphobic owner of the record store.

It's all people from Aster Street, from the downtown neighborhood. I'd been invited to other things before, parties and picnics friends and acquaintances have thrown, but I never went. Because of Bryce.

Now he's gone, and I have Ian—kind of.

I can't deny how natural and easy it's been to make the switch, but I'm not sure how comfortable I am, thinking I'm *with* Ian. Because I'm not.

Not really.

Yet in this moment, even if he weren't my Dom, I would still want to go and see everyone. Have fun for a few hours outside of work.

"Okay," I agree, forcing myself to unknot my hands. "Should I bring anything?"

"That's what we're shopping for. I'm getting the usual order, plus a few extras."

I follow him to the milk and eggs. "What's the usual?"

"I buy the basics for everyone," he tells me, loading up with multiple gallons of all different kinds of milk, whole, two percent, skim. Then he carefully lays packages of eggs on top of each other.

"Who is everyone?"

"Taryn and her crew, my kids, and occasionally a few things for Griffin, but he's anal retentive about food. Has to count his macros."

He rolls his eyes, and I bite back a laugh because Griffin and Ian are both in shape and muscular, particularly for their age, but Griffin is slimmer than his older brother, who is built like an ox. He works out every day, and it shows. On more than one occasion, I've envisioned him throwing tires and logs.

As we move on to the bulk drinks, I ask, "What do you do to work out?"

Right there in front of the crates of iced tea and juice boxes, the man runs his tongue along his front teeth. "You're curious, baby?"

My cheeks flame, and I pivot to leave him there, but he catches my wrist, a soft laugh whispering along the side of my face when he pulls me into him. "I like it. I like you looking at me."

When I finally meet his gaze, the humor dissolved from his eyes, I catch myself leaning into his hard-packed body, so I force myself to back away, clearing my throat. "Yes, I'm curious. I don't know much about fitness or lifting. I only walk when I can."

He easily slides a few packages of drinks onto the bottom of the cart, and that's what I mean. "Do you do that CrossFit kind of stuff, like lifting a car?"

He laughs again, and I like that his laugh sounds more like a wheeze. Unused. That means he doesn't do it often, but I can make him smile and laugh.

I do that.

"Even though I don't do CrossFit, I don't think they lift cars. I don't lift them either. Just regular old weights."

"Every day."

"Yep." He nods his head for us to continue on to the paper products. "Ever since my mom died, I've taken it pretty seriously. I always tried to take care of myself, but it really scared me. Both of her parents died young too, and I'm trying to do everything I can to make sure I live a long time."

I never met Violet Stone, but I've heard stories about her. The kind high school English teacher who took lots of side jobs like tutoring and summer camps to have enough money to raise her four kids. But other than that, she is a ghost.

After Ian tosses the biggest pack of paper plates I've ever seen in my life into the cart, I ask, "What was she like? Your mom?"

He smiles fondly to himself. "She was...pretty perfect." He's quiet for a while as we slowly make our way around the other aisles, strolling up and down each one. "Her dad, my grandfather, was originally from Iran. He was an engineer and exiled for being a dissident. He moved here and completely Westernized himself, married a blond white woman, and never taught my mom anything about her culture. I know she resented him for that as she grew older, and she taught herself as much as she could. Even learned some Farsi."

He pulls up the right sleeve of his T-shirt to reveal the name Violet inked with pretty flourishes along with a small dove. Underneath is some language I can't read, but I guess is Farsi. "What does it say?"

"Mother."

"Do you speak it?"

He shakes his head. "I'm not naturally academic like she was. She passed that gift on to Griffin. But that's what always impressed me most—she read everything she could get her hands on. Wanted to learn everything. I remember being a kid and thinking, *My mom is the smartest mom on the planet.*"

Reflexively, I brush my hand down Ian's back. "That's sweet."

He lifts a thick shoulder. "Don't all kids think their mom is the best, smartest mom?"

I suck air through my teeth. Because I don't think that about my mother.

"You don't get along with your parents?" Ian guesses, and I shake my head.

"Enough to talk to them every once in a while, but by the time I showed up, they were done raising kids. Four is a lot, and one who is the exact opposite of the others? I spent most of my time in the library. I was like *Matilda*."

"That movie about the little girl with powers?"

"You don't know how many nights I stayed awake trying to move things with my mind."

He plants his hand on my hip, gaze on my mouth. "I really want to kiss you right now because that's too fucking cute. I can't stand it."

I glance around, noting a couple who are complete strangers, and yet...

I step away from him, changing topics. "What about your dad?"

Again, I know the basics. He left Violet with their kids, and Ian pretty much became the head of the house way before his time.

"A piece of shit," Ian says easily, plucking up a pack of condiments—mustard, ketchup, and relish. "He married my mom straight out of college and knocked her up, but he never got over the fact that he wasn't drafted into the NBA. My first memories of that guy are how tall he was. He left the first time for a few years, trying to find work, but really, he was drinking and losing his paychecks to casinos. He came back when I was about six or seven, and still, I thought he was a giant. He stayed, played at being sober, but it didn't last. He left for good when I was fourteen. I never had the chance to show him how tall I grew."

Ian is taller than his father in every way. It doesn't matter if he ever reached the same height or not; I know Ian is a hundred times the man who gave life to him.

"I'm sorry about that," I say as we make our way back to the front of the store. "About all the loss you suffered."

He nods but doesn't reply, so I follow dutifully alongside

him. Until a jar catches my eye. I leap over to the milk-chocolate-covered almonds.

"Get them," Ian says, but I put the plastic jar back.

"I don't need them."

He picks it right back up. "No, but you want them."

"Ian."

He ignores me, adding a second jar to the cart then points to the dark-chocolate-covered almonds. "What about these?"

"You don't need to buy them for me."

"I don't need to. I want to. See how that works? Both ways."

I open my mouth to argue, but he holds up his finger. "Next, I'll give you my credit card and make you go shopping." When I zip my lips, he taps them with the side of his index finger. "Even if we weren't...us, I'd still want to buy these for you. I like taking care of my people. So, let me do that, okay?"

I give in with a nod, my jaw suddenly tight, eyes stinging at being named as one of his people.

Ian has claimed me in every way he can, as a friend, neighbor, lover, and now one of his *people*.

I am his. Through and through, and I've never felt more at home.

"After I pay for all this, I'm gonna buy you a slice of Costco's finest."

"Oh boy," I tease in a high, childish voice that earns me a stern eyebrow-raise.

"Or I could take you out to my car and edge you until you scream."

"I'll take the pizza."

"That's my good girl."

And that's how I have my first taste of Costco. With Ian at my side. Calling me *his* good girl.

Chapter 17
Ian

Nicole arrives to the picnic in a blue gingham dress and a red bow around her ponytail that is so fucking hot, I want to tie it around her wrists and flip up her skirt to take her from behind.

But since that's out of the question, I play it cool as she saunters over to Griffin and Andi to say hello and offer a small fruit salad before falling into conversation with Sloane about something that has her talking with her hands and leaning in to listen when Sloane speaks.

I pretend not to be annoyed that she hasn't acknowledged me or sought me out yet when I'm desperate for her attention. There are three dozen or so people scattered among chairs and under umbrellas, but she is the only person I care about right now.

My brother, who never misses anything, makes his way over to me, eyes squinted with interest. "That's a surprise."

"What is?"

He scoffs. "That's what you're going with?"

I play it dumb as my attention stays on Nicole when she

bends down to listen to Sloane's son, smiling so brightly at whatever he's saying—probably something about animals because his touch of the 'tism is an obsession with animals—it pulls the corners of my lips up too.

Nicole glows like the sun, and I'd love nothing more than to bask in her shine for the rest of my life. Warm myself under her rays.

Too bad my sister steps right into my line of sight, blocking my sunshine.

"You invited her, I assume," she says without pretense.

"Who is she?" I crane my neck around like I have no idea who Taryn's referring to.

"Don't be an ass."

"Me? You're the one who stomped over here—"

"I don't stomp."

Griffin adjusts the baseball cap on his head with his firehouse emblem. "You stomp occasionally."

"Fuck off, both of you. We're here to talk about Ian and Nicole."

I wrench my head back, my attention finally waylaid by the implication that this is some meeting to discuss my love life. "No."

Griffin and Taryn close ranks around me, both of them standing shoulder to shoulder as if they'd planned it. It's Griffin who pipes up first. "I thought she was still married."

I swipe my hand through my hair, my fingers catching on the elastic band, and I rip it out. "She is."

Taryn circles her hand. "And she's suddenly shown up here because..."

"Because I invited her."

"Where's her husband?" Taryn asks, glancing Nicole's way. She's now kneeling on the grass, talking with Sloane's daughter. Her smile is infectious with the shy little girl.

"Away." I hate even hearing the word husband in reference to Nicole. Talking about him leaves a bad taste in my mouth. "For a work trip or something. I didn't want her to be alone."

Griffin nods, all smug and shit. "Invited her out of the goodness of your heart. What a saint."

"You're right. I am." I make the sign of the cross over my two annoying-as-fuck siblings as they huff indignant sounds of amusement.

Taryn folds her arms, glaring at me now. As if she thinks that'll make me talk. "So, Saint Ian, are we supposed to believe Nicole has suddenly shown up to this picnic out of the blue when she's never shown up to any other party anyone else has thrown?"

"There's nothing to believe. That's what's happened."

"And you expect us to think it has nothing to do with you?"

I can't lie, too afraid to speak that into the universe, even if I should. To protect her and what we have. So I shrug instead.

My siblings both stare at me, but I refuse to offer them any more information. I'm walking a tightrope as it is, having to hide our relationship while wanting to shout it from the rooftops that she's mine.

Except that isn't true. She's not mine.

Not really.

Not in all the ways I want her to be.

"Look, it's just a picnic. Don't read too much into it." I clap Griffin on the back and start to walk away, but he stops me with a hand wrapped around my forearm.

"You sure about that? Because it looks like you're about to fuck up a good woman's life."

His voice is harder than I expect. Griffin has always been a stand-up guy, even as a kid. Never fooled around or did any stupid shit that children get up to. He always followed the rules, always did the right thing. I call him Captain America for a reason, but I don't like his insinuation that I'm doing something wrong.

Because I'm not.

My serious and straitlaced brother wouldn't be able to fathom the idea of what Nicole and I have or do. It's outside of society's norm, and it would blow his tidy little mind to know his big brother has finger-fucked some other guy's wife multiple times. Trained her to text him first thing in the morning and ordered her to face her fear and send him a video of her naked and masturbating.

He couldn't imagine how I wrestle with it every day.

Being her Dom instead of her man.

Settling for being a secret instead of walking over there right now to wrap her hair around my fist and kiss her.

Wanting her whole heart and accepting half.

Griffin could never be in my position, and I don't appreciate his judgment. I knock his hand away, lowering my voice so only he can hear. "Come down from your ivory tower before you open your mouth to me about that *good woman*. Because you don't know what the fuck you're talking about when it comes to me and her."

His reaction is faint, but it's there in the pinch of his mouth, and I step away, inhaling a cooling breath. "I'm gonna go grab a drink. You two want anything?"

They shake their heads, still looking concerned, but I don't care to stick around to listen to whatever else they have to say.

I help myself to a glass of the sweet tea Andi made and find a seat near Nicole as she chats with Dante, Clara, and Marianne. She offers me a smile and a casual, "Hey. Nice to see you."

As if we're passing acquaintances.

"You too, Nicole."

I hold her gaze, testing to see how long she'll last before it's too much. It's three seconds before pink blooms on her cheeks and another two before she nervously licks her lips. Ten seconds until her nipples pebble under the top of her dress, and I doubt she's wearing a bra.

Tease.

"Good girl," I mouth, and she bites into her bottom lip.

I jut my chin in a silent direction for her to go back to her conversation, and she does, so I keep myself busy by chatting with Taryn's son, Jake. He's sixteen and has been practicing his driving skills with Dante.

Before he came into Taryn's life, I picked up some of the slack her piece-of-shit ex-husband left, but since Dante has taken over, I've lost out on those day-to-day details from them. Like how Maddie, Jake's thirteen-year-old sister, has decided to try cheerleading, though he doesn't think she'll make it since she's not very coordinated.

And it's true.

With a check over my shoulder, I watch her fumble a catch of a beanbag June tossed to her. Poor kid.

I take in the rest of the picnic. Friends and family alike, all relaxed and happy. People I've known for decades, if not my whole life. They are everyone I care about.

All except Roman, and I slip my cell phone out of my pocket to send him a text. A single line.

Wish you'd come home.

Then I push away any melancholy thoughts about my baby brother and help myself to a plate of food and bury any remaining ire with Griffin over a game of basketball that draws a bit of a crowd, including Nicole. Every so often, I let my focus drift to where she's talking and laughing with Andi, and for a split second, my mind rockets into space, envisioning that she is mine, for real.

When she and Andi talk and laugh all the time because they're best friends, which is perfect for Griffin and me. I picture Nicole with me on every Costco run and at every family event. Holding her hand as we amble down Aster Street, taking lunch breaks together, and then going home together. Curling up in bed, listening as she reads her books out loud to me, forcing her to keep reading even as I go down on her.

It's bliss.

Pure, unadulterated bliss.

"That's game!" Logan shouts, jumping up to high-five his dad after I apparently spaced out so much, he hit his last shot for the winning point.

I clasp hands with Griffin, accepting his pat on the back of my head as a silent apology when we hug.

Another game starts with Jaybird and Cash playing Logan and Jake, and I take the opportunity to speak with Nicole.

I nod to the drink in her hand. "Is that Marianne's sangria? You better be careful. It'll knock you on your ass."

"I know. I'm sipping slowly, and it's my only one."

"Good." I make sure no one can hear when I say, "Because you'll need all your senses for later."

Her face turns as red as the bow in her hair. "Yeah?"

"Yeah. I brought your favorite little toy."

"My favorite...?" Her eyes go wide when she finally understands. "That's not my favorite. That's a torture device."

"Maybe *my* favorite little toy, then."

She moves in closer to me, the hem of her dress skimming my legs. "Thanks for making me come today."

"I'll make you come, don't worry."

She growls all cute. "You know what I mean. I'm having a really good time."

"As you should." I reach into my pocket to retrieve the small silicone vibrator, fisting it. "Now, I'm going to give this to you, so you can go to the bathroom and put it in. When you're done, I want you to play some cornhole with me."

She wrinkles her nose. "Do I have to?" I arch my brow, and she sighs. "Fine."

"Listen, brat, maybe knowing every point you score will get you an orgasm will motivate you."

That changes her tune, and she immediately accepts the little pink egg and hightails it toward the house. Ten minutes later, we're both positioned at the cornhole boards, her opposite me appearing flushed, maybe from the sun, but I'd like to think it's from anticipation.

"Remember the rules?" When she nods, I gesture for her to throw. "Ladies first."

She carefully plucks one of the beanbags from the ground, moving kind of funny, as if she's worried I'm going to power on the vibrator.

"Don't worry," I assure her. "We won't play until later."

With that, she takes a breath, swings her arm back, and tosses. Missing by a mile. "I told you. I'm terrible."

I wave her off. "You're still warming up. You'll get better. Just keep your arm in, closer to your body. You're swinging across. That's why it landed over here."

I throw my beanbag, sinking it, and she takes a sip of her sangria, snarking, "Show-off."

I laugh. "Try again."

She tosses and misses, and that's how it goes for the next five turns. So I move behind her. "Let's get you scoring some points here. Loosen up." I place my hands on her hips, wiggling them back and forth, earning a swat. "You're all rigid."

"Because I'm nervous."

"Of what?"

She doesn't have to say. The crinkle at the corner of her eyes and lips rolled over her teeth are enough. She's nervous people will find out about us.

I try to reassure her. "We're simply two people playing a game. That's all."

But that's not the truth and she knows it, so instead of lying to her or myself anymore, I wrap my hand around hers then guide her arm back behind us both. With a smooth swing forward, we release the beanbag. It doesn't go in the hole, but it does land on the board.

"That's one," I say, gratified, and she tilts her head back to meet my gaze.

"My only point."

"So? We're having fun."

"Fun for whom? You're scoring all the points."

With a squeeze to her hip, I cross back to my place at the other side. "And you're the one who's going to reap all the rewards. So, you better concentrate, huh?"

As the game goes on, her throws become more confident, but her aim doesn't improve much. Even as I try to extend the game and change the rules, she only scores two points by the time Taryn and Dante want to take over, their own apparent bet in place. But I am not interested in learning what the wager is. I can only assume it's something that will gross me out about my sister from the way Dante is warming up his legs with lunges while he grins lasciviously at her.

I hold out my arm to Nicole for a completely friendly side-hug. Or at least I thought so until June pops up out of nowhere. "You're a hugger now, Dad?"

I've never wanted to put a *FREE* sign around her neck and leave her out by the trash more than at that moment. But instead of doing so, I crush her to me, reminding her that, yes, I do give hugs.

To a very select few.

June laughs and fights my hold, eventually squirming away from me, only to stumble in Nicole's direction. She fixes her hair then turns to the woman who has my heart in her fist, covering her growing smile.

"Careful of that one," June says to Nicole, pointing at me. "He's got a wicked grip. Once he's got you, it's almost impossible to get away."

It's an innocuous sentiment from my daughter, and yet it is absolutely true.

I don't want to let Nicole go.

And from the way she's blinking repeatedly with her hands behind her back, probably clenched together in anxiety, she knows.

I'm just not sure if she wants me to let *her* go or not.

"Come on," June says, breaking the growing tension between Nicole and me, tugging on her arm. "Andi's gonna play."

My daughter pulls Nicole to the chairs fanned out around my brother's woman, strumming chords on her guitar, cowboy boots tapping to keep time.

Andi is a songwriter and spent a few years in LA before moving here, but she still makes trips out to California to work on whatever album she's attached to. Although, it's become common practice for her to pull out her guitar when we're all together like this. I'm not sure who started it, but we often throw out songs to see if we can stump her. Her repertoire is pretty big so it's not often she doesn't know how to play a song, but if she doesn't, she makes it her personal mission to learn it. Like the one I called out last time, "Damn I Wish I Was Your Lover."

"This one's for the guy who loves and respects all the great

'90s female singers." Andi aims the neck of her guitar at me with a dimpled grin. "Like every man rightfully should."

She plays the hit by Sophie B. Hawkins, and Clara raises her arms in the air, waving back and forth until a few more people join in, and suddenly, it's a concert. No one really knows the words until the chorus, and then everybody—even the kids—is singing.

Nicole drops her head back, laughing, free and completely unencumbered from worry about what people will think. She's simply having fun, singing off-key, and clapping along as she dances in her seat.

Andi moves on to other songs that I'm not familiar with, something with a Southern twang, and then a new pop song that Gracie, Griffin's daughter, joins her on. By the time they finish, it's dusk, and someone has pulled out a small speaker, playing music on there. Andi sets down her guitar to drag Logan out to the driveway to dance. Griffin and Gracie follow. Then Clara and Marianne. Taryn and Dante. And soon, the whole party has moved out to the street, singing, dancing, and passing out sparklers.

Nicole accepts a lit one from Jaybird, twirling it in front of her, drawing shapes that I imagine are our initials in a heart.

Wishful thinking.

Until she turns like she knows I'm watching and hits me with a smile so sweet, I feel dizzy.

Maybe I have it wrong. *She* is the one who has *me* wrapped up.

I am completely at her mercy.

Willing and ready to do whatever she wants.

For however long she wants.

As much as I want to control her, ultimately, I have to follow her lead. The only hope I have of keeping my heart intact is if she would choose me.

Love me.

Because all I have now is the ability to make her see stars.

Fireworks go off in the distance, and I open the app on my cell phone to activate the vibrator. Nicole jumps slightly but otherwise carries on as normal. I keep it on low for a while, allowing her to become used to the feeling before turning it up.

She leans back as if needing something to support herself and reaches out her hand for the mailbox. Even from here, I can see her white-knuckled grip when I hit it even higher, making it pulse. Her stance is tense, but no one would know she's close to coming.

The song on the speaker changes to Hozier, her favorite, but she can't even appreciate it with her chin down, eyes closed, and I smile to myself. She's trying so hard *not* to look like she has a vibrator in her pussy that she's starting *to* look like she does, so I change the setting one last time, hoping to push her over the edge.

She gives in to a small buck of her hips that could possibly pass as a dance move as she goes red all over.

I turn off the vibrator and wait until she catches her breath, slanting her head in my direction. I hold up my index finger, mouthing, "That's one."

Her lips form a small O, her chest rising and falling with her rapid breaths, the left strap of her dress drooping off her shoulder.

When I recall it tonight while I'm in bed and my hand is around my cock, I'll think about how I could rip that pretty little dress off her.

I'm not sure if she can translate my thoughts, but she glances down to the limp strap on her shoulder and pointedly leaves it there. Then she smiles at me.

Like the brat she is.

So I hit the power button again, turning the vibrator back

on. This time, she's expecting it and doesn't move. Even as I change the speed. She holds my gaze, twenty or so yards between us, but it might as well be zero. I can practically feel her breath on my neck, the coiling of her muscles. She licks her lips, and I taste them on my tongue.

"Almost there," I mouth, and she nods. "Eyes on me."

She keeps her eyes open the whole time, those blue pools expanding to an ocean as she comes again, her neck and back arching toward me, and I suddenly hate that we're here.

I wanted her at this picnic so she could enjoy herself, be with friends, but this fun little game is self-inflicted pain. Too many people and sounds—and not enough time to do all the things I'd like.

I need her alone.

And soon.

I shut off the vibrator and pocket my phone, holding up two fingers. She eventually rights her dress and fixes her ponytail, fanning herself.

Again, no one would know why.

She could be sweating from the summer heat.

But Nicole and I know better.

Our little secret.

Chapter 18
Ian

I t's been two days since the picnic and the game Nicole and I played while everyone around us went about their business, having no idea she had two orgasms. Right there in the middle of the party. It wouldn't be an understatement to say I've thought about those too-short moments at least once an hour. For the last two nights, I've stroked my cock, remembering it until I came all over my hand and stomach. Then I went back to the Jane Austen book, waiting on my nightly check-in text from my bookworm—an update that she's home safe and an answer to a question that I've started asking her recently: what was the best part of your day today?

Like some sad sack of shit, I always hope it'll be me. Seeing me or talking to me. Anything to let me know that I am the best part of her day, like she is the best part of my day, but it's usually something about her work, a kid she spoke to, or someone she helped.

And I despise myself all over again.

Because I was the one to put myself in this position. It is solely my fault that I am obsessed with an unavailable woman.

I thought I'd be able to compartmentalize like I usually do, but not when I see her every day. I've known her from afar for years, but I know her intimately now, and I can't do it. I can't pretend I don't hate how she goes home to the house she owns with her husband every night. Or that she still wears her wedding rings.

I told her I wanted to take her out on a proper date, but deciding on how I'd get her there was an issue. Being the stand-up gentleman I am, I said I wanted to drive her, but she didn't like the idea of me picking her up at her house, fearing neighbors might see and question her leaving with me. So, after some negotiation, she agreed that we'd go out later, after the bookstore closed. She'd sneak out the back door to my car.

I hate hiding, but I understand why she's uncomfortable, and I'd rather follow her rules than not have her at all. I knock on the back door, and after a moment, she breezes out in a light red dress with tiny white flowers all over. The thick straps and hemline that reaches her knees are not especially provocative, but with a slit up the side and a fit that hugs all her lithe curves, she might as well be walking the runway. I wolf-whistle through my teeth.

"Look at you." I take Nicole's hand, lift it up, then nudge her to spin in a circle, so I can see all of her. From the soft curls in her dark brown hair to the thin gold jewelry adorning her neck and wrists. "Stunning."

I guide her to where my 1970 Chevrolet Impala is parked and repeat myself. "You're stunning."

"Not so bad yourself." She flicks at the open collar of my white shirt, letting her fingers slowly drag down each of the buttons before resting on the waistband of my pants, toying with my belt.

This girl could be quite bold when given room to bloom.

A mistress of herself.

"Gonna be hard for me to keep my hands off you tonight," I say, and she smiles shyly as I wrap my hand around her waist and close the distance between us so I can whisper, "And I'm gonna need you to take your underwear off."

"*What?*"

I deliberately lower my gaze below her waist. "Underwear. Off."

She shakes her head, cheeks flushing underneath the street-lamp light. "I... You..."

"Want them in my hand."

In a poor attempt to throw me off, she taps the dark red roof of my car. "This is nice. You restore cars, right? How—"

"Now, Nicole." I hold my palm up.

She visibly swallows and teeters side to side on the heels of her sandals. "Now? Out here?"

"Just me and you here, baby. But if it'll make you feel more comfortable..." I open the passenger side door and then block it off so she's mostly hidden between it and me. "Go ahead."

She cranes her neck to look around, double-checking she's not being spied on, before dragging the skirt of her dress up a few inches as she reaches underneath. After a few wiggles of her hips, she slides the thin scrap of cotton down her legs, and I make sure she doesn't trip as she steps out of them. Then they're in my hands, and I can't wipe the grin off my face.

"Good girl."

"What are you going to do with them?" she asks, carefully sitting in the car, her legs together.

"Keep 'em safe." I stuff them in my pocket and shut the door to round the hood. Once I'm seated inside, I curl my hand around her neck, tugging her to me for a kiss.

It's been two days.

Far too long since I made her come and an eternity since I tasted her.

But before the night is out, I'm planning on devouring much more than her lips.

I steer with one hand on the wheel, the other on Nicole's left thigh, as we chat about the books we've been reading, my kids, and how I got into restoring cars, anything to fill the half hour it takes to drive to the restaurant, including the weather and sudden thunderstorm that hit last night, which led to her talking about how she's still paying off the loan it took to fix all the water damage she had a few years ago in her store.

"Sometimes it's hard to keep up the work on these old buildings," I say, waiting to turn at the green light.

"Guess you would know."

"Hm?" I glance over at her after making the left.

"You." She loses the battle of hiding her teasing smile. "You'd know what it takes to keep up with something old."

I squeeze her thigh. "Brat." I pull into the parking lot and tell her to wait for me to open the door for her. When I do, I slip my hand up her dress, palming her ass. "Careful, baby. This old man knows more tricks than you can imagine, and I'll use all of them on you."

At the expansion of her pupils, I press a quick kiss to her mouth, murmuring one last warning about being a good girl, then weave my fingers with hers, unselfconscious about being physical with her this far from home. I knew she wouldn't be able to relax if we stayed in West Chester.

Inside, we're seated at one of the circular booths on the perimeter of the floor that provides plenty of shelter. Excellent.

I scoot her right up against my side, my hand still on her thigh as we order drinks—a whiskey on the rocks for me and white wine for her—and I trail my fingertips up and down the soft skin of her inner thigh.

She clamps her legs together when the waiter arrives at our table once again, pad and pen in hand, but I don't stop touching her, enjoying how she tenses, trying to keep her voice even as she orders the risotto. I skate my fingers higher up her thighs, to the heat emanating from between them, only to stop a millimeter away to order the lamb.

Once we're alone again, I sip on my drink and remove my hand from her leg to rest my arm along the back of the booth, playing with her hair. Without her underwear, I know she already feels restless, and my goal is to keep her that way, on the edge.

"Tell me more about your family."

"What do you want to know?" She squirms beside me when I trace the shell of her ear.

"Everything you want to tell me."

She takes a sip of her wine before angling herself toward me, our knees touching. She doesn't wear perfume, the natural scent of her skin better than anything in this place. Absolutely delectable, and I lift her hand to my mouth to kiss her inner wrist then settle it in my lap, toying with the rings on her index and middle fingers. "I know you said you don't talk to them often, but was there a big rift?"

"Not really," she says, eyes on my hand. She uses her fingertip to trace the tattoo on the back of it. "We check in with texts more often than we have phone calls, but..." She meets my gaze. "We're not close. Not like you are with your kids."

I wouldn't call myself a perfect dad, but I love my children, and I try to make sure they know it. That's all I can do.

"How does Aunt Sue fit in?" I ask, flipping her hand up to trace over the lines of her palm.

"She's my mom's sister, and she and I always bonded. It's not that we were together often since she lived here, but I think she saw herself in me whenever the whole family got together for whatever holiday or reunion." She smiles to herself, her gaze somewhere in her mind as she explains, "There was a project we had to do in sixth grade. Interview a relative about our family history, and for some reason, I chose Aunt Sue instead of my parents. I got her email address, and since then, we kept in contact. She became my touchstone."

I'm the last person to understand female relationships, especially because I grew up with two brothers, but I imagine Nicole's mother might have taken umbrage at her sister and daughter being so close. "Is your mom okay with that?"

"She never said anything to me about it bothering her." Nicole shrugs. "Besides, I don't think I was what she expected."

"What do you mean?"

"I didn't fit in much with my family. I love them and they love me, but sometimes I felt like I was on the outside looking in. My mom has that kind of... Well, my parents were high school sweethearts, and she was a cheerleader. Growing up, she was into all the booster stuff with my brothers, and I think she expected a daughter more like her. Especially after they tried for a girl for so long. She's very outgoing and..." Nicole saws her teeth into her bottom lip.

"What?"

She tosses me a look, like she's reluctant to admit it. "Everyone in my family... They lived their best days in high school, you know what I mean?"

I suck air through my teeth. "They peaked?"

She laughs a little, covering her mouth. "That's awful. I'm awful."

"You're not awful." I pull her hand away from her face and nuzzle her palm.

She's basically putty in my lap with the way she leans toward me. I release her hand and curl my hand around her neck.

"What about you?" she asks, fitting perfectly against my side. "When did you peak?"

"Haven't yet." I sit back, forcing her to shift even closer to me. "The best is yet to come."

She studies me, eyes making a slow trek over my face, and I love how she is here—freely touching me, my beard, my chest, my arms.

Bold.

"What about your ex?"

Very bold.

"My ex?" I slide my fingers over the ink I gave Nicole. "You interested in learning about my marriage?"

It's wishful thinking to hope she's jealous of my past relationships. Because I'm downright envious of the motherfucker she's currently married to.

She nods. "I heard stories, but I want to get it straight from the source."

"What have you heard?" When she bites her lip, afraid to be honest, I give in to a rueful chuckle. "Whatever it is, it's probably true."

"So she really believes cell phones give people brain tumors?"

"Yeah, that is one of her more tinfoil-y beliefs."

I link Nicole's fingers with mine and lay it all out there. "I was working in an auto body shop when we met. She was from a well-to-do family. In hindsight, I think she liked me because I was different...dirty."

Nicole frowns. "What, like, the bad boy from the wrong side of the tracks?"

I run my hand over my beard a few times. "Yeah. Raised by a single mom, drunk for a father. I had no money and was working two jobs between the shop and learning how to tattoo."

"So what happened?"

"I fell for her. She was as eccentric as she was beautiful, and for a kid who'd worked every day since he was fourteen, she was a breath of fresh air. At twenty-two years old, she became everything to me."

From the set of Nicole's shoulders and the pinch of her mouth, I think maybe she is jealous, and I tug on a lock of her hair. "She was always into hippie-dippie shit. Was into crystals before they became cool and made her own deodorant. She loved nature and was truly granola-crunchy. Like, all these moms out there now on social media? Heather was the original. That's why our kids are named after things in nature. I didn't mind because her heart was in the right place."

Nicole is quiet beside me, listening intently, and even though we're talking about my ex-wife, it doesn't feel at all awkward. I want her to know about Heather, like I want to know all of Nicole's history.

"We were happy, and we had our three kids, but..." I shake my head in dismay of the past. "She ran this nature camp for kids with disabilities, and one day, she had June with her there. On their way home, a deer ran out into the road. Heather swerved off into an embankment. She had a concussion and a broken bone or two, but Juniper spent weeks in critical condition."

Nicole gasps softly, her fingers tightening around mine. "That's awful."

"Heather couldn't handle it. I don't know if she blamed herself or what, but she changed. She suddenly got really into bizarre, nonsense kind of medical stuff. She didn't want to listen to the doctors and tried all these off-the-wall remedies. At first, I thought it was a phase, you know? We had this huge scare with our daughter almost dying. It would shake anybody up, but she kept going further and further down the rabbit hole, and the more she tried to push it on the kids, especially June, the more impatient I got with her. Homemade cleaning supplies and fermenting your own yogurt is one thing, but starting to preach about the horrors of big pharma and how they have the cure for cancer but don't use it so they can keep making money is something else. She wouldn't even use sunscreen. Wouldn't put it on the kids. Didn't want them eating anything store-bought and freaked out about them playing with any other kids because they'd be 'poisoned.' She wanted them isolated, and when I gave her an ultimatum, thinking it would wake her up, she chose to leave."

Nicole slowly shakes her head, blinking like she can't believe it. That's how I felt when I was going through it. It's hard to believe. How a well-educated, capable person could fall for conspiracy theories.

"So, we divorced. I thought she'd fight me for custody, but I think she was so far gone at that point, she packed her bags and left."

"And opened up a wellness camp?"

I nod. "It's essentially a cult. She'd argue it's a healthy living commune—" I quirk my fingers over those last few words to quote them "—but she's making money off these people who really do believe they'll be cured of whatever ails them if only they eat a raw diet and shun Western medicine."

Nicole smooths her hand up over my chest to my neck, her fingers raking through my hair. "How do your kids feel about all that?"

"Each one of them feels differently about her, but now as adults, they know what her beliefs are. I never talked bad about her in front of them. I was very careful not to do that, but cell phones are banned at her camp. There is one phone in the whole place, and they can make calls once a week. She used to call the kids, ask them to visit, but they pretty quickly lost interest in her, especially when she wouldn't let them do the things they loved." I lift a shoulder. "My mom moved in with me to help when Heather moved out, and since then, I've always made sure to keep my family close. Keep everyone together."

Having my father leave and then my wife, it did something to my psyche. Made me adamant about doing everything in my power to keep those I love close. Because I don't think I'd be able to stand it if another walked out on me. It doesn't matter that my father is an asshole and my ex-wife has straw for brains, it hurts watching someone you love walk away.

"You're a good man, Ian Stone," Nicole says, brushing over my beard, her fingertips grazing my bottom lip with every stroke.

I am so gone for this woman, it will kill me when she walks away. And all my work to keep my family together will be for nothing if she's not part of it.

But I am unable to verbalize any of that. Not when she is still married and I'm terrified of hearing her say I am not what she wants. That I am simply a detour in her life.

So I allow myself a caress of her face, knuckles tracing the curve of her cheek and down to the line of her jaw, memorizing it for later. For all the days and nights I won't be able to touch her like this. When I'm a sad old man, I'll be able to remember what it felt like to sit next to Nicole at a fancy restaurant while she wore a red dress and gazed up at me like I was the center of her world.

Our food arrives then, and we shift topics to lighter things. But a new layer remains between us, a tether of understanding that holds us together. It binds us as easily as everything else has.

We share the house-made raspberry sorbet for dessert, and after I pay the bill, I lead her outside, my hand on the small of her back. From my teasing all night, she's practically vibrating, goose bumps rising any time I graze her with the mere tip of my finger.

She's primed, and according to the way she reacts when I kiss her against my car, she's desperate. I slip my hand beneath the fabric of her dress, spreading her pussy with my fingers, finding her wet and ready. She moans into my mouth, body arching into mine, and it takes almost nothing for me to make her twitch. I bring her right to the brink in seconds, only to stop.

I won't let her come. Not yet.

She whines as I pull away, but she doesn't say a word when I open the door for her. I get behind the wheel, sweeping my gaze over her, her parted lips, the outlines of her peaked nipples through the material of her dress, the way she's rubbing her thighs together.

"You ready to play?" I ask, and she nods.

Sweet as honey. "Yes, sir."

Maneuvering us back to the highway, I place my hand on her thigh, roughly pulling it toward me, forcing her legs open. "I want you to touch yourself." She hesitates, and I push her dress up higher. "Fingers on your clit to start."

She eventually does what I tell her to, slumping a little in her seat, her left hand holding up the hem of her dress, the other sliding between her legs where I can't see, but I know from her quick audible intake of breath, she's following my direction. I rub her leg as she works her clit. "Keep going, nice and easy until you come."

She whimpers, muscles tense under my palm, and a minute later, she's coming with a rushed breath and arched neck.

"Good girl," I rasp, wishing we could teleport, so I can finally have my mouth on her like I want. "Again. This time, I want your fingers inside. Use both hands if you need to. I want you to come again."

She swivels her head to me, as if she needs more of an explanation.

"You come when I want you to, whenever, wherever, and however many times I want." I squeeze her thigh. "Go on. Another one."

She shifts and squirms, her left hand moving between her legs, and I groan in the back of my throat, imagining her fingers circling her clit *and* pushing inside her. Warm and wet and tight.

I know exactly what she's feeling.

I wish I could feel it again.

"You like that?" I ask, even though I don't need to. Her moans are enough.

"Mm-hmm."

"You gonna come like a good girl?"

"Mm-hmm."

"Show me. Show me how well you listen to me."

Seconds later, she's coming like the good fucking girl she is. I grind my molars, my cock hard in my pants, and I carefully change lanes, heading toward the exit.

"Fuck, you're sexy, you know that?"

She huffs as if I'm kidding. I'm not.

"You know how amazing it is that you're so open with me? That you're not afraid? Turns me the fuck on. Now do it again. I want you so wet you're soaking the seat."

Which is fucking outrageous because I spent a lot of money on this leather. But fuck it.

I want Nicole more than I want anything else in my life.

She slams her head back against the rest, and I'm quick to find the familiar overlook I spotted on our way here as she brings herself to orgasm one more time.

"Give me your hands," I say, reaching for her wrists. She lets me pull them toward my mouth, sucking off the sticky arousal from her fingers. She tastes like salt and earth and all my favorite things, and I can't wait anymore. "Out of the car."

I damn near slam my door closed, my cock painfully hard as I meet her at the hood, putting my hands on her waist to lift her up on it. I toss her shoes off, place her soles on the hood, and push her dress all the way up. Under the night sky, I can see the outline of her body, though she's still mostly in shadow.

"You're my fantasy," I tell her, cupping my hands around her thighs, holding them open. "I've always dreamed of fucking a girl on my car, and now I'm gonna eat you out until you're screaming. I'm gonna give you as many orgasms as I want. You good with that?"

She breathes out a single strained laugh.

"I'm not kidding, Nicole. I need a yes or no. Because this is the easy stuff. What I'm about to do to you, it's nothing, but if you can't give me an enthusiastic yes now, you definitely won't later."

"Yes," she says after a stunned moment. "I didn't think you were serious—"

I don't let her go on, too fucking jacked up to care about how loud she is when I first put my mouth on her, licking up the length of her pussy. She can scream all night long, wake up everyone in a five-mile radius, I don't care.

I want her to.

I want as many people as possible to know that she's mine.

At least for right now, in this moment.

No matter what happens after this, I'll always have this fantasy brought to life.

Her fingers in my hair.

My tongue lapping against her clit.

Her cries filling my ears.

She comes with only my mouth, and I don't bother to clean off my face when I raise my head to swipe my fingers over her soaked flesh, sliding them inside to find that swollen spot to *really* make her scream.

"That's it, baby," I coo, both proud of her for letting go and grateful for her trust. "You're so sweet like this. Let me hear you."

She mindlessly pulls at her hair, hips bucking as she rides it out, and I barely let her come down before my mouth is on her again, relentlessly flicking at her clit and rubbing at the swollen spot inside her, squeezing her thigh so hard I think she might wake up with marks tomorrow. But she's wriggling all over, and I struggle to keep her still until I push my palm down right above her pelvic bone. It sends her over the edge, and she orgasms with a rush of liquid and a squeak of surprise.

"What was that?"

"You came again. Like I wanted you to," I say against the crease of her hip.

"No." She sits up, the whites of her eyes huge, her skin glowing in the moonlight. "What happened?"

That's when I finally wipe my dry palm over my mouth and beard. "You squirted."

"No, I didn't." She sounds mad about it.

I can't help my laugh. "You did."

"I didn't. That's not...a thing."

"It is a thing, and I made you do it." I incline my head with intention. "I'll do it again."

She holds both hands out, stopping me. "Ian."

"Don't be embarrassed. I like it. I—"

"I've never done it before," she interrupts quietly.

"I figured." I wipe at my mouth again, but it'll be a while before I get her flavor off me. *Good.* "I'll show you a lot of things you've never done before."

She moves, bringing her legs together, obviously working through something, so I give her a minute before I ask, "All right?"

Eventually, she meets my gaze, a pretty red stain on her cheeks. "Yes, sir."

"More?" I ask, and she nods before correcting herself.

"Yes, please."

I bow my head. "For as long as you'll have me, I'll take care of you."

And later, when I'm in bed with her scent and taste still all over me, I finally give in and come too.

Chapter 19
Nicole

It's been a week since my dinner and subsequent roadside orgasms with Ian, and I can still feel his phantom touch on me. In the days since, his daily tasks have turned more sexual. Like finding a pornography video I like then describing it to him via text, explaining why I liked it. Or writing down answers to questions on little pieces of paper—when I feel sexiest, what part of my body I like best—and putting them in my underwear. Three times, he's had me drop those notes in his mailbox at the end of the night.

It is the most delicious torture. Riding the edge all day, every day.

But it's also starting to feel like it's not enough. Not being denied orgasms, but keeping this to ourselves. I'd like to be able to go next door to Stone Ink and talk to him as if we're together and not only business neighbors. I want more than this cloak-and-dagger kink ride.

I'm not sure if Ian somehow understands this or not since I haven't been brave enough to admit it to myself, let alone say it out loud, but he texted me about an hour ago, and told me to go to Sweet Cheeks at 2:15. He'd just so happen to show up at the same time for a break.

So, here we were, sitting at the same table, almost like we're a real couple. It's only a few minutes over a cinnamon roll, but it's the best part of my day because any time I spend with him is the best part. He recounts his latest appointment, a woman who listened to a smutty romance book while getting tattooed, but she didn't realize how high the volume was, so he learned how a blue alien found his human mate on a snowy planet.

"It was pretty good," he says with a smile that lets loose a kaleidoscope of butterflies in my stomach. "Made me realize there's not enough sex in Jane Austen's books."

And I think—no, I know—what I feel for him is not some passing fancy. It's not an experiment I'll be able to forget about in a few weeks or at the end of summer or whenever we decide to call it.

What I feel for him is more than anything I feel for my own husband, which is all I need to know about my relationship with Bryce. If we can even call it that anymore.

He's been gone for about three weeks, and I've barely thought of him. Outside of a few texts, we haven't spoken. Clearly, he's not thinking about me, and yet I am not upset about that at all.

Though, if I reflect on the last few years of my marriage, I can see how the apathy had been building. How we'd slowly become less and less interested in each other until we became roommates instead of partners. Friends instead of lovers.

It never even occurred to me to want more.

Because I didn't know the difference.

But now, I've become conscious of what a relationship can really be.

Fun and exciting while still supportive and respectful.

Which makes me wonder if I'm enough for Ian. So far,

everything has been all one-sided. He's given me everything, and I've offered nothing in return.

"What do you have on your mind?" he asks because he knows me so well.

"I was thinking...when we're...together, it's all about me, and I haven't reciprocated at all. I should. I want to please you."

He takes a deep, audible breath, moments passing before he finally answers. "You please me every day, and the fact that you are even wondering about this shows me exactly how much you do care about pleasing me."

I fill with pride. "Yeah?"

"As for the physical side, what we're doing is more than enough for me. Believe me, baby, if I wanted more, you'd know it. So don't worry about reciprocating. What I want the most is to give you what you need."

Ian is nothing if not honest, but it's hard to believe that he would make it *all* about me. About my discovery. And want nothing in return. "Are you sure?"

He scowls, his silent reprimand. "Is this you doubting me? Second-guessing my directions?"

I shake my head, and he grunts before biting into the cinnamon roll.

"Have a little something," I tell Ian, touching my chin, indicating the icing on his beard.

The beard he had buried between my legs while I was laid out on the hood of his classic car.

The white cream clinging to the gray strands of hair makes my skin heat, and I cross my legs under the table.

As if he knows, he purposefully licks his lips. It's, like, a million degrees in here, and I glance over at Eloise behind the counter, nodding at her for a glass of water. When I turn back to Ian, he wipes a napkin over his mouth and beard. "Better?"

I clear my throat, yet my voice still cracks on the single syllable. "Yep."

He shifts his chair and grazes my knee with his hand, not-so-accidentally from the way his mouth hooks up in the corner. Before I can spontaneously combust, Eloise arrives with the water and the pink cardboard box of all the treats Ian ordered.

"Here you go," she chirps, grinning and bouncing her attention between us. "You two starting to take your breaks together?"

"N-no... Not...together," I stutter out, but Ian smoothly takes over.

"I needed to get out and stare at something prettier than those ugly mugs I work with."

"They're your kids." Eloise playfully knocks his shoulder, and I don't know why tension suddenly brackets my spine. As if I don't like my friend touching Ian. But that's ridiculous. I can't be jealous. I'm not a jealous person.

At least, I didn't think I was.

He shrugs, speaking to Eloise while keeping his eyes on me. "Might be, but they're still not as pretty as Nic."

Eloise pops her hand on her hip, evidently finding nothing odd about that statement. In fact, she smiles bigger. "Nicole is pretty. Far too pretty for you."

Ian nods in agreement. "Damn right."

I drink down the cold water as Ian and Eloise finish up their conversation, and she offers to take my dirty plate. When we stand, Ian places a proprietary hand on my back, and she clocks it, still having no physical reaction.

I'd been so worried about what other people would think if word ever got out about what was going on in my marriage—let alone if they found out about Ian and me—but with Eloise's indifference, it makes me wonder if the anxiety is all in my head.

While no one has ever come right out and said anything negative about Bryce, I always kind of had the feeling he put people off. He doesn't have much patience and doesn't enjoy community events like I do.

And I think my friends on Aster Street know it.

As Ian and I step out of the bakery and onto the sidewalk, I shield my eyes from the bright summer sun. It's been a long time since I put on a swimsuit, but the humidity has me voicing my thoughts. "I wish I had a pool."

"You ever go tubing?" When I shake my head, he says, "I used to take the kids when they were little. You want to go?"

"Tubing?"

"Yeah. Spend a couple hours floating around a river. I'll take you."

Floating in the water for a few hours? There is literally nothing else I want to do. "Yes, please."

"I'll make a reservation. You—"

"Hello, my friends!"

Ian and I both swing our attention to Clara, smiling brightly with a bouncing ponytail, as she flaps a fan open.

"How are you two today? I'm dying in this heat."

I step away from Ian. "We were just talking about how hot it is."

"I need an afternoon shot of sugar, but I'm already sweating from my two-minute walk here." She splits her attention between us. "You had the same idea, huh?"

I can't help but read into her words. Does she suspect that Ian and I were at Sweet Cheeks together?

"Not really," I say, rambling off an excuse. "I was here before he got here, and then he ordered stuff to go. See?" I point at the pink box like an idiot. "We weren't there together."

Clara nods slowly. "Sure. Okay."

Was that sarcasm? She doesn't believe me.

Oh god. If Clara suspects something, everyone will know by the end of the day.

"It was nothing," I mumble, pushing past Clara, who huffs a confused sound.

I practically sprint by Stone Ink to open the door of Chapter and Verse, but not before I hear Clara ask, "Is she feeling all right?"

"I think the heat's getting to everybody," Ian answers smoothly.

The heat of suspicion, yes.

My stomach flips as I think of the gossip that will be spread about me and Ian. My marriage. My whole life.

I force a smile at the worker behind the counter on my way to the bathroom, where I run the cold water, dousing my hands and wrists, rubbing it on my neck and across my forehead, uncaring about getting my hair wet.

The idea of being on display again makes me nauseous, and I lean against the sink, taking deep breaths until my anxiety passes and logic sets in. Clara doesn't know anything. She was simply being her usual friendly self. But the fear of being caught and judged lingers in the back of my mind.

It's there as I complete reports, pay a few bills, and stress out over hitting next month's sales goals until my phone buzzes with a text from Ian.

IAN

Are you okay?

I'm fine.

IAN

Don't lie. What are you worried about?

People finding out.

IAN

I am not trying to downplay your fear, but
Clara didn't seem to suspect anything.

Sure, the logical part of my brain wants to agree, but the overly emotional, cat-backed-into-a-corner part of my brain wants to run and hide. Instead of answering Ian, I go in search of Mr. Darcy. Which is where Andi finds me, sitting on the floor in the corner by the poetry books, petting my cat.

"Hey, Nic." She bends to stroke Mr. Darcy's head. "Hello, handsome."

He purrs, loving the attention from two people, and we both coo and smile at him for another minute before I set him down to ask Andi, "Here for anything specific?"

She shakes her head. "Just looking. We're taking the kids to the beach for the weekend, and I thought I'd come and see if anything calls to me."

Since Andi moved to West Chester about two years ago, we've gotten to know each other pretty well since she comes in every few weeks to buy a new book. Griffin is a huge reader, but he orders all his books online to be delivered to his house, while Andi enjoys browsing in person. She loves poetry, celebrity memoirs, and the occasional romance or women's fiction, so I point her to the table of "Beach Reads" that features the newest summer releases in those two genres.

As she flips through them, she tells me, "It was so nice having you at the picnic. I hope you can come around more often."

My heart starts to pound again, and I wave my hands. "Oh yeah, it was fun, but I don't know."

Her perfectly shaped and laminated brows inch up in a silent question that puts me on the defensive. I take a step back.

"It's just that... I mean, I have no reason to. Show up. That was a one-off."

She opens and closes her mouth, eyes drifting toward the left, to the shared wall with Stone Ink.

And I can't shut up. "I'm not with Ian or anything."

She slants her gaze my way once again, a slow smile spreading across her features as if talking down a crying toddler. "That's okay. I didn't mean to imply you were. It was nice seeing you, that's all."

I feel a pang of guilt at misinterpreting her words, but with panic fogging my mind, it's impossible to see anything clearly.

I need to escape, to find some semblance of control.

As if on cue, my phone buzzes in my pocket. I pull it out, seeing Ian's name on the screen. The message is simple, commanding.

IAN

Go into your office and text me when you're there.

The words send a rush of heat through me, a mix of desire and relief. This is what I need, something to ground me, to remind me who I am. I look up at Andi, forcing a smile. "I'm sorry, Andi. I have to go...deal with this email."

She nods, her smile understanding. "Of course. I'll see you later."

I wave, already hurrying toward the back of the store, to the small office tucked away in the corner. I close and lock the door behind me, my heart still racing, but now it's not merely panic —it's anticipation.

Here.

IAN

Get yourself off.

I set my phone down on the desk to move the hem of my dress, pulling it up, revealing my thighs, my hips, and panties with the note I wrote myself this morning. I remove it, reading, "I am mistress of myself. I am strong. I make my own decisions."

Closing my eyes, I remind myself of all those things. No one can make me feel bad about my choices because they are mine. No one else's. No one's business but my own.

I am mistress of myself.

I slip my hand inside my underwear, my fingers finding warmth and wetness, the ever-present need as my mind fills with Ian, his touch, his voice, his orders. I can hear him in my ear, whispering, guiding, controlling. I can feel his hands on my waist and thighs, his mouth on my throat and between my legs, his body hard against mine, leading me to the filthiest kind of heaven I've ever known.

I stroke my clit, my fingers moving in quick, desperate circles. Pleasure builds, sharp and intense, a coil tightening deep inside me. I'm right there on the edge, dancing on the precipice. So close, so close...

My phone buzzes, and I glance at it, my breath hitching at the message.

IAN

Give me an orgasm.

His command sends me over, fireworks exploding behind my eyes, a wave of heat and light and sensation. I cry out, my fingers pressed tight against my fluttering inner muscles as I ride the waves of the orgasm before slumping into my chair.

As my pulse slows, I can finally parse out my emotions. The panic is gone, replaced by a warm, languid calm. This is what I needed—my release, his control, our connection.

I clean myself up and straighten my dress before typing out a message to Ian.

Thank you, sir. Just what I needed.

I hit send, and I can imagine his smile, his satisfaction, his pride.

And I am happy to give that to him because he gives the same to me.

While I am the one making the decisions for myself, he's the one who showed me I can. He's given me the confidence to be mistress of myself.

Chapter 20
Ian

"Honestly, I don't know how you do it." Nicole flicks her foot, spraying me with water. "No one should look good wearing a life jacket while sprawled out in an inner tube. But you..."

I lower my sunglasses and grip her delicate ankle to keep her from splashing. With the sun high above and sounds of nature all around us, it's the perfect day to laze away on a river. After she freaked out the other day, she had to be reminded that even though she was scared, I would take care of her. Knowing her history, I understood the root of her fear, but she needed me to take away the option of thinking about it.

And so far, my girl is enjoying herself.

I am thoroughly enjoying her.

"You're one to talk," I say, tugging her inner tube closer to mine. She's naturally tanned, but I still took the time to slather her up with SPF. Her bikini is plain navy blue, quite modest compared to others I've spotted, but Nic's beauty is the kind that blooms, a flower bending toward the light. She's soft and willowy—and so fucking pretty, I'm tempted to drag her out of this river and find the nearest campsite. Show her that I can give her everything she needs and anything she wants.

"When we're done here, I want to take your top off and suck on your nipples until you come."

She snorts a laugh that quickly fades. "You're serious."

"I'm always serious when it comes to you."

She nibbles on her lip as her already rosy cheeks darken even more. She adjusts her sunglasses and tugs at her life jacket, and I like how uncomfortable I can make her. Even more pleased at how she pushes herself to work through her shyness.

She will not kowtow or be intimidated by anyone. Not even me.

Because even though I can't see them, I feel her eyes boring into me. "How did you get into all the, uh, lifestyle stuff? Did you take a test or something?"

"A test?" I scrape my fingers over my beard. "You been doing some more research?"

"Of course."

I tip my head back to the sky for a minute as I gather my thoughts. No one's ever actually asked me before.

"Well, it wasn't a test," I say. "Although I know they exist. You do one?"

"I might have."

I grumble my approval as I move our inner tubes so we're side by side. "What did you find?"

"I got a really high submissive score."

I trail my fingertips over her thigh, and her skin dots with goose bumps. "You don't say."

"And I'm apparently 73% brat."

I dip my hand under the water and snap the elastic of her suit at her hip. "Accurate."

"You like when I'm a brat," she retorts, and I nod, placing my hand on her knee, tickling the soft skin underneath.

"So I can make you pay for it later."

She wiggles, permitting my fingers to lower to the apex of her thighs.

"But mostly, I like when you realize you don't have to put up with anyone's shit and stand up for yourself."

She widens her legs enough for me to trace the shape of her over her soaked bathing suit bottoms. Up and down. Up and down.

"How did you learn?" she asks, returning to our conversation. The curious little thing will not be satisfied until she has answers, so I lay it all out for her.

"It took me a long time to be interested in a relationship again after Heather left. I'd go out with women and have some one-night stands here and there, but I started seeing this one woman, Cynthia. She was the one who introduced me to it."

Nicole listens intently, even as I continue to pet her, making her squirm a bit.

"I always liked being in charge when it came to sex, but Cynthia had dabbled in the lifestyle for a while. She asked if I wanted to go to a party with her, and I'm up for whatever, so I went and... You know you hear about stuff like that, but seeing it in real life? My mind was blown."

"You liked it," she says, smiling as if I'm telling her some well-guarded secret. Though at this point, I think I would tell her anything she wanted to know.

"It was eye-opening, and then... I don't know, I started picking things up."

"Where? How?"

"You can occasionally find classes somewhere, at private clubs or parties. Sometimes, it's trial and error. It's a lot easier to find information now than it was when I started."

"When was the last time you were with someone?"

"Dated or in a Dom/sub relationship?"

She shrugs. "Both."

"Last time I had a real sub was two or three years ago. It lasted a few months. Last time I dated anyone was a woman Clara set me up with. We went out a few times, but that was it."

"What happened with Cynthia?"

"She was into things I wasn't. We went our separate ways a long time ago."

"What was she into?" Nicole asks in a near whisper. "Paddles and whips?"

I move my hand from between her legs to palm the back of her head. "You keep bringing that up. Is that what you want?"

"No, but it's easy to spend a few hours on Reddit threads."

I lightly grip the hair at her scalp. "So then you know it's not always about pain."

"And you don't do pain," she says, calling to mind a myriad of images and things I do want to do with her.

"It doesn't particularly turn me on, but if that's what you wanted..."

She thinks on it for a while as I stroke my fingers over the nape of her neck. "I liked when you gave me my tattoo, but not because of the pain. I don't think I'd like to be flogged or anything like that."

Even as she's telling me she doesn't like it, simply having the conversation is turning me on. That she's adventurous and willing to be open to new ideas.

"Is there anything you would like to try?"

She turns her head side to side, making sure no one can hear us. "When you make me find videos to watch, sometimes I have to look through a lot."

"You have my attention," I murmur, and when she rolls her

lips over her teeth, hiding her smile, I squeeze her chin. "Tell me."

"I think I would like to be handcuffed. Can you do that?"

I don't hide *my* smile. "Yeah, baby, I can do that. What else?"

"There was another one when he trained her to come on command."

My gut burns with excitement. "That's my favorite thing."

She grins. "Yeah?"

"Yeah. You'll let me train you?" I conveniently ignore the fact that it takes months to train someone to control orgasms with verbal commands. I don't know if she'll still want to do this with me in a few months, but for now, a guy can dream.

"Do I get special treats for a handshake or begging?"

I don't get it at first, but when I gather she's talking about a dog, I slide my hand under the back strap of her bikini top, holding on to it. "What have I said before?"

"Not sure, sir," she replies, all attitude, really living up to the results of whatever the fuck bullshit quiz she took. I like it anyway.

"Act like a brat, and I won't give you what you want, even when you shake and beg," I remind her. "But be my good girl, and you'll get rewarded."

She folds her hands together, all angelic. "I'll be good. I promise."

"I doubt that," I tease, though my smile slips as I let the undercurrent of this conversation settle over me. I've had some romantic relationships with kink, and I've dated some of my subs, but more often than not, that part of my life has been relegated strictly to play.

I don't want to pressure her when she's in the middle of a traumatic period in her life, but what we're doing is a lot like dating, and if she's looking strictly for play without emotion, we've already crossed a line. At least, for me.

I'm not sure about what she's feeling, except for that stricken look of fear in her eyes yesterday when we ran into Clara together. She's so afraid of being seen with me, it's a blow to my ego. Even as I fully comprehend it, my heart kicks and bucks at the thought of letting her go. At not being able to claim her like I want to.

I'm older and more experienced than her, but I'm not driving the ship here.

She is.

And as much as I hate giving it up in the bedroom, she is in control of where we go.

She is the one who defines what we are. Which, for now, seems like she still only wants me to be her Dom. Not her man.

Unfortunately for me, this isn't a casual fling or experiment. I don't want to try her on like a shirt, only to return her later.

This isn't some trial period for me like it is for her.

Once she figures herself and her future out, all I'll be left with are memories of her sweet laugh and delicious taste. Like a refund receipt.

But if I've learned anything in this life, it's to be grateful for what I have, and if this time is all she'll give me, then I'll enjoy every last minute of it.

"You okay?" she asks, and I startle, my mind having wandered away.

"Hm?"

"Are you all right?"

"Yeah." I notice that I've floated away from her, lost physical contact, and she's frowning. "Just thinking."

"Good place to do it." She splashes me again. "What're you thinking about?"

"You never stop asking questions, do you?"

She shakes her head, teeth in her bottom lip keeping her grin from spreading wide. "Means I'm comfortable with you."

I grunt, immensely glad, and wishing she weren't so goddamn cute. It would be a lot easier to draw lines between us.

Keep this to only sex. Dominant and submissive.

Or make this a committed relationship like…boyfriend and girlfriend.

Although, I'm fifty-one years old. Far too fucking old for a girlfriend.

"Shit," I grumble, needing to get out of my head. With a gruff sound, I snag Nicole's inner tube. "Come on. We're outta here."

"You have plans?" she teases, and I wade us to shore. My plans involve a lot fewer clothes and a lot more orgasms.

"Let's go, brat." I all but push her out of her inner tube. We hand over our gear then make the short walk back to my car, where I tug on the strap of her bikini top, pulling her closer to me. "Did you do what I told you to this morning?"

"Yes, sir."

She wants to find out what I'm really like? She's gonna learn today.

"Get in the car and take off your bottoms. Sit on your hands." I close the door once she settles in her seat. She complies immediately, and I don't waste any time pulling out on the road. She's naked, save for her bathing suit top, and I turn the vents directly on her, so she's blasted with cold air the whole drive.

And I don't say one word.

Riling her up.

I imagine her still-damp skin freezing, and with nothing but her bare ass and pussy on the leather, she's shifting all over the place.

I'm gonna torture the shit out of her.

"We're going to my apartment. I'll park in the back, so no one will see." Except it's the last thing I want to do. I'd rather parade her down all of Aster Street. Claim her as *mine*.

She shoots her eyes to me, worried, and while my muscles clench in hesitation at the thought of hurting her, *I* am the one in charge in this instance. If she wants to see how far I can take her, then we have to stop fucking around, running and hiding. I've reached my breaking point, and I need her in my bed.

At my place, I inform Nicole that June is out, working at a summer camp, and toss her cover-up to her so we can head inside, right up to my apartment. I waste no time directing her to my bedroom. The less time I allow her to get mentally organized, the more she'll live in the moment. The more compliant she'll be.

I tell her to give me the brush she bought this morning then get undressed and lie on my bed with her feet on the mattress. Her wide blue eyes follow me as I adjust the air, keeping the room cool. Her skin is already covered in goose bumps, her nipples tight beads, and when I have her where I want her, I stand at the edge of the bed, lightly brushing the soft bristles across her stomach.

I'd texted her this morning and told her to go shopping. Pick out an item, something soft and small that she liked. Originally, I'd planned on using it strictly for sensory overload, maybe blindfold her and tease her skin with it or anything else I might like. But now that I know what she really wants, I'll use this brush to teach her that I can and will completely control her.

"Any time you want to orgasm, you need to ask me. Any time you even touch yourself and you're about to come, you need to ask me. If you're at home and masturbating, you'll call me and ask. Got it?"

She nods, and when I arch my brow, she offers a small, excited smile, her hips shifting as she says, "Yes, sir."

"Good girl. Now…" I drag the brush—probably some kind of makeup brush that's wide and flat—over her sternum. "I believe I said I wanted to suck on these pretty little nipples." I spend a few seconds sweeping the brush over each of them. "What do you think of that?"

She's already whimpering, and I fucking *love* it.

"And when you want to come, what are you going to do?"

"Ask."

"That's my perfect girl." I bend, closing my mouth around her nipple, her skin cold and clammy and oh-so perfect against my tongue. She smells of sunscreen and tastes of salt, and her hips buck up off the bed. "No, no. Stay still."

"I can't," she moans, and I move to her other breast, flicking at her nipple with my tongue before sucking on it.

After a moment, I lift my head, telling her, "You can, and you will."

She tries to settle down, but I can feel the electricity simmering under her skin. A live wire.

"Please, Ian."

"What, baby?" I skim her side with the brush. "What do you want?"

"Make me come."

I continue caressing her ribs and waist as I hum around her other nipple. "That's not how you ask."

She squirms, and it's near impossible for me to ignore the heat of her pussy with every absent lift of her hips. She continuously fists and unfists the sheet, so close to coming, it makes my own skin break out in a sweat.

"Please, please, please," she moans. "Can I come?"

"Already?"

When I bite the underside of her breast, she nearly screams, body completely restless.

"You're not doing a very good job of keeping still. I don't think I should let you come."

"Ian!"

"Yes, baby?"

"Please, can I come?"

I give her nipple one more long suck as I swipe the brush back and forth across the other before straightening, watching as her body flushes red. "Come, baby. Come for me."

She shakes and groans and falls over the edge with complete abandon and utter beauty. I palm the soft and wet skin between her legs as she settles down from the aftershocks. Still, I draw the brush over her body, write my name across her stomach, spend a minute going over her tattoo, even make a little heart over her real one.

I'm a fucking child.

A love-sick puppy.

And yet, I stay here, captivated by the woman who has no idea she's tattooed my own heart with her name.

"Let's try that again, hm?" I slide my hand around her thigh, pushing it open farther. "Keep them like this." When I swipe the brush up and down the length of her pussy, she shudders. "Don't move."

She freezes immediately, save for her fingers clutching the sheet tighter and the rapid rise and fall of her stomach when she breathes. I continue to brush along her slit, as gently as possible. I know the barely there touch is working as her legs begin to tense and tremble. She's trying so hard to be good and still for me, doing what I want, and it makes me hard. I reward her by sliding my middle finger down the wet seam of her flesh, parting it to reveal her clit. Then I brush the tender, swollen bud.

Nicole gasps. "Oh my god."

"Feel good?"

"Never felt..." She shivers. "Anything like it."

I turn my wrist and crook my finger, giving love to the tender, swollen spot inside her.

All of her is tender.

All of her is swollen.

And pleading.

And shivering.

And glistening with sweat, even though her skin is cool to the touch.

She is completely under my control, and I can't help but take a moment to kiss her, licking my gratitude into her mouth.

With every stroke of the brush, she climbs higher and higher, her cries growing louder, and I watch in pleased satisfaction, my cock tenting my swim trunks.

Maybe next time, I'll climb over her and put it in her mouth, but not today. Today, she needs to learn what it means to be mine.

Her arms and legs start moving, forgetting about the position I want her in, and I can tell I'm losing her. Before I'm able to give her any other direction, the telltale pulsing of her inner walls gives way, and she orgasms without asking.

I immediately step away from her. No matter how much it pains me—her wetness all over my fingers and the brush still in my right hand, fisted at my side.

When she recognizes what's happened, her eyes fly open, and I cluck my tongue. "You didn't ask."

She licks her lips. "I'm sorry."

"Me too."

"Is it... Are we done?"

I nod, and she wrenches upright, not bothering to cover up. "What? No."

My chuckle is gruff. Like it's been through a cheese grater. "You aren't in charge."

She darts her gaze around as if she can find help.

I offer her a reprieve and kiss her mouth. "We'll try this again another day, but we're done for now."

"What about—"

"And later," I say, nibbling on her earlobe, "you will call me while you're touching yourself, and you'll ask me to come."

"But—"

"I know. It won't be as good as when you're with me. But that's part of your punishment."

She heaves a sigh even as she reaches for me, and I help her get dressed, ignoring my hard-on still raging and begging for attention.

But more than that, my heart kicks around my chest as I walk her downstairs and kiss her goodbye before she gets into her car to drive home. Drive away from me.

Fuck. I'm toast.

Chapter 21
Nicole

For the last two nights, Ian's talked me through an orgasm on the phone, voicing when and how to touch myself until I've teetered on the edge, and then the awful man has told me to, "Hold it. Yes, good girl. Not yet, not until I say..."

Only after I started begging and keening did he order in his raspy voice, "Come, baby. Come for me."

And if this is what Pavlov's dogs felt like, I understand why they drooled. We're only a few days into this training, and already, I crave to hear those five words in his deep rumble.

As much as he says he loves control, I love it too. The more Ian controls me sexually, the more I learn about myself and how to control my own life.

I learn what I like, to speak up for myself, and—most importantly—not to feel bad about any of it.

I am finally learning how not to give a fuck.

Clearly, other people are noticing.

Aunt Sue smiles at me from her backyard in Maine on our video call. A few years ago, she and an old high school classmate reconnected online. One thing led to another, and she is now married to the owner of the biggest recreational fishing company in Maine.

"It sounds like everything is going well for you," she says after I fill her in on the bookstore business. Aunt Sue isn't involved anymore, but I often still ask her for advice or to be a sounding board for new ideas. "And you look really happy."

"I am happy." I adjust my headphones, figuring now is as good a time as any to tell her. "Happier than I've been in a long time, and I wanted to talk to you about it."

She sets her chin in her fist. "Okay."

"Bryce has been away for a few weeks doing fieldwork."

She purses her lips, nodding, but keeps quiet, waiting for me to gather my courage and spit it out.

"While he's been gone, things have sort of crystallized for me."

"What kinds of things?"

I lick my lips and rip off the Band-Aid. "I don't love him anymore. I haven't for a long time."

She's not surprised in the least, and while I appreciate how she never jumps into conversation—as some people do, trying to problem-solve—I expected some kind of reaction. I tell her so, and she laughs quietly.

"I'm not really sure what you want me to say, hon. I've been front and center for your entire relationship, and I remember very clearly what you were like on the day you married him, so I'm not shocked."

But *I* am shocked. "What?"

"You were so calm..." She tips her head side to side as she thinks. "Maybe calm isn't the right word. Resigned? Or... It was like you were there because you were supposed to be, not because you wanted to be. I remember seeing you in the dressing room with your hands folded in your lap like a school-girl. Like you were waiting to be told what to do next."

I don't know whether to be offended or grateful that she's so honest.

Looking back, I suppose that's what it was like. Bryce and I dated, he asked me to marry him, and one foot in front of the other, I did.

I did what I was supposed to do.

But now, I'm doing what I want to do.

"Is there someone else in the picture?" Aunt Sue asks, and I find myself biting back a smile. Answer enough.

I've been afraid of other people finding out about Ian and me, but Aunt Sue would never judge me.

"Who is it?"

"It's, um—"

"Ian Stone?" she guesses, and my jaw drops. She merely waves away my surprise. "The two of you always did have... something. That man could scare away people with one look, but when you were around, he was different. Went from a bear to a cub. And you..." She laughs to herself. "The number of times I caught you watching him. I always knew you liked him."

Hearing her outside perspective makes me feel better, braver about my decision.

On-screen, she shrugs. "Maybe you more than like him."

Do I?

Do I love Ian?

Is it even possible to come to love someone in a few weeks?

"Are you okay?" She frowns at me. "Why do you suddenly look upset? I didn't mean to insinuate anything. If you're—"

"I'm not upset." I blink a few times to clear my blurry vision. "I'm happy, really."

"But...?"

I sniff. "I'm scared."

"I understand. It takes a lot of courage to go after what you want, especially when what you want is not set in stone. Do you know what you're going to do?"

I shake my head. "I need to talk to Bryce when he returns home, but I haven't thought much beyond I know I don't want to be with him anymore."

"I'm sure it'll be hard, and you'll have uncomfortable conversations, but I'm proud of you for making your decision. A lot of people settle for less because they're afraid to admit they want more."

Knowing my aunt understands and is in my corner gives me the boost I need to face another one of my fears. After we hang up, I tell my worker that I'm going on a break, head out of Chapter and Verse, and stride right next door to Stone Ink.

I don't care who sees me.

Because soon, I'll be here as often as I want to be. Might as well start now.

Jasper's at the check-in desk today, leaned back in a chair, a well-worn paperback in hand. He lifts his gaze from the page to offer me a jut of his chin.

"Hey. How's it going?"

"Good. I'm here to—"

"Dad," he calls over his shoulder. "Nicole's here."

I'm not sure what it means that he knows I'm here to see Ian, but I can't even begin to make an excuse or explain it away because *I* don't even know what it all means.

That I very possibly haven't hidden my growing feelings for Ian as well as I thought.

Jasper merely raises a brow at me, so much like his father, then turns back to his book.

When Ian appears a moment later, I'm flustered and still stuttering. He wraps his hand around my neck, and while he doesn't kiss me, he does lean down so close I can feel the scratch of his beard. "Did you eat lunch?"

When he might as well have asked, "Are your panties soaked?"

And, yes. The answer is yes.

"Mm-hmm." When I comprehend he's waiting for more of an answer, I ignore the feel of his fingertips squeezing my neck and fumble for one. "I had a salad. It was good. Then I talked to my aunt. It was a good talk."

"*Good.*" He grins because he knows exactly what he's doing then walks me back through the shop. It's not very busy, with Cash the only other one working. He offers a quick and quiet greeting as he continues tattooing.

"I only have twenty minutes until my next appointment," Ian says as he rushes me upstairs. As soon as the door is closed behind us, he takes my head in his hands and kisses me like he hasn't seen me in ages.

Like he's stealing my oxygen.

Like he's claiming me as his.

"We don't have time to play." His lips skate over the pulse point in my neck. "But I've been dreaming about your mouth all day."

With his hand still in my hair, he unbuckles his belt and undoes his jeans with the other, pushing them down his thighs. He reaches past me to the couch and grabs a pillow to throw on the floor. "On your knees, baby."

"Oh, so you get all the fun today," I say as cheekily as possible, even though my mouth waters at the idea of finally tasting him. I haven't been allowed to touch him yet, and I have no idea how he's lasted this long, giving me orgasm after orgasm while not wanting me to return the favor.

At least until now.

And I am more than happy to do so.

I sink to the floor and tilt my head back to stare up at him. He lightly cups the back of my head. "What did you talk about with your aunt?"

"Mostly the business and how she's started playing pickleball."

"Oh yeah?" His voice is steady and even. "Anything else?"

Mine sounds like a leaf shaking in the wind. Especially when he tugs his boxer briefs down, revealing his erection, long and thick. "I told her that all these weeks have helped me figure out what I want."

"What do you want, baby?"

"You."

His dark eyes flare with something I can't comprehend at the moment. Not when his fingers grip my hair deliciously tight, and he drags the tip of his shaft to my chin. "We're both going to get off today. I'm going to tell you how I like it, and you're going to pet your pretty little pussy. But you're not going to come, right?"

"Not until you tell me."

"Good girl. Now wrap your hand around my cock."

I curl the fingers of my left hand around his girth, amazed by the bead of moisture forming at the tiny slit. I want to lick it, but I don't dare. Not until he tells me.

When I raise my eyes again, I find his hard eyes focused on my hand.

I assume I haven't done anything wrong. I did what he told me to, but his jaw is working beneath his beard. He's mad. Or, at the very least, annoyed.

That's when I see what it is.

The only pieces of jewelry I'm wearing on my left hand.

My wedding bands.

I open my mouth to explain that I have no attachment to

them anymore. They're only on my finger as a habit. It means nothing. In fact, I'm ready to take them off for good.

But he doesn't let me get that far. He thrusts his hips forward and shoves his cock into my mouth.

I gag, and he backs off, his features at war. One second appearing apologetic and the next frustrated. I think I see jealousy in his gaze, followed immediately by lust.

"Use your hand and mouth," he instructs. "Take it as far back as you can. I don't care if you're sloppy." When I do as he says, breathing out of my nose but still gagging a little, he nods. "In fact, I like it that way."

I find a rhythm that works, alternating between working him with my hand and mouth. When I lean back to catch my breath, a line of spit keeps us connected, and he wipes it away, thumbing my swollen lips. "Now get yourself off. I want you rubbing your clit hard and fast."

I pull the hem of my shirt out from the elastic waistband of my loose, floral-print shorts. Of course I'm not wearing a dress today, making everything so much more difficult. Adrenaline has my blood rushing in my ears, my hands shaking in my haste to please him and get myself off.

Ian, though, is in complete control. Not one hair out of place. His breath steady and even as he praises me. Instructs me.

Brings me swiftly to the edge of orgasm without even touching me. Besides where his hands hold my head, he's getting *me* off getting *him* off.

"You want to come, don't you? Not yet. Wait," he orders with a soft voice, almost cooing at me. "Wait, baby. Not yet."

I whimper around his length, my fingers flying over my clit. I'm soaked and hot and need to come. I drag my mouth off him, stroking my fist up and down. "Can I please come?"

He shakes his head, even though I can see his muscles tensing, feel the heat wafting off him. "Not yet. And don't stop sucking my cock. *Hard,* Nicole. Do it."

I slide him back into my mouth, sucking hard and pulling fast. As fast as I'm circling my fingers over my clit.

"Don't you fucking come yet," he grits out, yanking on my hair at the scalp.

I whine and suck him to the back of my throat, my mouth full and watering, jaw aching. I'm about ready to ask him again when he finally says, "Come, baby. Come for me."

I go from being soaked to being completely drenched, my fingers covered in my wetness, as he comes in my mouth. It's sensory overload—his salty taste, his hoarse voice, and the echo of my orgasm crashing around inside. It ripples through me, head fuzzy and vision blurry. My heart tumbling in my chest with the knowledge that, yes, I think I do love him.

But I don't have time to contemplate this new revelation because Ian hauls me up to standing, his pants already zipped, before sticking my fingers in his mouth, licking them clean. Then he's kissing me, our flavors mixing on each other's lips and tongues.

And, still, I feel outside of myself.

It isn't until the door flies open a mere five feet from us that I'm forced out of my orgasm haze.

"What the hell?" Ian shouts, startled at the commotion that is his son.

Jay's eyes widen, obviously bemused to find us here.

"What are you doing?" Ian pushes me behind him.

The younger Stone's eyes float between his father and me, interested and full of mischief. "I'm hungry."

"There's food in the break room," Ian says, but Jay shakes his head.

"No, there's not."

"You ate all of it?"

"I'm a growing boy." He grins. "What are *you* two doing up here?"

"*I* live here," Ian growls, like only an irritated dad could.

His middle son nods and crosses his arms, entertained by all of this. "And the two of you are up here…"

"Taking a break," Ian fills in.

Jay's smile grows another inch, and I already don't like whatever is going to come out of his mouth next. He shifts over a few inches and theatrically brings his hands to his chest like he might break out in a rousing rendition of "Tomorrow" from *Annie*. "Are you my new mommy?"

I cover my blazing cheeks with my hands, hoping he can't tell how mortified I am. For his part, Ian pulls his son into a headlock. "Don't be a jackass." Then he ruffles Jay's hair and tells him he can make himself a sandwich. "But," he says, reaching for my hand at the same time as he raises a stern finger toward Jay, "don't try to embarrass Nicole again. Or you're gonna be a lot hungrier after I put new locks on the door."

Jay attempts to swallow his smile. It doesn't work. But he does salute his dad and wave to me. "I'm just giving you shit, Nic. Tell me to fuck off anytime, okay?"

I shrug, take a breath, and say, "Fuck off, Jay."

Father and son both crack up, and I realize it's been a long time since I've felt like I've had any family besides Aunt Sue in my corner. But these guys? The whole of the Stone family, I think I might belong with them.

If only they'll have me.

Chapter 22
Ian

I lean against the doorframe of Chapter and Verse, arms crossed over my chest, one foot kicked up. Jasper's out on the sidewalk, Cash is at the back of the store, while Jay sits with the other children, cross-legged on the floor in front of Blue Betty as she reads aloud from a brightly illustrated children's book, giving life to each and every character with different voices. Meryl Streak stands off to the side with big glasses and a caftan, playfully admonishing children who talk out of turn—mostly Jay.

While we're not officially security, I wasn't going to chance anything happening to the bookstore or the workers because some asshole thought he'd be a hero. Especially after I perused the online comments about the event. Funny how the term "degenerate" is thrown around by people threatening violence and causing emotional harm to those they dislike. We're just here having some fun with books.

A man and woman probably not much older than me but a lot more beige slow their stride as they approach the bookstore, faces curled in obvious distaste, and I straighten from my position, letting my arms drop to my sides so they can read my *Support Your Queens* T-shirt. Jasper sidles up next to me, tipping his head to the side, silently dismissing them with a shake of his head.

My eldest child doesn't talk much, but he sure as shit gets his point across.

Our tattoos and muscles probably help too.

The man grabs the woman's hand, nearly dragging her away, past our shop to Sweet Cheeks. If they don't like Nicole's drag queen read-aloud hour, I'd bet my entire savings they won't enjoy Eloise's pride flags and name tags with pronouns listed.

Turning back to the store, I spot a few familiar faces. Jude Grey, of Grey's Candy. Nate, one of the co-owners of Tabby Cat, the wine bar across the street, and father of a feisty little one. A woman, who I'm positive is Maddie's dance teacher, and the mechanic I take my car to when it needs a tune-up. There's also another couple, attempting to stop a kid from putting a bucket on his head after upending it so all the small notebooks and pens fell out.

Nicole bends, laughing quietly as she picks it up, waving away the parents' worry and apologies. As usual, I study her, from the top of her ponytail, to the bright blue boa around her neck that she accepted from Betty, to the hand she's holding in the air, pointing something out to the dad in the kids' section. I notice she's not wearing her wedding rings today, and for a moment, my breath stalls, my heart beating in my ears so loud, it's the only thing I hear.

During our very short conversation upstairs, before she gave me the best blow job of my life, she'd said she wanted me.

Sure, she wants me for sex and some fun for a few weeks, but she's never made any declarations.

At least, not until today.

With her bare finger.

That's a *statement*.

One I hope means she wants me in her future. Or at least that she's not going to go back to a man who doesn't make her happy. Because that's all I want.

Her happiness.

As much as it would pain me to let her go, I would if it made her happy. I just don't think that weasel in a sweater vest can give her what I can. He can't make her happy like I do.

And no one would make me as happy and fulfilled as she does. There's never been anyone in my life who's made me consider the possibility of love and marriage again until Nicole. When I picture the rest of my life, she is in it, and if it were up to me, I'd drive over to her house right now and pack up all her stuff myself. I'd move it all to my place.

Then again, I'm not sure she would want that.

Jay was being his usual pain-in-the-ass self the other day, teasing Nicole about becoming his new mommy, but I felt her body go rigid. So, she might be ready to step away from her marriage and still not be ready to take a step forward with me.

If I'm even reading this right. I could be jumping to conclusions, according to what I want to happen. It's just...

Fuck.

I love her, and I want to be with her.

I want her in my house and in my bed. Out to breakfast with my kids. At picnics with my family. My kiss good night and first smile in the morning.

My new normal lately has been following these imaginary journeys in my mind about Nicole, and by the time Jas hits my shoulder, gesturing with his head that he's headed next door, I blink into awareness that the story hour is over. Cash and Jay filter out with the families, both of them wearing a few stickers on their shirts from Betty and Meryl.

After the crowd is gone, I stay behind to help Nicole clean up. I gather discarded paper cups and toss them into the recycling bin then straighten the chairs.

Mr. Darcy slinks out from behind the counter, his tail swishing as he approaches me. I crouch down and extend my hand, letting him sniff my fingers before he butts his head against my palm, demanding attention. I oblige, scratching behind his ears as he purrs contentedly.

"He likes you," Nicole remarks, a smile playing on her lips as she watches us from across the room.

"What can I say? I have a way with pussies." My joke earns an eye roll that bleeds into a blushing grin, and I give the cat a final pat before standing up. "Why doesn't he live at your house?"

When she hesitates, I already know what she's going to say. *Who* she will name. "You know Darcy's been around a long time. Aunt Sue got him, and he was used to having the run of the apartment upstairs and here. When she moved, she didn't have the heart to take him, but Bryce wouldn't let me bring him home. He's allergic to cats."

"Allergic... Like deathly ill—or the sniffles?"

Her shrug is minuscule, and I've seen this reaction out of her before. Like she's tired of fighting with him. "It was just easier to keep Darcy here. He's the shop guard cat. Vicious."

I can't smile at her attempt at levity because this is bigger than the cat. "He belongs with you. You're his home."

Nicole nods as the cat completes a figure eight around her ankles as if he knows we're talking about him.

"And you belong with someone who will make that home for you."

"Are you..." She closes the short distance between us, mouth opening and closing in stunned silence until she finally rasps out her question. "What are you saying?"

"I'm saying that I want to belong to you. We've never talked about what your plans are with...him." I can't even say his name. It's a lump in my throat that's almost impossible to swallow around. "But I want you to know I'm here. I'll be here if or when you're ready for something more than fun."

She considers my words, her fingers fisting the sides of my T-shirt. She's no longer afraid to touch me in public, which could only be a good sign. Along with her missing jewelry.

And my hopes are up.

Until she frowns. "You want to...date me?"

I touch my index finger to her bottom lip. "I want to do whatever you want. However much you'll give me." Her tongue pokes out to wet her lips, licking my finger, and a jolt of lust shoots through me. "I know I was the one who told you not to give any fucks about anybody but yourself, but I want you to give a fuck about me."

She bites back a smile, her bratty attitude shining through her whispered words. "You mean you want me to fuck you."

I lift a shoulder. "That too. I want you to give lots of fucks *about* me. Because—" I stop myself, ready to tell her how I feel, but I doubt she's ready to hear it yet. So I backtrack. "I like you, and you can have every last one of my fucks."

"So romantic."

"Baby, I will give you all the romance you want." I curl my hand around the nape of her neck and place one soft kiss on her mouth, laying all my dreams at her feet. "But I can't pretend it's not killing me anymore. I'll give you all the time you need, I just need to know if at the end of this journey you're on, you're going to want me with you."

She backs away a few inches, and her pretty blue eyes drift back and forth between my own, searching for meaning and very possibly reading between the lines. Of course my brilliant and curious girl would study all the possibilities closely. No matter how much she's grown over the last few weeks, she will never stop being cautious, and I'm glad of it.

"What if I said I wanted to get another cat?" she asks, as if *that* will make me change my mind.

"Is that supposed to turn me off? You want another cat? Okay. You want three more cats? All right. I'll build you a whole goddamn cat castle, if that's what you want."

Her throat bobs on a swallow, her eyes alight like she might start laughing or crying. But she doesn't respond, and I hold my breath.

Waiting for long seconds.

Fucking days.

I would wait as long as she told me to, but right now, I have trouble keeping my impatience in check. I tell myself to relax my muscles and release the grip on her neck to play with the ends of her ponytail.

She fixes her gaze on my eyes, and when she finally speaks, her voice is gentle but firm. "Ian, I hope you know how much I care about you, as a person and friend, but especially as a man who's shown me what life can be like. What relationships can be. You've made me realize I know myself better than I thought, and you helped me to be braver than I ever suspected I could be." She gently scratches at my beard, and this feels like a breakup even though technically we were never even together. "I want you to know that I will always cherish you and what we have together. I've never felt anything like it. But..."

I work to keep my features smooth, refusing to let on to the fact that I'm most likely having a heart attack.

"I can't make any promises yet. Not until I officially end things with Bryce." She reaches for my hand, threading our fingers together. "It wouldn't be right for me to jump into something new before properly closing that chapter of my life."

I nod, even as irrational frustration wells up inside me.

She's doing the mature, responsible thing, but the jealous caveman in me wants to throw her over my shoulder and take her upstairs to my apartment right now.

"Yeah, no, I get it. Absolutely. You're right," I mumble, hoping I sound somewhat coherent.

She gives me a small smile, maybe because she thinks me losing my mind is funny. Or maybe because she knows how she's waltzed into my life and shaken it up like no one and nothing else has been able to. Or maybe she knows I'm not telling the truth.

Because I want all of her *now*. I don't want to wait.

She brushes her thumb over my knuckles. "I want to be able to give you—give us—my full attention. You deserve that."

"You deserve to do this at your own pace," I reply because it's true. But also...

Tell me you love me.

Tell me you'll sleep in my bed.

Tell me you're mine for good. Forever.

I tug on her hand, pulling her against me. "I'm yours, Nicole. Whenever you're ready."

A blush stains her cheeks, and I can't resist dragging the tip of my nose over the warm flush, inhaling the familiar scent of her shampoo. She offers me a kiss, her lips brushing against mine when she murmurs, "Thank you for being so understanding."

I don't feel all that understanding, but I'm glad I can at least pretend I am. "Don't give me too much credit. It's the least I can do. It's the least anyone can do. Start expecting more. Your bar is too low."

Her laugh is muffled against my chest. "The bar is in hell."

Which makes me want to roar. As far as I'm concerned, her husband doesn't deserve her maturity. What he does deserve is the middle finger spray-painted on his walls as the goodbye note. Nicole doesn't need to explain herself to anyone, but it goes to show what an amazing woman she is that she'll give him that.

"I just need a little more time," she says, tipping her head back.

I ignore the rising pain in my chest, a mixture of jealousy and desire and love. "Take all the time you need."

Come home to me.

Make me yours.

"Soon," she whispers. "I promise."

I close my eyes, breathing her in, willing myself to be patient. To trust her promise that she's not going anywhere.

When she draws back, the affection in her gaze steadies me. She knows how I'm struggling, yet she's still here.

I take her hand again, running my thumb over her bare ring finger. A silent promise of my own. That, when she's ready, I'll be here to give her everything. My heart and my future, it's all hers.

"I know," I say simply. And I do. However long it takes, she's worth it.

We are worth it.

Chapter 23
Nicole

I walk into my house on cloud nine. The day was amazing. The drag story hour went off without a hitch, we made a ton of sales with all of the publicity, *and* best of all, Ian told me he wants to be with me.

I'm so relieved and giddy, I don't notice the car parked out front or the luggage in the hall.

"Hey, there you are."

I jump back, right into the wall, hitting my head, and Bryce reaches for me with a wince.

"Sorry. Didn't mean to scare you."

He rubs the back of my head, and that bubbly happiness that made me practically float in here evaporates. I am not so much set down into reality as dropped.

"You're home."

My husband steps away from me once I'm upright again. "Yeah. We finished a few days early."

"You didn't text me."

"Didn't think I needed to."

"Well… I could've…" I glance around, looking for an escape. Not finding one, I flop my hands. "Planned."

"Planned for what?" He huffs a laugh. "A welcome-home dinner? That would be nice."

After a month of having no expectations put on me—other than the ones I've asked for—I can't help the roll of my eyes. He's so accustomed to my going with the flow, doing what he wants, that of course he thinks I'll take his suggestion and get my butt in the kitchen to make him a dinner, even though I've just come home from a twelve-hour workday.

He doesn't care, though.

Never has.

He's never once made me dinner, and he long ago stopped asking me when I'd be home. He stopped caring about me altogether.

Not that I am any better. When he spent weekends grading papers, I didn't mind. I didn't bother to check up on him or adjust my schedule to match his so we could spend more time together.

We've become strangers to each other, and now that I've had the opportunity to see the person he's become, I am not interested in learning any more. I don't want to be married to someone who is more excited about his work than having a conversation with me over coffee. I want someone who looks forward to spending time with me. I want someone who makes me want to leave work early because I know they're waiting for me.

Marriage is more than sex, and passion may fade, but I shouldn't have to settle for someone who thinks all our problems will be solved by a hall pass for the summer.

This month away from Bryce has opened my eyes to exactly how much time I spent convincing myself that I was content, as opposed to actually *being* content.

Ian has given me the time and space to figure out what makes me happy, and it's him. Plain and simple.

"It's after nine," I say, going back to his suggestion of dinner. "Didn't you eat?"

"I had a snack on the plane."

I turn to the living room, where I set my purse and keys down on the table. "What time did you get in?"

He follows behind me, tossing himself on the sofa. "A few hours ago."

I blink around. "A few hours ago? What were you doing all day?" I wave my hand toward the kitchen. "You could have made yourself something."

"Yeah, but I didn't know when you would be home, so I thought I'd wait."

"Because if I made something, you could eat. But you would never make me something to eat for when I got home."

He tips his head. "Ah, come on. I'm not trying to start a fight."

"But you are, though. I've been working all day, yet you expect me to make you a meal."

He motions to the hall, where he still hasn't moved his luggage. "I've been traveling."

To think I went from a man saying he'd *wait for me* to a man saying he'd *wait for me to make him dinner.*

I take a deep breath, steeling myself for a conversation I'm not ready to have but cannot avoid. I clear my throat and take a seat across from him. "I feel like I should ask you about your trip, but that would be disingenuous." At his confused expression, I explain, "I did a lot of thinking while you were gone, and I've come to the realization that for the last few years, that's *all* we've talked about."

"What do you mean?"

"We ask each other about our days, and that's pretty much

it. Aside from an argument about dinner or some boring lecture you want me to go to, we don't *talk*."

"Boring lecture?" He sits up, offended, having missed my actual point. "You're calling my lectures boring?"

"Yes, Bryce. Some of your lectures are boring, but I meant all of it. All of the conferences and speeches and award ceremonies, I attend them all for you, but you've never once come to things I've invited you to."

"Because why would I care about some fall street festival?"

I shoot my arm out at him. "Because I care! I care, and you don't. I went to all of your lectures, because you asked me to. Because you wanted me to support you, and I have, but I can't expect that in return, and I'm tired of pretending like we care about each other's days when you obviously don't care about mine."

"Wow." He rubs his hands over his face. "Didn't expect to come home to this."

"I didn't expect you to come home," I say, which only annoys him further. "I thought I had a few more days until you returned."

That has his brows rising. "Oh yeah? Did you have something special going on?"

If he only knew.

"No, but I wanted to have more of an idea of what I'd say to you."

He snorts. "You've said quite a lot."

And I am not done. "I want a divorce."

He shoots up to standing. "You *what*?"

"I want a divorce."

He begins crisscrossing the room, repeatedly raking his hands over his hair. "Why? Where is this coming from?"

I shake my head, confused by his level of shock. This honestly can't be *that* surprising. "Why? You asked for an open marriage. You've been gone for a month, and we barely talked. You can't honestly tell me you're surprised."

"Yeah, the fuck I can."

I don't know what else to say, so I stay quiet and cross my arms, waiting for him to stop pacing.

"Are you punishing me? Is that what this is? I wanted to try something new, so you want a divorce?"

"No, this isn't a punishment. This is me being honest with you and myself. Neither one of us is happy."

"Yeah, but I've never seriously considered divorce."

"No, only an open marriage."

He stops and pivots to look at me. "Is this about someone else? Were you with someone else while I was gone?"

I don't feel like now is the time for that particular conversation, so I veer around it. "This is about how you wanted to try something else, so we could both find what makes us happy— and I did."

"A divorce? A divorce would make you happy?" When I nod, his answering laugh is pure derision. "Oh, okay. Yeah. That makes sense."

I don't want to be pulled into a more of a fight, so instead of giving in to my growing ire, I snatch my purse and keys back up. "You can't have it both ways. You can't ask for an open marriage and then be surprised when I want more than what we have."

He catches my elbows, preventing me from walking away. "This is a rough patch. We can work through it."

"A rough patch was us needing to go to marriage counseling. You wanting to have an affair by calling it an open marriage is black-hole territory."

He tightens his hold so I don't try to turn away. "You agreed to this!"

"You're right. I did. I did research, and I—unlike you—was

careful about my decision. I wanted rules and boundaries and to understand what your goals were out of all of this, but you simply wanted to have sex with someone else. You don't care about *our* relationship."

"That's not true."

"Then tell me why you want to stay together."

"Because I love you." Although, he says it like an instant callback. There is no real emotion behind it. No thought or action to back it up.

"You don't love me. You're simply afraid of losing me. And what's funny in all of this is you could've saved us this trouble by being honest with yourself and me. Years ago." I wiggle my arm free. "I'm going to spend the night somewhere else. We can talk more tomorrow."

He follows me to the door, standing in my way. "So you don't care about what I have to say? What I want?"

I shake my head. "I do care about you. I want you to be happy, and I know you're not. You said so yourself before you left. So, all of this—" I wave my hand around at him "—it only goes to show you don't care about what I want or how I feel. *You* wanted an open marriage. *You* don't want me to leave. It's all about you. It was your idea to see other people because you assumed you'd be happier, and I went along with it. I'm telling you now that I've been happier this summer than I have in a long time, and I'm asking you to try to understand where I'm coming from."

"I can't. Nicole, we're *married*. You're my *wife*." He sounds destroyed, and I look away, guilt racking my bones.

"I'm sorry. The last thing I want to do is hurt you, but I need to put myself first."

"That's fucked up. I didn't know you could be so selfish."

It is the one thing he could say to make me stay. To bend

me to his will. But I'm done people pleasing. I squeeze my eyes shut, willing the stinging in my eyes to subside.

"I'm sorry, Bryce. I really am, but I'm leaving."

He doesn't make a move to stop me as I walk out, and I exhale a shaky breath into the warm night sky before pulling out my phone to call Ian. He picks up immediately. "Hey, baby." When I sniffle, his tone changes. "What's wrong?"

"Can I come over?"

"Yes, of course. I'll be waiting at the door."

Chapter 24
Ian

I watch Nicole drive her little Nissan into the space behind our shop and jerk to a stop. She jumps out, her eyes scanning the area until they land on me. I'm already walking toward her, my arms open, and she runs to me, her body crashing against mine. I wrap her up, holding her tight as she buries her face in my neck.

"I've got you," I murmur, smoothing my hand down her hair. "It's okay."

I'm not sure what happened, but when I heard the telltale waver in her voice, I about burst out of my skin. It was all I could do to wait for her here. I would much rather have gone to her. Protect her. Take care of her. Make sure whatever it is that she's upset about never hurts her again.

But all I can do now is take her upstairs into my apartment. After I close the door behind us, I point her toward the living room, where her still red-rimmed eyes take in the art on the walls, including a framed photo of my mother that Andi found a while ago and printed for all of us—Griffin, Taryn, Roman, and me.

"Never took you for someone to put up kids' artwork on the walls," Nicole says, nodding toward a drawing that's probably fifteen or so years old. A crooked and thinly drawn picture of a very tall figure with two circles on their arms that are supposed to be biceps and three more small figures all holding hands, wearing various triangles or squares of clothes and lengths of hair. It's us, my three kids and me, as illustrated by a young Juniper.

"That was my first Father's Day after Heather moved away," I explain, smiling to myself. "I loved it so much I got it tattooed."

Nicole's mouth pops open, eyes searching over my body. "Where?"

I pivot and pull at the back of my T-shirt, gathering the cotton in my hands until the hem is high enough to reveal the ink between my shoulder blades.

"I love that," she says quietly, her hand brushing over it and then down, to right above my pants. "Your family is everything, aren't they?"

I turn and nod, letting my shirt settle back into place as her eyes slowly make their way to mine, her chin tilted up. I hold it in place between my fingers, allowing myself one quick, reassuring kiss for the both of us. She's here now, and I will take care of her.

"I'd do anything for them. My kids. My brothers and sister."

You too, I don't add.

"How is he?" She points to a smaller photo of Roman and me at his high school graduation with my arm thrown over his shoulders. I'm sure my mother took the photo, but at this point, my memory is hazy about that day.

I shouldn't be surprised Nicole's asking about my baby brother. There are probably as many stories whispered around town about him as my ex-wife, but I am much more protective of Roman.

"He's okay."

She steps closer to the wall to study the photo. "You two look a lot alike."

I'd rather talk about what made her upset instead of my family issues, but I assume she's only trying to sidestep it, so I take her hand and pull her down to the couch next to me.

"You get half an hour to decompress, and then we're talking about you."

With her head settled on my shoulder, she tips it back to meet my gaze. "Thank you."

I pop a kiss on her temple then lounge against the corner of the cushions, so we're both relaxed, her back against my chest, my arms around her middle, her head lolled against me. Then I ask, "What do you want to know?"

"What happened?"

I take a deep enough breath that she rises when my chest does. "He was still pretty young when Dad left—about two years old—and I always felt responsible for him. Mom was working so much, I was left to take care of the three kids, but especially Roman. Griffin and Taryn took care of each other."

I smile to myself as I continue, "Griffin was born a forty-year-old. He taught himself how to make dinner when he was eight. Swear to god, the kid found one of Mom's cookbooks one day, turned on the stove, and made a lasagna. And Taryn, she was easy. But Roman was young, so I took care of him. Whenever I wasn't working, I was with him. He started helping me fix up cars when he was, like, in first grade. By the time he got his driver's license, we'd finished this gorgeous 1986 Monte Carlo."

"That's not the one you have now?"

"No." I snort a rueful laugh. "That little shit banged it all up the first chance he got, so I made him fix it up before we sold it off."

"So that's what you did? Restored the cars and sold them?"

I hold her closer, resting my cheek against her temple. "Yeah, it was a hobby, but I don't do it anymore. The Impala that I have, that's the last one I did and kept it for myself."

She skims her fingers over my arm, raising goose bumps in her wake. "When did you stop?"

It takes me a minute to do the math. "About seven or eight years ago, I guess. It's time-consuming and costs a lot of money. I needed to put all my energy into my shop, and with everything going on with Roman, it kinda lost its luster for me."

For a while, she's quiet, tracing over my tattoos until she presses up to face me, one hand next to my head, the other on the center of my chest over my heart. "What's the truth about Roman? He seems to be a mystery."

I huff. "Yeah. Even to me."

She lies back down, her ear against my shoulder, curled up on me like I'm her personal sofa. I idly rub my hands up and down her back, play with strands of her hair.

"Roman had a full-ride football scholarship to Penn State, which we were all ecstatic about. He played defensive end, and he could've made it to the NFL. His coaches were all behind him, and I think that's where he would've ended up."

Nicole tucks herself up tighter as if expecting the bad news. I deliver it quickly for her sake and mine.

"He tore his quadriceps during practice camp his junior year, so he had his surgery and was doing his rehab. He was good. Until Mom had her stroke."

Nicole gasps quietly, and I repeatedly wind and unwind a strand of her hair around my finger, focusing on that so my mind doesn't conjure up all those awful memories of that time.

"She collapsed outside the grocery store. She was buying a few things for me and my kids."

A kiss is pressed to my throat when I close my eyes tight and throw my arm over my face. "She was in the hospital for a few days in a coma with brain swelling. She had a couple more minor strokes while she was there and passed a few minutes after I left her room."

"I'm so sorry," Nicole says, voice shaky.

It takes me a little while to swallow past the sand in my mouth and blink open my eyes from their stinging. "Roman took it the hardest. We were all devastated, but he... He lost it. He went back to school but ended up failing out. He got real into partying, and I didn't know at the time, but he was taking any and every pill he could get his hands on. He moved home for a year or so and lived with me and the kids, but..." I go back to petting Nicole's head, soothing myself with the repetitive motion. "He's lived all over the place, was in Philly for a bit, then New York City, and somehow ended up in Buffalo. He'd stop home every once in a while, and I saw him slipping away but I couldn't do anything about it. I gave him money, I set him up with appointments for therapists, got him into a drug and alcohol rehab, but he didn't want it. He just..." I blow out a big breath. "I haven't seen him in person in a long time, and I feel like I let him down. I'm letting my mom down."

"No. No." Nicole stretches up, kissing my temple and cheek and mouth. "You're not letting anyone down. You're doing the best you can, and you have nothing to feel bad about."

"Except that I have no idea what my brother is doing with his life. I know he's restoring cars, but beyond that...nothing."

She tucks her face into my neck, murmuring words about how I'm a good brother and a good man. And I want to be that for Roman and for her, but there are times when I doubt it. Though it's reassuring to hear it from her.

That she believes I'm a good man.

Because she is the best person I know, so if she thinks I'm anywhere close to her level, I must be doing okay.

"All right, baby," I say after a while, sitting up and taking her with me. "Your turn. You need to tell me what happened tonight."

She nods a few times, her teeth sawing into her bottom lip as she scratches her fingers over my beard. Then she takes a deep breath, forces her ocean eyes to me, and spills it all. About Bryce coming home early. About how she was straightforward and honest. How she told him she wanted a divorce, and that he didn't take it well. Tried to turn it around on her. Called her selfish.

Pain drips from each of her words. Emotional torture she's putting herself through because she is so afraid to hurt anyone's feelings, she'd rather stay quiet than rock the boat. Yet, I'm so incredibly proud of her for being open and putting herself first, because after all these years, she should. She's spent too long going along to get along. It's her turn to finally have what she wants.

To be happy.

And I have a clawing desire to drive over to her house and punch that son of bitch in his motherfucking face for all of his offenses, not the least of which being the dick who won't make himself a goddamn sandwich because he expects her to do it.

I kiss her cheeks, catching the tears as they roll over her pink skin. "You're not selfish, and you have nothing to feel bad about. You're doing what's right for you."

"I know, but—"

"No buts. You are doing what is right for yourself. He's made you upset and caused you to cry for far too many years.

Don't let him take this away from you either. Be proud of your-self. You were very brave tonight."

She sniffles, wiping the back of her hand over her face, but it's useless. She needs a shower and sleep, so I scoop her up and carry her to the bathroom, where I turn on the shower. She starts to argue about doing this with Juniper here, but my daughter is out for the night with that boyfriend of hers who I'm not a huge fan of, which earns a quiet giggle from Nicole when I tell her so. Her smile is the first sign that she's coming down the other side of the mountain she climbed tonight, and I help her into the shower before removing all my clothes as well.

It's a tight fit in the stall, but we make it work. I use my soap and loofah to gently scrub all of her creamy skin until it's covered in suds, from her shoulders to the tips of her breasts to the soft skin between her legs. I even kneel to wash the bottoms of her feet, teasing at her arches until she laughs about being ticklish. Then it's her turn, giving me the same treatment as she asks about each of my tattoos, lovingly smoothing her fingers over each one. Then we take turns massaging shampoo and conditioner into each other's hair, joking about how I always have an extra hair tie on my wrist if she ever needs it.

After, we dry off and share a toothbrush before she excit-edly finds my beard oil, saying how much she loves the scent and insists on combing it through with her fingers.

It is beyond anything I could have envisioned. Every day that started or ended this way would be perfect.

Sharing my home with this woman. Laughing and kissing and falling into bed naked.

We don't have sex because she's still too emotionally wrung out, and I don't want to take advantage of her while she's working through so much in her mind, but I do hold her close, under the covers, up late as we talk about everything and nothing special.

Like it's another Friday night with the love of my life.

And the next morning when we wake up, we start the process in reverse. Except when she gets dressed again, I don't let her put her underwear back on and insist she wear one of my T-shirts today.

No, I can't officially stake my claim on her, but I'll take my last name across her chest with the Stone Ink logo. She tucks it into the skirt she wore yesterday and uses one of my elastics to tie her hair up. Her face is clear of makeup, she smells like me, and it's the most beautiful version of her.

We walk downstairs together, where I kiss her palm before we part ways, her to go to work and me to meet my kids for breakfast.

Like it's any other morning with the love of my life.

Chapter 25
Nicole

I'm not sure if the sun really is brighter and the bird chirps happier or if it's merely my mood that makes it seem that way. After spending the night with Ian, I feel so much calmer about my future. I know divorce is not easy, but having him in my corner will help me overcome all the emotional hurdles that I know will be in my way.

As I flip on the lights in Chapter and Verse, I reflect on how much has changed this summer, and how even if Ian weren't in my life, I think I still would have eventually come to the same conclusion about my marriage. There is simply no way for me to ignore the red flags anymore.

Darcy meows at my feet as I refill his food, and I remember how easily Ian agreed to me wanting more cats. Not that I plan on testing him anytime soon, but I have reason to believe that if I—somewhere down the road—brought home a few cats, he'd shrug and tell me to take off my shirt.

I unlock the front door to my store and wave to a few people meandering down the street, all the shops on Aster Street opening up on this quiet summer weekend. The humidity is nowhere near its height, and I think we're all enjoying the reprieve for a little while. One of Eloise's workers at Sweet Cheeks calls out a greeting to me, and I smile back in time to see my husband storming down the sidewalk.

Trying to act as normal as possible, I tug the sandwich board out and continue the process of opening up until he's right in front of me.

"Where have you been?" he demands in a voice that is much too loud, and I dart my gaze around, holding my hands out in front of me.

"Keep your voice down, Bryce. It's nine in the morning."

"I'm not gonna keep my voice down. Tell me where you've been all night."

I purposely lower my volume to a near whisper, hoping he follows suit. "I told you, I slept somewhere else."

He shoots his arms out to his sides. "Yeah! Where?"

"Keep quiet. Everyone can hear you."

"I don't give a damn!"

I turn, planning on taking this conversation inside, but he stops me, slamming his hand on the door so I can't open it.

"Where the fuck do you think you're going?"

"Bryce!" I've never been afraid of him before, but this behavior is so out of character, I'm not sure what to expect, and I back into the window behind me, trying to put as much space between us as possible.

He looms above me, angry gaze raking over me from head to toe before settling on my chest. "What is that?"

I look down, tugging at the too-long sleeve of Ian's shirt. "What?"

"That shirt. You never wear T-shirts like that." He aims his thumb over his shoulder. "But all of a sudden, you're sporting something from *that* shop?"

Caught off guard by these questions about my clothes, I don't know how to answer. "I... Yeah."

He must put two and two together because he takes a few steps back from me, his voice raised even louder. "So, which one are you fucking? Which one of those tattooed assholes gave you their shirt?"

My jaw drops, stunned at the viciousness in his voice. "I'm not having this conversation with you. Especially if you're going to continue yelling at me."

"Oh no. We're having this conversation now. Or we can walk right next door so I can figure it out for myself."

I pull on his arm when he makes as if to pivot. "Don't you dare. You're acting ridiculous. Where is all this coming from?"

"Where is this coming from?" He huffs a sarcastic sound. "Gee, I don't know, Nicole. Could it be that I left for a month, only to come home and find out my wife has been cheating on me and wants a divorce?"

My sudden intake of breath is actually painful, and I place my hand on my chest. "I am *not* cheating on you."

"What else would you call it?"

With the way he's grilling me, lobbing question after question with that callous sneer, I have a hard time keeping this civil. All I want to do is scream back at him, but that would make this more of a scene than it already is. With a peek around, I notice people staring out of windows from the stores across the street, and I press my hands together.

"Please, Bryce, can we talk about this inside?"

He ignores me. "So, it's true. You are fucking somebody else." He spins around, throwing his arms up in the air. "You hear that, everyone? Your favorite little book lady is having an affair!"

I am not proud of myself, but I push him, my eyes stinging with tears as my whole body feels as if it's on fire. "Stop! You need to stop right now! You're embarrassing yourself. You're embarrassing me!"

I hate the way my voice cracks on the last word.

I hate how he would so carelessly make the worst moment of my life public.

But he has the gall to laugh at me, taking steps backward out of the alcove in front of the door to the sidewalk. "I'm embarrassing you? Good. Because you deserve it for what you did."

"What I did?" I wipe at my wet cheeks, failing at my attempts to drag him inside and away from prying eyes and ears. In my peripheral, I notice people coming outside, obviously watching this all go down. "I didn't do anything except agree to what you wanted. You wanted to see other people, remember?"

He jerks his arm out of my hold, his face inches from mine, his brown eyes on fire with rage. "That's not what I meant, and you know it. I wanted us to experiment together, not *separately*."

He can't be serious. We never discussed anything like that. Hell, he never discussed anything unless I brought it up, and he can't suddenly pretend he meant something else.

"That's absolutely what you said," I tell him, my voice trembling with indignation, and while I don't like having this fight out in the open, I'm not going to let him walk all over me. "You asked for an open marriage, plain and simple. You said you wanted the freedom to see other people. You wanted us to experiment and explore and find what made us happy, so—" I hold up my hands, crooking my fingers in air quotes "—we could be happy. Don't try to rewrite history now and claim you meant something different. It's not my fault you aren't happy with *your* decision."

Bryce's jaw tightens, a clear sign he knows I'm right but

won't admit it, and he glares at me for a moment while I drag him back to the bookstore's door. Once we get there, he plants his hands on the frame, his chest right against my back so he's once again blocking me from opening it. He hisses his next words, his mouth right next to my ear. "I didn't think you'd be fucking the first guy you ran into. Have some goddamn dignity."

Tears stream down my face as fury boils in my veins. He is *not* going to speak to me like that. I push him with every ounce of my energy, sending him back a few feet, and then I do it again, so we're out on the sidewalk. Out in the open, in front of the small crowd that has gathered. "How dare you! You don't get to judge me or talk about dignity after the way you've treated me. You checked out of this marriage a long time ago. I won't apologize for finally living my life the way I want."

Bryce's eyes dart between me and Stone Ink and then out to the few scattered people around us, including Clara and Marianne, who jog over this way.

"You okay?" Marianne asks, and I raise my hand, knowing there is no way to save this—the marriage or my reputation. Bryce hung out our business for everyone to see, and I am utterly humiliated, but before I can answer, he butts in.

"She's fine."

"She's not fine," Clara says. "You're screaming at her."

"Because she's cheating on me with one of these bastards," he says, flinging his hand out to the tattoo shop. Then he juts his chin at me. "So, you gonna tell me which one it is you want to divorce me over?"

Before I think better of it, I point my finger at his chest, speaking through gritted teeth. "I don't want to divorce you over Ian. I want to divorce you because you treat me like shit, like I'm dispensable, and then you blame me for finding someone who treats me better."

He sets his hands on his hips, shaking his head like I'm some misbehaving schoolgirl. "That gray-haired one? He's, what? Sixty? Seventy? Never took you for someone into geriatrics, but I never thought you were stupid either."

Clara gasps, jumping up in his face. "You better watch yourself before I smack the shit out of you."

Marianne pulls her away, her cell phone up. "Go home, Bryce. You've done enough damage for today."

He puffs up his chest like he's some tough guy, though his gaze sharpens on Marianne's hand when she says, "I will call the police."

He runs his tongue over his teeth, a visible war in his eyes, wanting to stay and humiliate me more or leave because of Marianne's threat. For a second, he seems like he might keep arguing, but he gives in with a shrug, as if it makes no difference to him. Then he aims his last parting shot at me with a cruel smile. "You think you can walk away from this marriage and keep your bookstore? My name is on that loan agreement. If things go south, you might lose more than just me. You'll lose your precious store too."

I never thought my husband would be vindictive, but after this, I have no reason not to believe he won't try to drag me through the mud. Even fight me for ownership of my store. And the risk of losing Chapter and Verse is worse than any public humiliation he could put me through. As he walks away, I inhale a stilted breath, my body racked with a shiver despite the temperature, and Marianne loops her arm around my shoulders. "It'll be okay."

Clara claps twice for the attention of the gathered crowd. "All right, everyone. The wicked witch is dead. You may all go about your day." She flaps her hands, shooing them away. "Go on and spread the word that Bryce Kelly is no longer welcome in any of our stores."

I might laugh at her cheerful tone if not for trying to choke back a sob. Marianne ushers me inside my shop with Clara soon following, hanging the *Closed* sign on the door. I lift my arm, intent on telling them I can't close, but Marianne quiets me. "You can't work in this state."

"You can barely breathe." Clara gently pushes on my back. "Head between your legs. We don't want you passing out."

I follow her directions and work on catching my breath, slowing my heart rate while they busy themselves around me. I can't focus on anything they're saying, but when I sit up after a few minutes, I'm greeted with a cup of water and a box of tissues.

"You don't have to tell us what's going on," Marianne starts, smoothing out my hair. "But feel free to let us know how to help."

I blow my nose a few times. "I assume everyone heard what's going on."

Clara winces. "I know I can be gossipy, but I swear, Nicole, I would never say anything about what went on today. What he did was way out of line, and whatever you want us to do is what we'll do."

Her wife nods. "We're on your side. No matter what."

It's nice to hear, but I can't muster any desire to defend myself. So I let it all out. "I didn't cheat on him with Ian. He asked for an open marriage earlier this summer."

Marianne snorts. "And now he's pissed no woman actually wanted him, while you found yourself a hot silver fox."

"Men are trash," Clara says on a sigh before backtracking. "Except for Ian."

"And Griffin," Marianne adds.

Clara points her finger up. "And Dante."

"All Stone and Stone-related men are kept from the trash

heap," Marianne declares, and I breathe out a watery laugh that turns into full-on sobbing.

They surround me on either side, murmuring encouraging words I appreciate, but I have never felt so stripped down with mortification since college. No matter that logic tells me I didn't do anything wrong, I *feel* like it.

I feel like everything Bryce accused me of being.

Selfish.

A cheater.

Stupid.

Someone unworthy of happiness.

Which is why I flinch when Marianne shows me her cell phone screen. "I think we should call Ian."

"He's having breakfast with his kids," I say, not wanting to intrude on his time with them, even though it's just an excuse.

"He won't be upset," Clara assures me. "In fact, I think he'll be more upset if we don't call him."

They're right, and yet Bryce's voice lingers in my head.

Selfish.

Cheater.

Stupid.

How could Ian want anyone like me?

Chapter 26
Ian

I surreptitiously rub my palms on my jeans as the server sets down our plates. It's the usual breakfast with my kids, but I've got a knot in my stomach, knowing I have to tell Jasper, Jaybird, and Juniper about Nicole.

I don't know why I'm so nervous. It's not like they think I'm a monk. I've dated before—some women they've known, some they haven't. But what I have with Nicole is special, and I need my kids to know this time is different.

And, truth be told, I am worried about their reaction. I think any single parent has a sticker in the back of their mind, a thought that hangs around, making itself known every so often that their children won't approve of their new partner.

I poke at my pancakes. "So I, uh, got something I wanna tell you three."

"You took us out for breakfast to give us bad news?" Jaybird readjusts his black-framed glasses, a smirk on his face. "Bad form, Dad."

"It's not bad news, and I don't know why I take your unappreciative ass out at all. Next time, I'm leaving you home."

"He'll just follow me," Jasper says around a bite of bacon. "Like a lost puppy. I can't get rid of him."

Jay tosses his arm around his brother's shoulders. "You love me."

Jasper doesn't push his arm off, but he also doesn't answer. This is how it's always been between them. Jaybird desperate for his older brother's attention, and Jas begrudgingly giving it to him. Then again, my middle child is desperate for anyone's attention.

A puppy is an accurate description.

"So, what's up?" Juniper asks, smiling. She's my favorite child for a reason.

For a second, I lose myself in her dimples, the same ones as my mother, and stroke my hand down the back of her head. I'm tactile with all of my children, but especially Juniper. I need to remind myself that she's here. My baby is still with us. She steals a bite of my pancakes because she can never not eat other people's food and always *just wants to try it.*

And maybe that's why my eldest child is my favorite.

I clear my throat and move my plate farther away from my daughter. "I wanted to let you know that I've started dating someone."

The three of them blink at me, completely unsurprised, and when I raise my brows expectantly, Jay's the one who gives me a reaction. He throws his arms up. "Oh my god! I can't believe it!"

I heave a sigh and rub at my forehead. Honestly, I don't know why I take him out in public.

"You're *dating?*" he goes on, garnering the attention of every single other patron in the place. He places the back of his wrist against his head like a Victorian woman about to faint. "I cannot believe you would keep this from us."

Jasper shakes his head. "Shut the fuck up, man. I'm trying to eat, and you're making it weird."

"*I'm* making it weird?" Jay motions to me. "*He's* the one being weird. Announcing he's with Nicole like he needs a kidney." He turns to me. "Do you need a kidney?"

I ignore him. "So, you know already? You all know?"

Jasper barely glances up from his omelet. "Yeah."

"Kinda hard to miss the way you've been acting lately," Jay says around a bite of toast. "All smiley and shit."

I huff, leaning back in my seat. "Well, damn. Thought I was being subtle."

Jay snorts. "As a sledgehammer."

I turn to June for confirmation, and she shrugs. "I could tell something was going on. You were extra diligent about making sure everything was clean."

"That's because of you." I aim my fork at her. "For someone who's never home, you still somehow leave the place a mess. And why the hell do you need so much makeup? There are bottles all over the counter. I'm gonna throw them in the trash."

She shoulders me. "If you throw them away, you'll be throwing away your money."

I hit her with a glare. A real one. "I gave you that credit card for emergencies."

"My primer being discontinued is an emergency."

"Primer?" I ask at the same time Jaybird says, "Like for paint?"

"You put primer on before foundation," she explains, and Jasper curls his lip.

"I still don't understand. What's the point of all of it?"

My daughter waves her hand at the three of us. "What's the point of your tattoos? Because you like them? They make you feel pretty?"

When Jasper and I don't answer her rhetorical question, Jay shrugs. "I think I'm pretty without them."

She rolls her eyes. "Nothing can help cover up your face."

Jay throws a sugar packet at her, and I put my hand out, stopping the fight before it can begin because even in their twenties, they still act like toddlers.

I get back on track. "So you're really cool with me and Nicole?"

Jas nods while June smiles. "Of course. We're happy for you."

"As long as you keep all your kinky shit away from us," Jay mutters, and for a moment, I lose my breath, afraid I've accidentally let something slip or given them a peek into my sexual lifestyle, but no. He's merely being a turd.

I've always been open with my kids about sex. A person has to be, raising two curious boys, let alone a girl. The nightmares of what women have to deal with keep me up at night. But I've never discussed *my* sex life with them, and I wouldn't. Though I have shown them pictures of a dick infected with gonorrhea. Gotta know what they're dealing with if they don't take their shit seriously.

"If you're referring to what happened the other day, that's your fault for walking into *my* house," I tell my troublemaking son.

"What happened the other day?" June asks around a bite of French toast.

"I walked in on Dad in a...*delicate* situation." Jay puts on a French accent, and Juniper gasps.

"He's overexaggerating, and it would never have happened in the first place if you didn't walk into people's houses without knocking," I say, lifting my coffee cup to my mouth.

"That's *my* house," he replies, offended.

"It was never your house since you never lived there." June

and I moved in to the apartment when I bought the building. By then, Jay had already graduated high school and was well on his way to living independently.

"You live there, ergo, it's my house."

I polish off my coffee and set the empty cup on the table. "You are exhausting."

Before he can respond, June perks up. "I think I should move out."

I whip my head to her. "What?"

"I think I should move out."

"And go where?"

She lifts her shoulder. "Things are getting serious between Easton and me, and—"

I shut that idea down. "No."

"Absolutely not," Jasper says in follow-up.

"I don't think so," Jaybird agrees.

She frowns at all of us, color rising in her cheeks. "Why not?" She gestures at her brothers. "You two were living on your own, and—"

"You're not moving in with Easton," I say. "You're not even done with school yet."

"What does that have to do with anything?"

"You're too young," Jasper replies.

"I am not."

Jay nods. "Junie, you—"

"Don't call me Junie," my daughter snaps. "Don't tell me I'm too young when you guys are the ones treating me like I'm five. I'm a grown woman."

"You're twenty," Jasper points out, earning an irate huff.

"And what were you doing at twenty? Driving across the country on your motorcycle? Fucking strangers? Selling drugs? No one knows because you won't ever tell anyone, so don't come at me like I'm a child when you refuse to be an adult."

Jasper told me what he did in those years after he graduated high school, which was mostly a lot of soul-searching, but I doubt June wants me to point that out at this particular moment.

I drape my arm on the back of her chair. "Juniper, I understand you want to move out, but I'd like you to—"

"Oh, you can stop patronizing me, Dad," she says, pushing her plate away and crossing her arms over her chest to fume. "But keep treating me like a know-nothing child, and one of these days, you won't be able to say shit to me about it because I'll go off and do something without saying a word to any of you."

Admittedly, I'm a little overprotective of her, as are her brothers, but it's hard not to be, with her past. She's my little girl, and she's their baby sister. There's no way for us to shut off our instincts. But I could listen better.

"Can we talk about this later?" I try, moving her plate back in front of her. "After your school year starts. We'll talk about it. I promise."

She eyes me suspiciously, though the hard line of her mouth melts easily when I poke my fork into a piece of her French toast and hold it up like an airplane. "Stop," she says with a laugh, smacking my hand away as I fly it to her mouth. "Dad!"

I eat the French toast instead then I tell my boys, "Your sister is smarter and more mature than either one of you was at her age. Don't be dicks."

Jasper inclines his head in agreement as Jaybird raises his hands, so full of innocence. "It's not her. It's Easton."

"Jaybird," I warn as June kicks him under the table.

"You're such an asshole."

Jay snaps back. "You know how it is between him and Cash. I still can't believe you'd ever go out with him."

Putting my hand over June's mouth, I stop the argument by asking, "Speaking of, where is Cash this morning?"

"With his grandma," he says, going back to his breakfast, so I let go of June.

Cash's grandmother lives in a nursing home, but he visits her regularly. He's a good kid, dedicated and loyal, and basically one of my own since he and Jay first became best friends in elementary school. He also happens to be the guy my daughter has had a crush on since she was little, although she doesn't know I know. Whatever she's got going on with Cash's stepbrother Easton, I don't get, and clearly, I won't. So I keep my mouth shut and hope everything will turn out all right.

"What about you?" I motion to Jas with my fork. "What you got going on today?"

"Not much. Working on some stuff."

"New pieces?"

He nods but doesn't give anything more. Not that I expect it. He's quiet. Lives in his head a lot. So, I drop it and lean back in my chair. With everything out in the open, I throw out an idea. "Now that you three know everything, what would you say to a dinner with all of us and Nicole?"

I'm met with agreements and pull my phone out of my pocket to text Nicole when I notice a missed call and voice mail from Marianne, which is weird because while we're friends, we don't call or text each other without reason, and my pulse stutters at all the possible reasons rushing through my mind.

"Back in a minute," I tell my kids then head outside, where I settle under the cover of the awning to listen to the voice mail.

"Hey, Ian," Marianne starts quietly. "I wanted to let you know that Clara and I are here with Nicole at her store. There was a...confrontation today. Bryce showed up and..."

I don't hear anything else as anger sends blood rushing in my ears. If that piece of shit hurt her, I will fucking murder him. I shove my phone into my pocket before the message is even over, and I'm moving without having consciously thought of it, spinning on my heel to stalk back inside the diner.

"Everything okay?" June asks, probably noting my thunderous expression.

"No, something's come up with Nicole." I drop a credit card on the table. "I gotta go."

Jasper's brow creases in concern. "What happened?"

"I don't know yet, but I need to get to her." I'm already heading for the exit when Jay calls out behind me.

"Go get her, Pops!"

I lift a hand in acknowledgment but don't look back. Right now, my only thought is getting to Nicole.

And I'm barely aware of my surroundings as I drive home, to my shop, to the bookstore that shares a wall with it, to the woman who owns my heart.

I don't mean to, but I bang my hand on the back door of Chapter and Verse harder than I intended, and Clara opens it a few seconds later, eyes roving over me. "Hey, whoa. Chill out on the bear mode. You're gonna make the situation worse."

"I am chill."

She barks out a laugh. "Chill like a feral animal with rabies. Seriously, take a few breaths before you go in there. She's been through a lot."

I grumble a litany of curses as I comb my fingers repeatedly through my hair, taking deliberate breaths, attempting to still my racing pulse. But it's like putting a bull back in his cage after he's seen the red cape.

"She's physically okay," Clara tells me. "He didn't touch her."

That only makes me feel marginally better. He can keep his fingers.

"More than anything, she's embarrassed," Clara says,

ripping my goddamn heart out. "He made a big scene out front, screaming and yelling at her."

"About what?" I lock my hands behind my head, squeezing my eyes shut as I remind myself that aggravated battery is a felony.

"You."

I hunch over like she kicked me in the gut. This sorry excuse for a man verbally assaulted Nicole because of me. Over *me*.

Fuck it.

I could sell the shop to pay for lawyer's fees.

I pivot, reaching for the door, but Clara catches my wrist. "Don't you dare go after him. He is nothing. Don't make your anger more important than your love for Nicole. She needs you."

It takes a few moments, but her words sink in.

He is nothing.

And Nicole is everything.

I shake out my arms, my hands tingling from how tightly I had them curled in fists, but I force them straight now and inhale a deep breath. Clara rubs my shoulders like a boxer in the ring. "That's it. You got it now. Go in there and get your girl."

She pats my back twice, and I march down the hall to the main floor of the store. When Marianne spies me, she whispers something to Nicole that has her raising her bloodshot eyes to me. My old friend says something to me, but I don't hear it, all of my focus on the woman curled up on the chair with used tissues strewn around her.

"Baby." I kneel in front of her. "I'm so sorry."

She falls into me, her face in my neck, tears wetting my shirt. For the second time in less than twenty-four hours, she's crying, and as much as I hate to admit it, I wonder if this is worth it. Putting her through all this pain. Would it be easier if I let her go?

But then she winds her arms around me, clinging tight, and no. I could never let her go. Even if I wanted to, she wants me here with her. And I am nothing if not in service to her.

"I should have been here." I kiss her head, her ear, pull her back to kiss her wet cheek and chapped lips. "I'm sorry I wasn't here."

"You couldn't have done anything," she says between sniffles, and I use my T-shirt to wipe her face dry. "You're gonna have my snot all over you."

"I don't care."

Her responding smile is wobbly, but it settles my wrecked nerves, nonetheless. When she's breathing normally, I hold her face in my hands, stroking my thumbs over her cheekbones. "What happened?"

"I was opening the store, and Bryce showed up. He looked like he hadn't slept at all, and he started yelling at me, demanding to know where I was all night, who I was with. And then..." She slants her eyes away from me, and I know whatever it is, it's gonna make me go apeshit. "He saw your shirt—" she plucks at the Stone Ink tee I put her in this morning that is more like a dress on her "—and figured out I was with you."

She drops her gaze to her hands, clutching at her long skirt. The same one she wore yesterday, because I could give her a shirt to wear but not anything else. "He got even more mad?" I guess, and when she nods, I release my gentle grip on her to move away. The tingle in my hands is back. This time with a desire to strangle him. "What did he say?"

"That I cheated on him. People were all watching him as he screamed about me cheating on him."

I growl and turn away, fighting with myself, knowing I

should stay with Nicole but needing to go confront him. Let him say to my face what he dared to yell at her.

"He called me stupid."

I whirl around to her. "He *what?*"

With eyes as big as dinner plates, she stands, tugging on my hand, preventing me from fucking slamming through the wall like the Hulk and heading straight to him. "Please," she begs, crying again. "Don't leave."

"He insulted you. On top of everything that son of bitch put you through, carrying on in front of our friends and neighbors, he's going to insult you? No. No. I'm not gonna let that stand."

"*Ian.*"

I stop at her broken plea, and she presses her front to my back, her cheek against my shoulder blade, her hands on my waist. "If you go, you'll only make it worse."

I hang my head, clenching my fists at my sides. "I don't know how else it can be worse."

Images of my childhood flood my mind, memories of my belligerent father yelling at and insulting my mother. My good and kind mother who Nicole reminds me so much of. I couldn't physically stand up to him then, but I can certainly stand up to the ghost of him now in Bryce fucking Kelly.

"He threatened my store," she says so quietly I almost don't hear her, and I circle around to face her.

"Say that again."

"When my store got damaged in the hurricane a few years ago, he put his name on the loan note with me, so I could get the money. He's just trying to scare me by bringing that up, but if you go fight with him, I *know* he will use it against me."

I sigh, jaw sore from grinding my teeth so hard. "You can't let him bully you."

"And I can't let you fight my battles."

"The fuck I can't."

"Stop." She pushes my hands off her and pulls her shoulders back, standing tall for the first time since I stormed in here. "You need to stop. You can't protect me all the time. I appreciate that you want to, but you can't be the one to make my decisions and fix things. That's the greatest gift you gave me." She shuts her mouth, rolling her lips over her teeth like she's trying to keep from crying, her chin trembling for a few moments. Then her throat lifts on a swallow and she speaks, low but firm. "You taught me no is a complete sentence. You taught me to ask for what I want. You taught me that I am in command of myself, so I am asking you not to confront him. I am telling you that I need to figure this out on my own. For once in my life!"

It's only then she breaks, heaving out a ragged breath, tears rolling down her cheeks, and my heart cracks in two.

"I'm sorry," I rasp, wrapping my arms around her middle, towing her into me. "I'm sorry. I don't know what else to do. I can't sit around while someone I love is hurting. I need to—"

She wrenches back. "You love me?"

It takes a few seconds for her and my words to register. Then I shrug, because... "Of course I love you. I fucking love you, Nic, and I need to do something to help."

The smile that shines through her tears knits the lacerations of my heart back together and kisses the bruises on my soul better. She lays her head on my shoulder, her fingers digging into the muscles on either side of my spine. "Then go home. You need to calm down, and I need time to figure out what I'm going to do."

"No." I dip my chin down, my beard tangling with strands of her hair. "I'm not leaving you to face this alone."

She laughs like I'm stupid. "I'm not facing this alone." Leaning back, she slips her hands around my shoulders and up to my neck, sinking her fingers into my loose hair. "I know I have you, and you have me, but you showed me how strong I can be. So let me be strong."

Well, when she puts it like that, how can I deny her?

She tugs me down to meet her lips, tasting of salt, and I gather the cotton of her skirt in my hands, pulling her up so she's on her toes. Still, it's not close enough. I speak all the words into her mouth that I can't say out loud.

I'm proud of you.

I love you.

I want you in my life forever.

You are tattooed on my heart.

Carved in stone.

Then I let her go. To be mistress of herself.

Chapter 27
Nicole

Clara and Marianne reappear from where they'd been hiding away in the back, apparently tidying up. As if they don't have their own business to run.

"You didn't have to do that," I say, motioning around the newly cleaned storage room. "And you didn't have to stay so long. I'm sure you have things to do."

"Yes, like make sure you're okay," Clara says at the same time her wife produces her cell phone.

"I'm texting you the name of my attorney friend who specializes in business contracts, and if you need the name of a divorce lawyer, Taryn has a good one."

I rub my clammy palms down the sides of my skirt, thinking of Ian's sister and how she's been put through the wringer with her ex-husband over the custody of her kids, but she seems really happy now with Dante.

"Yeah, thanks, I'll reach out."

Marianne slides her phone back into her pocket. "What else can we do?"

"Nothing. Really. You've helped me so much already by being here."

She slips her arms around me for a hug, and Clara follows so they've got me in the middle. And that's how it stays for the rest of the day. My friends and community showing up for me, over and over.

After Clara and Marianne leave, I take a deep breath and turn the sign on the door to *Open*. While it would be easier to close up shop, crawl into bed, and hide under the covers, I can't afford to lose business. Not when my future hangs in the balance. I need every customer I can get.

It starts off as a slow trickle, but it seems word—Clara—has spread fast about what happened. Everyone from Aster Street and the downtown area stops by, offering words of encouragement and support. Eloise is one of the first to arrive, bearing a box of cinnamon buns and other baked goods. "I thought you could use a pick-me-up."

Then it's the Kanekos, who own the sushi restaurant, and their daughter Mio, Ned from the record store, Pat and Helen from the pet store, Lori from the secondhand shop, and the Palacios from the high-end furniture store with the gorgeous armchair I've been drooling over for a year but never bought because Bryce thought it was dumb to buy such an expensive piece of furniture. "You're never home to sit in it," he'd said, but I'd come home just to curl up with a book and read in it now. It'll be my first purchase post-divorce, I decide.

Andi strolls in with Logan and Grace in the afternoon. The kids look around while she approaches me at the counter. "I heard about what happened earlier, and while I've never met your husband, I know you, and I know you're a good person. You don't deserve that kind of treatment."

She's about a decade younger than me but has probably

seen and done more in her life than I ever have, since she was born in Texas, lived in California, and now resides here. She's also sweet as her homemade tea and cooler than I could ever hope to be.

With her hand pressed to her chest, she leans in close. "I might not be an official member of the Stone family yet, but I think I can speak for the entire family when I say, we're behind you one hundred percent."

"Thank you. I appreciate that."

"And for what it's worth, I know how it feels to be put into the middle of an embarrassing situation. You don't need me to tell you this because you're a smart woman, but in case you need the reminder... How everything went down has nothing to do with you and everything to do with the ego of a fragile man."

Isn't that how it always goes? From the downfall of societies to violence against women, it's always because of the fragility of men.

"I actually did need to hear that."

She nods and offers me a squeeze that belies her short stature. She has more strength than anyone might assume, and I am grateful for her friendship. For everyone's.

About an hour before close, Dante Moretti arrives with a few boxes and a tool kit. "I come bearing the tidings of Taryn for your husband to quote, contract gangrene of the dick, end quote—" he grins widely, obviously proud of his girlfriend "—and a new security system." He sets down the boxes, explaining, "Ian has tasked me with setting it all up for you, so don't mind me. I'm following the big guy's orders."

Yes, Ian might have done what I asked and left me alone to sort myself out, but he has once again proved that he is never far away from me, physically or emotionally. I am always on his mind.

Like he is always on mine.

Especially as I close up the store and find a text from him.

IAN

Dante should have explained how the security system works, and I want you to use it. Text me a picture or video of you using it to lock up.

So I do, earning a **Good girl** in return, but once I take a seat in my car, I realize that I don't want to go home, to the house I shared with Bryce, but I also don't have anywhere else to go. If I asked Ian, he wouldn't hesitate, but I'm not sure that's a great idea either. Not when my argument with Bryce is so fresh, the sting of humiliation still trailing after me. Ever since college, I've been so worried about becoming *that girl* again, only to have made the conscious decision to put myself into a situation that made me *that girl.*

I can't say I regret being with Ian, but the pain of having an old scar ripped open is still too new to be able to pretend like it's not. I can't go on with my life with him until I am sure I won't crumble under the weight of my fear of disappointing everyone. I've spent my life trying to please others, and that necessity to feel worthy doesn't suddenly up and disappear. I know I'll continue to second-guess myself about all of my choices if I don't take a step back.

I have to get out of the eye of the storm for a bit.

Which is exactly what I tell Aunt Sue when I call her, more tears falling as I rehash everything that transpired within the last twenty-four hours. She listens patiently as I pour out my feelings, and when I finally run out of steam, she softly asks, "Are you regretting your decision?"

There is no question. "I know divorcing him is the right thing for me to do. I just need time to figure everything out. What I'm going to do about money and the loan and—"

"Why don't you take a few days off and come stay with me?"

"What?"

"You said it yourself—you need some time, so take it here. Stay with me for a few days, and we'll work it all out, the attorneys, the money, the loan stuff. And maybe you can see some whales too. If anything, that's worth it."

I stare at the back door of Chapter and Verse, wondering if it's possible. If I could take a vacation. I mean... I am my own boss. I wouldn't have to shut down completely, only change the hours and make sure my staff could cover it. I—

"I practically hear you overthinking it. Come on, hon. You know you need to. It's take a break now or have a breakdown later."

Well.

When she puts it like that...

"Okay. I'll come."

"Good. Now go pack your bags and tell that handsome bear of a man you'll see him in a few days."

I hang up and head back into the store to make some calls and send some emails, setting myself up to take a few days off before texting Ian that I need to talk to him. We meet outside by my car, his hair tied back, his glasses on.

"Are you in the middle of an appointment?" I ask, knowing his work habits, and he nods. "Then what are you doing out here?"

"You said you needed to talk."

I shoot my arm out. "Not while you're in the middle of something."

He waves me off. "It's a big piece. We both needed a break anyway."

"Ian."

"Nicole."

"I could've waited."

"And so can Batman." At my quirked brow, he shrugs. "I'm tattooing Batman on this guy's arm. The Robert Pattinson version. I personally would've gone with Michael Keaton to get the traditional yellow symbol, but..."

When I laugh, he grabs hold of my shoulders and hauls me to him. "I love that sound. I was worried I wouldn't hear it again with so much crying."

"I know. I think I'm dehydrated."

"You need to drink water."

"I will."

He kisses my forehead, cheek, then mouth. "We'll have to go back to basics. Daily proof you're drinking and eating."

I wrap my hands around his wrists, his big hands bracketing my face, and lean into his palms. "I need you to do me a favor."

"Anything."

"Can you take care of Mr. Darcy for a while?"

"Sure, but why?"

"I'm going to visit Aunt Sue."

He doesn't answer right away, merely tenses his fingers, lengthening them a bit more, the tips extending under my hair to my scalp. "Okay. I'll bring Mr. Darcy next door to my place for a few days. Hold him hostage. Make sure you'll come back to get him."

I turn, smiling into one of his palms, kissing it. "Don't worry. I'll be back in a few days."

He bends, lips brushing against mine. "Promise?"

"Promise."

We don't say anything more. At least, not with words. I speak with my tongue sliding along his, fingers curling into his shirt, my heart beating wildly against my rib cage, an echo of his, banging so hard, I can feel it against my chest when I stand on my toes, aligning my body with his, trying to get as close as possible.

I'm so grateful for you.

I love you.

I want to be in your life forever.

Tattoo your name on my heart.

Carve my blessings in stone.

Chapter 28
Ian

I arrive at Cuppa Jo fifteen minutes early to meet my brother and sister because I'm a sad sack of shit after everything that's happened, planning on staring at my cell phone, waiting for Nicole to text me. She's been gone exactly three days, and while I know she promised she'd come back to me, I'm doing my very best to give her the space she asked for, even if it's killing me. Between the few messages and nightly calls, I should be satisfied, yet I'm not.

I'll never have enough.

I'm insatiable when it comes to that woman.

Especially with her sending me selfies every morning, proof she's drinking water. I could use a few more, naked, and then another video or two, but it's nothing compared to having her in person.

Having her in my arms soothes my stress.

A smile, and my day is better.

Hearing her voice, and I'm reminded all over again of why I love her. That soft-spoken yet cheerful tone is a cool lake on a hot day, the first snowflake in winter, shelter from the rain. She is comfort and beauty and my sanctuary.

A memory hits me as I sit at our usual table with the order of coffees, and I close my eyes to sink into the vision playing out in my mind. It was a long time ago, when Nicole was probably just out of college and working for her aunt next door at Chapter and Verse. We almost never spoke then; I was newly divorced and she was so young, but there was one day she met me out front on the sidewalk with my mail—an occurrence that happens sometimes when our envelopes make it into each other's piles.

I remember her standing there, dark brown hair catching the sun, a timid smile slow to grow on her face. I don't recall what she said to me, if anything at all, and I certainly don't know if I had any words for her, but I do know my mother witnessed the brief interaction.

She was there to pick up June, and it's as if it happened yesterday. The way I can see Mom tip her head in curiosity as she watched Nicole turn back to the bookstore. "I like a girl who reads," she said offhandedly. "She seems sweet."

I thought nothing of it then, but my heart lurches when I hear my mother's voice in my head, her bright smile when she looked at me. "Pretty eyes too. Matches my necklace."

She lifted the small pendant. My siblings and I put our money together to gift it to her when we were younger, a simple chain with an aquamarine gemstone because it was her favorite color. She wore it every day after.

I don't know why that memory stands out to me now, except it wasn't long before she passed, and there were so many times this summer I wished Nicole and my mother could have met. But I guess they kind of did. And Mom liked her.

Goose bumps rise on my arms, and I scrub my hands over them as I think of the box I have Mom's jewelry stored in.

When we went through her belongings after the funeral, each of us took something—Griffin pictures, Taryn *I Love Lucy* baubles, and Roman a blanket and pillow. I chose the few pieces of jewelry she wore, including that necklace, some bracelets, a ring that belonged to her father, which he brought with him from Persia, and her mother's wedding ring, a thin gold band inlaid with tiny diamonds. Mom had sold the engagement ring my father had bought for her, but she kept her family heirlooms.

They're mine now.

To do with what I'd like.

And I believe my mother wouldn't mind seeing her mother's ring on Nicole's finger.

"Hey," Taryn says, breaking me out of my thoughts, and I move to make room so she can sit next to me.

Griffin follows, taking a seat opposite us, and accepts his coffee with a nod. "We thought we were gonna be early."

I eye my siblings. "Why were you coming early?"

"To make sure we understood the gossip before we asked you about it," Taryn says, completely unrepentant.

I roll my eyes. "There is no gossip."

"Okay," my brother mumbles sarcastically. "Even I heard it, and I don't usually hear anything."

I rub the heels of my hands against my eyes. "Clara's got a big mouth."

"She's trying to protect Nicole," my sister points out, and I know that, but she also doesn't know how claustrophobic being in the spotlight makes Nicole feel.

"It would be better if everyone stopped talking about it. Nic hates being the center of attention. She's had some bad experiences in her past with rumors, and I don't want her traumatized any more than she already is."

"So you know about those past bad experiences?" Taryn

asks, alluding to a second unasked question. *Why do you know about them?*

Since I told my kids, and it feels like the entire town watched what happened the other day, I guess it's time to set the record straight. "Her husband is an asshole."

My brother and sister don't argue. In fact, they have no reaction whatsoever, as if I'm stating a fact.

"And before he went away on a work trip, he told Nicole he wanted an open marriage."

That earns a tic of Griffin's brows and a narrowing of Taryn's eyes.

"Nic and I...we were always friends, but then..."

"Come on, man," Griffin says after a sip of coffee. "You've always liked her."

"Yeah. You didn't hide it especially well," Taryn agrees, and maybe I did always like her. But I never let myself imagine anything could ever actually happen.

"So, you two got together, and now her husband is home, and he's pissed," Taryn guesses.

"He confronted Nicole at work because she asked him for a divorce, and that's what all the rumors stemmed from. And so you both know the truth, I love her. I love Nicole, and we're going to be together. I know it's messy, but I'll deal with whatever comes my way. I don't care what people say about me, though I do care what they say about her. I'm not asking you to defend me, but if you hear anything about her, I am asking you to speak up on her behalf because she doesn't deserve it. She is a *good* woman."

I aim that last bit at my brother because of the tiff we had at his picnic, saying I was ruining her life, and he turns a bit sheepish, curling his hand around the bill of his cap, sucking air through his teeth.

"I know I apologized already, but I didn't realize it was so complicated, and I'm sorry. You are a good man, and I'll always have your back. Nicole's too."

Taryn knocks her elbow into my side for my attention. "And I wouldn't be worried about what people are saying, because it's basically all about how much they love Nicole and her store and how Bryce was the biggest dick for screaming at her like that."

The reminder of it makes my blood boil all over again. "I wish I'd been there. God... I would've liked to..." I mime wrapping my hands around his neck.

Griffin agrees with a nod, though he says, "It's better you weren't. Because I'm not sure you would've listened to reason, and it would've been like a bear versus a raccoon. I'm glad I didn't get a call to attend some kind of mauling downtown."

Taryn raises her coffee cup in a silent cheers. "I rather like having you around and not in prison."

"Yeah. I guess the trade-off is better." I release a tired sigh and scratch at my beard before leaning back against the booth. "So... Now that we got that out of the way, one of you tell me something good."

After a sip of her coffee, Taryn tells me that her pitiful ex-husband has stopped fighting her and has given her full custody.

I throw my arm around her. "Holy shit! Why didn't you say anything before?"

"Because you're going through stuff."

"Yeah, but this is amazing. He's finally out of the picture."

She winces. "Not quite. He's still their dad, and I told the kids I won't keep them from seeing him if they want to."

Griffin huffs. "They don't want to, and I don't blame them. We know what it's like to have a piece of shit for a father."

We go quiet after that, the happiness about Taryn's win dimmed a bit, even as we chat about the day-to-day events of our lives. Plans for the fall and the kids going back to school, and after we all finish our drinks and say goodbye, I'm still feeling uneasy and decide to take a walk.

My limbs buzz, and it could be the afternoon hit of caffeine or my impatience at Nicole not returning my text, asking if she's decided when she's coming home, but either way, I've walked two miles before I'm conscious of it. My mind a million miles away—or, more accurately, 608 miles away in Bar Harbor, Maine.

I want Nicole to stay there as long as she needs. I want her to be happy.

And I also could probably walk from here to there without stopping for how badly I need to be by her side. Feel like I'm doing something other than sitting on my fucking hands.

She didn't want me going to talk to her motherfucker of a husband, fearing it might turn into a physical altercation, and that's fair, but asking me to simply wait is like asking a wolf to stay on a leash.

Nicole is my girl, my family, and she's hurting. Yet I'm supposed to let her handle it. She can—I *know* she can—but she also knows that I will always give her anything she asks for. And by making me stand on the sidelines, she's taking me out of the fucking game.

Cutting my knees out from under me.

As much as I hate the toxic alpha bullshit, I don't know what to do with all this pent-up energy from not being able to defend her. To protect what's mine. So I walk another mile and imagine Bryce Kelly's head on a spike.

And suddenly, I'm out front of my childhood home, the house where I spent the first fifteen years of my life. The one my parents bought together and the one my mother eventually sold to pay off all the bills. We moved in to a tiny apartment, where I slept on the couch so Taryn and Griffin could share a room, while Roman slept with our mom.

I stick my hands in my pockets and rock back on my heels, taking in the run-down ranch with the cracked driveway, dirty siding, and ugly brown paint on the window frames. The grass is patchy, the garage door is dented, and the rain spout is missing.

But there is a For Sale sign stuck in the yard, and I snap a picture. Roman wanted to know what became of our house, which holds a lot of good memories despite the bad ones, and I send it to him, along with one single line.

Come home.

Then I spin on my heel and head back the way I came, toward Aster Street, where I make a stop at the pet store to buy more treats for Mr. Darcy since he's running low and my newly adopted son has taken a liking to the homemade ones in the shape of fish.

I plan on spoiling that little dude like I spoil his mother.

Till death do us part.

Chapter 29
Nicole

After a week with Aunt Sue in Maine, I am more excited about my future than I've ever been. She was right—the whale watching did put me in a better mood, and the hours of talking, planning, and making phone calls to attorneys have helped me set everything in order.

But it doesn't make me any less nervous walking into my house, knowing what I have to say. Having no idea how Bryce will react.

I find him in the kitchen, slumped at the table, his laptop open while his gaze is fixed outside of the window, and the very last thing I ever expect him to do is to inhale swiftly and audibly when he spots me. Pushing up to stand, he roves his eyes over me, face going slack before he offers me a smile. "You look beautiful."

I glance behind me as if he might be speaking to someone else. Of course, he isn't, and I fidget with my bracelet, the same one Ian toyed with the day he implied I was stronger than I appeared.

"Thank you." I clear my throat, casting my focus around

the room, dishes piled up in the sink, takeout boxes stacked on the counter, a tied-up garbage bag by the back door, probably because it needed to go out last night but he never got around to it.

"You look like you got some sun," he says with two steps toward me, and I tug on my plain T-shirt, the V-neck collar revealing my tan from the afternoons I spent outside, enjoying the sunshine and salt air.

"I did."

"Where did you go?"

Before I left, I texted him one message that I was going away and we would talk when I got back. He didn't respond until midweek, when he apologized profusely for yelling at me. I didn't reply.

"I stayed with my aunt."

He nods and motions for me to sit down at the table, clearing it of the empty coffee mug and half-full glass of water.

My hands tremble slightly, and I wrap my left fist around my right, reminding myself I am strong. That I can take *this* step because I've chosen to.

I perch on the edge of the chair as he sits across from me and smiles hopefully, as if we didn't have a blowup in the middle of Aster Street and this summer has been business as usual for us.

I'm not sure if he's delusional or merely that arrogant, assuming I won't actually leave him.

"We need to talk."

He rubs a hand over his stubbled jaw. "Yeah. Okay."

Silence settles between us because all the words I've practiced have slipped from my brain. So I reach for the closest ones. "I haven't changed my mind. I want a divorce."

He blinks a few times, showing no emotion for a full minute, which I only know because I watch the seconds tick by on a big decorative clock hanging on the wall opposite me. "I shouldn't be surprised, but I am."

My rehearsed lines come back to me, and I sweat like an actress under stage lights. "Why? We might as well be roommates, and I'm not sure what other outcome you expected when you decided you wanted to open our marriage."

"I didn't expect you to cheat on me," he says with no trace of heat in his voice. It's all hurt.

But I don't feel an ounce of sympathy. Not anymore. "By definition of what we agreed to, I did *not* cheat on you." Flicking my hand out to him, I let my irritation loose. "Besides, you were doing the same thing."

"I wasn't!" He explodes from his position to stalk across the room. "I didn't cheat on you. I didn't sleep with anyone."

Now *that* surprises me. I have no words.

He tunnels his fingers through his hair, turning in a tight circle, his eyes on the ceiling. "While you were fucking your tattoo artist, I was drinking and regretting the decision."

I cover my gaping mouth with my hand, truly gobsmacked. He was the one who wanted to go out and meet other people, have sex with other people. And he didn't do any of it?

"I was bored, I guess," he admits, shoulders drooping, chin to his chest. "I thought it would be like when I was younger, go out and sow some oats and get over it. But apparently..." He raises his head and meets my gaze. "No one wants a forty-year-old with oats to sow."

If I weren't so angry, I might laugh because I was right about all of it. "You were bored? With me?"

He lets his arms flop down at his sides. "With life in general. I thought I could find some excitement. It was never about you."

"We're married. Of course it's about me."

He takes his seat again, showing every one of those forty

years on his face all of a sudden. "Yeah, but it's not like I don't want you anymore. I want to be married to you."

"You're bored," I reiterate with a sardonic laugh, feeling like I'm the only one living in reality. "And I'm your wife. So, if you're bored with your life, you're bored with me."

He scrubs his hands over his face then takes a deep breath. "I think, maybe, it was never about finding excitement with someone else." He licks his lips, jaw working like he's psyching himself up for something. "I think I was hoping that was the answer, because the real answer is I want a baby."

I shake my head ruefully. I *knew* it. I felt it in my bones.

"Why? We agreed."

"My colleagues at work are always talking about their kids, and I've been thinking a lot about my childhood and how I think I would like to give my experience to someone else."

I can understand that, but it's not what I want. It's not what I ever wanted. Not having kids was one of the things that brought us together. At a time when twentysomethings were dating to find their life partner, usually being a parent is at the front and center of their preferred qualities. Bryce and I agreeing we didn't want any made it easy to pair off together.

Still, he asks, "You think you might change your mind?"

I shake my head with an aggravated huff. "You know I had my tubes tied. You were there, in the hospital."

"Yeah, but you could get it reversed." When I start to argue, he cuts me off. "Or we could adopt."

"*Bryce.*"

He frowns, and finally hearing the truth sends the fight straight out of me. For how smart he is, I can't believe he'd make such a dumb assumption. "So, you decided you wanted a baby, and instead of having a conversation about it with me, you thought we'd have an open marriage and that would fix your wanting a child?"

"Essentially, yeah." His eyes turn glassy, and the show of emotion seeps some of the ire from my chest, replaced with a sentiment that's not quite pity but close to it.

Fuck around and find out.

"You understand that both of these choices were yours, and you're regretting both of them. You are right. This isn't about me. This is about you not knowing who the hell you are. What you want in life. And it is certainly not me."

He sniffs and clears his throat a moment before he drops his head into his hands. "God, I've ruined everything."

A part of me wants to comfort him, while another part of me—a bigger part—hates him for putting me through so much pain. I'm not sure what the outcome would have been if he'd talked to me about what he was feeling, but we'll never know. There is no going backward. He wants a child, and I have a relationship with Ian. This isn't something we can work through with counseling.

This is the end for our marriage.

Despite the anger still simmering in my belly and the resentment flowing through my veins, I'm cloaked in sorrow. I know my future is bright, but it's never easy to say goodbye. My eyes burn as they fill with tears, and I preemptively wipe at them.

My voice cracks when I tell him, "I think deep down I've known for a while that we weren't right for each other."

He swipes the back of his hand over his eyes and nose, blinking over at me. "But we were happy once. Weren't we?"

The truth is that I'm not sure, but I don't know if I have it in me to say so. This is hard enough as it is; there is no need to make it worse. I wipe my cheeks. "I guess, somewhere along the way, we stopped talking and having fun and putting each other first."

We're both quiet for a while, accepting our new reality and

drying our tears. Ten years ago, I never would have expected I'd be here having this conversation with my husband, but then again, I never expected to fall in love with Ian Stone.

All of this has taken me by surprise, and while it's hard right now, I know it will get better.

"I wouldn't take it back," Bryce says, meeting my gaze. "All my time with you, I wouldn't take any second of it back."

I nod because I wouldn't take it back either. Being with Bryce was part of the reason why I decided to move away from home permanently, and marrying him taught me a lot about myself. Breaking up with him taught me even more.

Going through this terrible time led me to the person I know is right for me. So, I can't take it back. I can't take any of my choices back, even the ones that hurt.

I bite my lip, finding words I hope comfort him. "I want you to find what makes you happy. We both deserve that."

Bryce's shoulders drop in defeat. "I really am sorry, Nicole. For everything."

"I know," I whisper. And I do. Despite the pain he's caused me, I know Bryce is struggling in his own way. We both made missteps in this marriage. But staying together out of guilt or obligation isn't the answer.

I rise slowly to my feet. "I'm going to pack up some of my things. I've already made arrangements with a lawyer for the papers, and the loan—"

"I'm sorry about that too." He shakes his head at himself. "I shouldn't have said what I did that day. I didn't mean it, especially about the loan."

I shrug. "In any case, it's taken care of."

He doesn't need to know the details about how my aunt lent me the money to pay it off, with the backing of her new husband. "What's the point of marrying someone with money if you don't use it?" she said.

Bryce merely nods, seeming small and lost, and he stands from the table. "I'm going to go out for a while, give you space to...do whatever you need."

He takes a hesitant step toward me, and I think I know what he needs. The same as I do. Closure.

I hold my arms open, signaling him to meet me halfway in an embrace. Both of us begin to cry again, holding each other tight, rocking slightly.

"I'm sorry," he whispers into my hair.

"Me too," I say, if only because I'm sorry we're both in this very difficult place in our lives.

When we break apart, I see his eyes are red-rimmed, and I offer him a smile, one I hope conveys that I'm not going to harbor any hard feelings. "I'll be out of here in an hour or so, and I'll come back to get anything else another day."

He nods a few times then combs his hair back from his face. "I guess I'll see you around, then?"

"Yeah. I'll see you around."

I watch him walk to the front door and grab his keys from the hook. He pauses before opening the door, glancing back at me one more time. I offer him a small wave, and that's it. The door shuts behind him, on the life we had together.

Alone now, I let out a long exhale. That was one of the hardest conversations I've ever had. But it's done now, and I straighten my shoulders to head to the bedroom, breathing deeply, attempting to loosen the tight feeling in my chest.

I pull my large suitcase out of the closet and neatly fold my clothes into it. Shirts, pants, dresses all get packed away as I repeatedly count to ten in my head. I grab underwear, socks, and pajamas too, all while speaking the words for the clothes out loud, keeping myself tethered to reality. Once the big suitcase is full, I zip it up and move to a smaller one for things like shoes and toiletries, stretching my arms up high, my ribs constricting around my organs, like they might crack.

It doesn't take long before I've packed up as much as I can fit, and my face hurts from crying. The empty space in the closet and dresser reminds me that even though this chapter of my life is ending, a whole new one is beginning. There will be new closets and dressers for me to fill. And I'm really looking forward to it, but right now, I need help. I need comfort.

I need Ian.

After zipping up the last suitcase, I pull my phone from my pocket to call him. It rings a few times then goes to voice mail.

"Hey, it's me. Just wanted to let you know… I'm back home in West Chester, at my house, and I'm packing up. I'm going to stop by the store and then check in to a hotel." I breathe a few times through my nose. "I really want to see you. I…" My voice breaks. "I really need you, Ian. Please call me back when you get this. Love you."

I end the call and wipe at my eyes. I know he's probably busy at the shop, but I was hoping to hear his voice. To have him reassure me that I'm doing the right thing. That everything will be okay.

I take a minute to catch my breath and clear my vision then move my bags to the back door. Each trip reinforces my choice. This is the right path, even if it's hard. Even if it hurts in this moment.

I only wish Ian could be here next to me as I take these steps. So they don't feel like giant leaps of faith.

Chapter 30
Nicole

The door to Chapter and Verse bursts open violently, and I shoot up from where I'd been slouched behind the counter. Ian towers in the doorframe, face contorted into a mask of fury, his jaw clenched and eyebrows drawn together. He looks ready to tear something apart with his bare hands.

But the moment his blazing dark eyes land on me, his entire demeanor softens. "Are you okay?"

I nod.

"Are you hurt?"

I shake my head.

"Come here, baby." He strides across the room, ignoring the curious eyes of the patrons, and opens his arms to me. I run into them, jumping up to wrap my legs around his waist, and he catches me without moving a millimeter. As if it's nothing to hold me up as I sob against his chest. The warmth and strength of his embrace immediately make me feel safe, like nothing can touch me as long as I'm with him.

"Shh, I've got you." He presses a kiss to the top of my head then says something to my assistant manager that I don't catch, too busy breathing in the scent of cloves and securing my arms around his neck. A moment later, he carries me to the back room.

He sits down on an old office chair and lets me curl up in his lap like a cat. I cling to him as he caresses my head, the steady rise and fall of his chest soothing me more than anything else ever has in my life.

He doesn't press me to talk, simply holds me close, occasionally kissing my temple and whispering soft words about how happy he is that I'm home. After several minutes, I lift my head from the comforting crook of his neck to meet his eyes. "You stormed in here like you were gonna break something."

"I got a voice mail with you crying. Of course I'm gonna smash some shit."

"Sorry."

He thumbs away my tears. "No. I don't want to hear that. You don't apologize for crying. *Ever.*" Then he pulls my hair back into a ponytail, fisting it in his hand, tilting my head back to keep my eyes on his. "What I do want to hear is why you're upset."

I swallow the lump of emotion in my throat. "I talked to Bryce."

Ian's jaw tightens. "What happened? Did he say something?"

"No. Well, yes." I set my hands on his bearded jaw. "He was upset and got a little angry, but it was civil. He didn't say anything to make me cry. I'm just... It's hard."

My nose burns, and when the tears flow again, Ian presses my face to his throat, his fingers still in my hair, rubbing my lower back with his other hand. "I know, baby. I know. You're okay."

"I was honest, and so was he, and..." I hiccup. "It was really hard to hear."

"What'd he say?" he asks, this time without a temper.

"He wants a baby."

A few minutes pass before Ian guides me to sit up straight. We've never spoken about this, and I can see the questions in his eyes. "We decided we weren't going to have kids, and I was sterilized, but he apparently changed his mind. He thought he'd be able to get over it if he had some more excitement in his life."

"What a dumbass motherfucker," he grumbles. "I hope you don't feel bad about that."

I lift my shoulder, tucking my hair behind my ears. "Yes and no. We both agreed together, but I feel bad that we wasted time. Because that's what it feels like...a waste."

"Nothing in life is a waste."

I rub at the tip of my nose, knowing I must look a mess. I pluck at my top and take a deep breath. "We were together for a long time, and it's over now."

He kisses my temple. "Endings are hard."

"That's why I called you." I dip my gaze down to his chest and scratch my fingernail on the lettering of his dark gray Stone Ink T-shirt. "Because even though this is what I want, I'm still sad."

He doesn't reply, only lays his hand on the back of mine, flattening my palm against his chest, right over his heart.

"He told me that he hasn't been with anyone else and thought we could get back together."

Ian's brows furrow, his fingers digging into my hip as if to keep me in place. I have no plans of moving. "You said you were packing up. Does that mean you moved out?"

"Yeah. I took some of my clothes and toiletries, but I left most of my things there. Books and personal items."

"Okay. Do you need help with that?"

"When the time comes, yes."

"When the time comes? The time is now. I can get the boys to move whatever you want. I'd rather get you set up as soon as possible. I need you in my bed, Nic. I—"

"Wait." I lean away from him. "Do you think I'm moving in with you?"

He frowns at me. "Yes. Are...you not?"

"No. I made a reservation to stay in a hotel for a few days until I find a place. Don't make that face."

"I will make a face. You're not staying in a hotel or anywhere else besides mine."

This stubborn man. "No, Ian."

"Don't use that voice on me."

"What voice?"

He flaps his hand at me, annoyed. "*That* one. When you think I'm being unreasonable. I'm being perfectly fucking reasonable that I'm not letting you spend money on a hotel or apartment when you can live with me for free."

I close my eyes, lowering my forehead to his shoulder. "Yes, who doesn't want to live with a growly bear?"

"Don't you want to live with me?" he murmurs against my ear, suddenly sounding very un-Ian Stone-like. All his confidence gone.

Though I've thought about living with Ian and all that would entail, I need to be on my own for a bit. I lift my chin, meeting his gaze. "Yes, of course I do, but I need to get myself sorted first."

He deliberately lets his gaze wander over me. "You seem sorted to me."

I refuse to laugh. "I can't leave the bed I shared with my husband for—"

He places two fingers over my mouth. "I can guess what

you're about to say. And I love you so much, I want to understand you, but I really don't want to hear about where you were sleeping before my bed. Call me a dick. Call me jealous. I don't care. I don't want that image in my head. Not when you're in my lap and *mine*." He rolls his forehead against mine. "You do what you need to. Doesn't mean I won't be trying to get you in my bed every night."

I finally give in to that laugh and press a chaste kiss against his mouth. "Our relationship can't be based on sex, you know."

He shifts me back an inch so he can dig into his pocket to tug out his phone. "No, our relationship can't be based on sex." He presses on the screen a few times then holds it between us, my shaky voice coming from the speaker in the voice mail I left for him.

"Why are you—"

He shushes me with his finger on my lips again, eyes on mine as the message ends with me saying, *"Please call me back when you get this. Love you."*

He grins and rewinds a few seconds to play it again. *"Love you."*

And again. *"Love you."*

He slants his head and mouth at a cocky angle. "What'd you say again?"

I refuse to answer.

Because I didn't realize I'd said those two little words. They were involuntary but true. I wouldn't have thought it was possible to come to love someone in a matter of weeks, though it's undeniable, and yes, I love him.

Instead of asking me again, Ian curls his hand around the nape of my neck and pulls me to him, his lips brushing against mine as he says three of the best words I've ever heard. "I love you."

A warm, resonant hum fills every corner of my being as this

man—all muscle and ink—lays himself bare at my feet. "I love you, Nic."

I've never heard anything sweeter, never felt anything more profound than to have someone I respect so much choose me. *Love* me.

I cup his face, the roughness of his beard a delicious contrast to the softness of his lips. "I love you too," I whisper into his mouth, the depth of emotion making it almost too difficult to speak with my heart in my throat. "I love you so much."

His answering kiss is hot and hungry, with his hands gripping my hips to pull me closer. I can feel his heart pounding in his chest, matching the frantic rhythm of my own. "I need you."

He nods and stands with me in his arms, maneuvering me in front of him to open the store's back door, only to push me next door once we step outside. Then he unlocks the back entrance of the tattoo shop and practically carries me up the flight of steps and right to his bedroom, kicking the door shut behind us.

He flings my shirt off. "I'll give you keys." Then he undoes the button on my shorts to pull them down my thighs as he kneels in front of me. "They'll unlock the front and back doors."

He stares up the length of me, gaze predatory even as he's the one on the floor in the position of submission. Even though he is the dominant one—my Dominant—he is offering himself to me. I rake my fingers through his hair, and he closes his eyes, head loose on his neck and moving according to how I want. "What if I show up early in the morning?"

"I want you to." He tilts his face to rub his beard and mouth on the inside of my forearm, along my tattoo.

"What if I make a mess of your things?"

"I want you to."

I wouldn't. I'm not a messy person, but the idea of my

toiletries next to his and my clothes in his closet is too tempting to deny. I fear I'll be here more often than I planned. Especially with how he's the one offering himself to me.

"What if I—"

"Anything," he says. "Anything you want, you can have. Anything you need, I'll give you." He kisses my thighs, hands skimming up to my backside, squeezing, showing me how he could easily overpower me, yet doesn't. He remains on his knees, worshipping me, kissing my hip bone, flicking the tip of his tongue over the small brown birthmark by my knee, murmuring sweet words about how perfect I am and how he's waited a long time for me.

And maybe that's what this is, each of our happy endings. We've both had difficult experiences, but we are what we deserve. We are what we've been waiting for.

Our blessings carved in stone.

He finally stands, his eyes practically black as they trail over the length of me. "You're so fucking beautiful," he murmurs, brushing his thumbs over my nipples through the thin fabric of my bra. I gasp, arching into his touch, and a slow, wicked curve twists his lips. He unhooks my bra, freeing my breasts to his hungry gaze. "You gonna be my good girl?"

I nod, and he raises a brow, pinching my nipple as if to test me. I moan, my knees weak, skin hot, and I reflexively wrap my hands around his wrists, though I'm not sure if it's to hold him closer or push him away.

He makes a tsking sound. "You think you're in charge here all of a sudden?" He shakes his head, forcing my hands to my sides. "I don't know where you got that idea." He bends and captures my nipple in his mouth. "Keep it up, and you'll get cuffed."

If he thought that would deter me, he thought wrong.

Or maybe it's exactly what he wants me to do. Be his brat.

I move, wrapping my hands around his neck. "Make me come."

In one smooth motion, he has me in the air so he can toss me on his bed. "You know the rules."

I do, but I'm tired of waiting, so after pushing my hair back from my face, I tow my underwear off and throw them on the floor by his feet. He takes his time, pointedly staring at them before lifting his eyes to me once again. "Oh, you're really asking for it, huh?" Without taking his gaze off me, he steps toward a small chest and digs out two sets of leather handcuffs. "Let's see how much I can make you regret that."

I bite into my lip, excitement sending goose bumps up my arms, tingles settling so low in my belly that my inner muscles flutter and contract, desperate to be filled.

"Feet on the bed," Ian orders, then nudges them wide so he can secure one pair of cuffs around my left ankle and wrist together before doing the same to my right ankle and wrist, keeping my knees bent and me bound in this position. Then he shows me the brush I bought a few weeks ago, the one he'd tortured me with, training me to orgasm on command. I immediately groan, remembering the feeling of the bristles on my most intimate flesh.

"So fucking pretty," he says, hovering over me at the edge of the bed, lazily drifting the brush over me, down my cheeks, across my collarbone, teasing my nipples, and skimming it down my stomach. "Let's review the rules and see if you can follow them. What are you supposed to do in order to come?"

"Ask."

"Mm-hmm." He swipes the brush along the length of my sex. "And when can you come?"

"When you tell me."

"Good girl," he praises, then holds his palm up to calm me. Maybe I look as feral as I feel. "And when I ask what color you're on, you need to be honest. If you're good, you say…?"

"Green," I answer with an eye roll, earning a hard tweak of my nipple that makes me squeak in protest.

"If you need me to slow down…?"

"Yellow."

"And stop…?"

"Red."

He nods and drifts the brush back and forth across my clit, revealed because of how he has me positioned, unable to close my legs. I'm completely open and at his mercy. "You should also use it on your own if you ever need to stop or slow down. We can't have fun if you're not honest with me."

When I nod, he deliberately presses the brush down harder on me, changing the friction. A test. So I tell him, "Green."

He smiles down at me in satisfaction. "Look at my little brat. She loves being so submissive." He hums, enjoying how he can torment me. "I'm going to have this pussy begging for me. Weeping for my cock."

I squirm, trying to angle my hips away from the godforsaken brush, so good yet too soft and not near enough. "Please."

"I like when you beg, but you don't really want it yet, do you? When you really want it is when you'll give me the magic words."

Back and forth.

Up and down.

Stroking.

Brushing.

Slowly taking me higher and higher.

I'm panting and writhing, my nipples so tight they're painful, my arousal dripping out of me. At least, that's what it feels like when I clench around nothing but air.

"Fuck me!"

He shakes his head. "No. Not yet."

I try to kick out of the cuffs. Of course, it doesn't do anything but make Ian heave a sigh. Then he sets the brush down on my stomach. "You want it? Go ahead. Try to use it. Get off with it if you want it so bad."

I clench my jaw. "You...are..."

"What?" He bends over me, nipping at my lips as he curls his fingers around the handle of the brush once again, his knuckles skating over my pelvic bone, so close to where I need him. "What am I?"

"The worst," I whine, but he only sucks on the skin of my throat.

"You love it. Tell me you love it." He goes back to brushing over my clit, sending me nearly to the ceiling, my overly sensitized nerves unable to take much more.

"I love it. I love you!" I arch my back. "Please, please let me come. Can I come?"

"That's my good girl." He slides his thick index finger into me. "You want to come?"

I whimper and nod, my words lost to the feel of a second finger entering me, stroking me. Spots fill my vision as I cry out.

"Not yet, Nicole. Don't come yet."

He's brushing and stroking and brushing and stroking.

"Oh, please," I rasp, wheezing for air.

"Not yet. Not until I tell you. You need to hold it."

A third finger.

I think I'm dying.

"You ready to come?"

I squeeze my eyes shut.

I'm on fire.

"Three..."

I shake my head back and forth.

"Two..."

I fist my hands.

"One..."

I grit my teeth, hanging on by a thread.

"Come, baby. Come for me."

All at once, everything releases. My mind spins, and I let go of the scream I was holding back, giving in to the orgasm. Jumping headfirst into the fire. Breaking up through the ice to fill my lungs. Rolling into the comfort of Ian's chest.

I don't know how or when it happened, but he removed the cuffs and took me in his arms, my head tucked up under his chin, his hands roaming over my back. It takes me a minute to come to, shifting around, bringing life back into my limbs.

"I touched the stars," I rasp, and he chuckles, rolling so I'm on my back, but that's when I notice the big wet spot under my calf. I lift my head. "Did I...?"

He nods. "Yeah."

I'm too relaxed to care or be embarrassed. Not like that first time after our dinner date. "I'm not sure I've ever come so hard in my life."

"Sounds like a challenge." He kisses my ear before levering over me. "What color are you on?"

I blink a few times, taking in this position he's holding over me, with his hands on either side of my head, his knees on either side of my hips. And suddenly I'm not tired anymore. "Green."

He leans back and does that super-hot thing men do and strips off his T-shirt with one hand by pulling it from behind his neck. I barely have time to admire his chest because he hops up to remove his jeans and underwear, and then there is *too* much for me to admire.

His tattoos.

The bulging of his muscles.

The way he swipes his hand over his beard, eyes roving

over me as if considering whether to lick the ice cream in the cone or bite right into it.

The breath he lets out when he fists his cock, stroking slowly up and down like he could be content to stare at me while he gets himself off.

But it's not enough for me.

I spread my legs in silent invitation, and he wastes no time settling between them, but instead of giving me his hard length, he leans to the side to slide his fingers back inside me. "Did you like that? You liked being handcuffed?"

"Yeah. I really liked it."

"We can do more," he tells me conversationally, like he isn't stretching me out, readying me for him. "But now, I'm going to fuck you hard. No more playing."

"Okay," I whisper, and he bends to press a tender kiss to my mouth.

"We've never talked about condoms, but if it's all right with you, I don't want to use them. I'm healthy."

"Me too," I manage to say with the building tension in my muscles. "Please. Just do it. Make me come again."

"You don't tell me what to do," he says and pinches my nipple in reprimand.

I gasp. I'm already so close to coming again that he only needs to flick his wrist to make me cry out. I'm taut as a bowstring and feel like I could snap in half. As I'm about to tumble over the edge, he pulls back, a wicked grin on his face. "Not yet, baby." He positions himself at my entrance. "I want to feel you come around my cock."

He pushes into me, a slow, steady slide that fills me completely. I inhale deeply, my nails digging into his shoulders as I adjust to the sensation. He stills, giving me a moment, his eyes locked on mine, this emotional connection now a complete physical one.

I only have enough time to take one more breath before he angles his hips back, pulling out to the tip then plunging back in. He takes my thighs in his hands, pushing them up and back so they bracket my ribs, and he fucks me. *Hard.*

Each thrust wrenches the air from my lungs and hits so deep, I'm not sure if it's in pleasure or pain. Either way, I beg for more.

"Yes, fuck," he grunts, but I don't hear much more than that, the sounds of our panting breaths and hard slaps of flesh filling my ears. It's all I can concentrate on. Besides the building pressure inside me.

I'm full and floating above the earth, so high I can't string together the words I need.

A question.

Something to ask him.

But it's too late.

I can't bear it anymore.

"Come, baby," he says, touching where I'm slick and swollen, sending me to outer space. "Come with me."

I do. We fall together, our mouths meeting in delirious touches, both of us unable to coordinate our lips to actually kiss each other. All we can do is breathe into each other, scrape his teeth along my chin and brush my lips over his beard.

I'm drowning in sensation, drowning in him, and it isn't until he flips us so I'm on top of him that I can take a full, deep breath. I shudder as I lie on him, a sweaty, panting mess, my heart beating so hard beneath my rib cage I'm sure he can feel it.

He presses a kiss to my forehead, his arms tightening around me. "I love you."

"I love you too," I say, tracing the lines of his tattoos with my fingertips. "And I want another tattoo."

He chuckles, the sound rumbling in his chest. "You're addicted now?"

I lift my head to meet his gaze, a slow smile spreading across my face. "You said I would be."

He nods, one hand splaying on my back, the other on my thigh. "I'll mark you whenever and wherever you want me to."

I press up a few inches so I can touch my chest, tap on the space over my heart. "Let's start here."

"Put my initials there," he says, full of honesty and certainty. "Since your name is already carved on my heart."

Chapter 31
Ian

With the newly picked-up cake in my hands, I march closer to Chapter and Verse, catching sight of Nicole through the window as she moves about the bookshop, confident and at ease. And my chest swells with pride.

After everything she's been through, here she is kicking ass. And looking so good doing it.

After another minute of watching my woman, I push open the door, announcing my arrival by saying, "There's the birthday girl."

She turns, her face lighting up with a smile that hits me like a punch to the gut. Every damn time.

"Hey, you," she says, voice soft and warm before I steal a kiss.

"How's business?"

She sighs, running a hand through her hair. "It's been a slow day. I'm a bit nervous about meeting the sales goal this month."

I can see the stress in the lines of her face, the slight furrow of her brow. I want to smooth it away, to take her worries and make them mine. But I know better. Nicole needs to stand on her own two feet, and I respect the hell out of her for it.

"You'll get there," I tell her. "You always do."

She juts her chin out to the box I set down. "What's that? Is it a cake?"

"Listen." I wrap my hand around her biceps to keep her from sneaking a peek at it. "You need to learn to have a little patience."

She locks her hands behind her back, hopping on her toes like she's Little Miss Innocent. "I'm really patient."

I cross my arms, frowning down at her. "Are you now? Last time we played the *Nicole needs to be patient game,* you lost."

"That's because you cheated."

I cluck my tongue. "I make the rules, baby. That's not cheating."

"Well," she starts, dragging the word out, rubbing her tits against me like that'll make me give in. And she's goddamn right. It will. "Maybe next time, I'll tie you up and turn the vibrator on, see how patient *you* are before you come."

The vision of Nicole, needy and naked, rubbing her sweet little pussy all over me while I'm tied up assaults my brain. And... "Okay."

Her eyes widen. "Really?"

I shrug. "I can be a good submissive."

She snorts. "We'll see how long that lasts."

When she spins around, I smack her ass. "Hurry up. We don't want to be late to your own party."

Nicole finishes and locks the door behind us as we step out onto the sidewalk, the early February air making our breaths puff up in miniature clouds in front of us. Though we only have to walk a few steps, I pull her into my side, my arm over her shoulders to keep her warm.

We closed Stone Ink early to put a little party together for Nicole's 40th birthday. Everyone is here—my siblings, all the kids, Clara, Marianne, and others from the neighborhood—the music on and their laughter filling the place up. I've been Nicole's since that day I walked into Sweet Cheeks to find her crying, but over the last few months, my family has brought her into the fold. Nicole would never and has never attempted to "mother" anyone—no matter how many times Jay teases her about it—but I know all the kids respect her as my partner, and also as someone they can talk to. June and Riley ask her for advice, and she's become close friends with Sloane and Eloise.

She is part of the Stone family. And eventually, I will make it official.

Juniper spots us first. "Happy birthday, Nicole!"

"Thank you."

The rest of the crew greets her with similar sentiments and hugs, both of us immediately enveloped in chatter, plenty of jokes and laughter to go around. I set out the small, special-ordered cake after we all eat pizza, and Nicole gasps at the open book with wild flowers sprouting from in between the pages. "It's so gorgeous, I don't want to eat it."

Jay raises his fork in the air. "But I will."

I knock him upside the head.

June lights the candles, and we all sing to Nicole before she blows them out, offering me a mischievous smile. And I will, without a doubt, make each of her wishes come true. No matter if it's for that cat she's been eyeing on the adoption website or a trip somewhere. I told her one of these days I'll take her to an all-inclusive vacation resort where we can float in a lazy river all day, drinking margaritas.

While we eat the cake, she opens gifts, including packs of her favorite pens—because my girl does indeed have favorite pens—a gift certificate to a spa, and matching T-shirts for her and me to wear from Jaybird. They say *Homie Lover Friend*. I actually like them, because I like anything that claims her as mine.

When it's my turn, I hand her the flat rectangular box. "Ian," she chides, guessing correctly that it's jewelry. "You didn't need to get me anything."

I ignore that and point to the gift, which she opens to reveal a delicate gold necklace with a diamond. One that is suitable enough until she's ready for me to put one on her finger.

"It's beautiful." She removes it from the box to hold it out to me, then lifts her hair up so I can fasten it around her neck, placing a kiss there.

"Remember what I said? Might look pretty and delicate, but it's really strong."

She loops her arms around my neck, kissing me with too much enthusiasm for the kids because they all start gagging and booing and throwing things at us.

"Get a room!"

"You heard what they said." I guide Nicole to stand up, slipping my hand to her lower back. "Let's get a room."

"I'm going to Riley's tonight," June calls. "I don't want to hear whatever it is you're gonna do."

Nicole covers her furiously blushing cheeks, and I toss a wave over my shoulder. "All you clean up, huh? I have things to take care of."

Another round of gagging and booing and throwing things ensues, and I usher Nicole upstairs, making sure to lock the apartment door behind us. She officially moved in with me on the first of the new year, after spending a few months on her own. While she did worry a little bit about what others might think of her moving in with me so quickly, I was more nervous about making sure she was confident in her decision. I hated every night she wasn't with me, but thankfully, I didn't have to wait too long.

Now, I turn on the table lamp in the living room, casting everything in a warm light as I shoo Mr. Darcy away, whispering to him that his mother and I have important things to discuss, which makes Nicole giggle. I tell her to have a seat while I open a bottle of champagne and carry it back out to her, along with two glasses.

She sips, lips tipped up flirtatiously. "Is this when I get my real present?"

I lounge on the couch next to her, pulling her into my lap, grabbing a handful of her ass. "You mean when I finally tattoo my name here?"

She laughs, so sweet. "Yeah."

"Tomorrow," I say, capturing her lips in a slow, deep kiss. She melts into me, her body fitting perfectly against mine, her tongue tasting like sugar and champagne.

The day she signed the divorce papers, I inked a matching piece to the one I have on my ribs. *Write your troubles in the sand and carve your blessings in stone.* Because tattoos are addictive, she said she wanted another one for her birthday, joking that it would be my name. But I am nothing if not a man who will give her anything she wants. Including my name on her skin.

Truly, nothing would make me happier.

Until then, I'll mark her in another way, and I bend to suck on her throat. She whines, pushing at me, but I don't let up until there's a red bruise on her skin. I down the rest of my champagne as I drift my fingers over the mark and along her throat, toying with her new necklace.

"One day, I'll give you a diamond for your finger. The one from my mother," I inform her, the first time I've spoken my desire to marry her out loud. Knowing how I can overwhelm her, I'm always careful to make sure she is in charge of her own decisions, but I need her to know what I want.

And it terrifies me that she might not want the same thing.

She finishes her champagne then takes my glass to set both of them on the coffee table before placing her hands on either side of my face. "One day, when you give me a diamond for my finger, I'll say yes."

I let loose a breath and press my forehead to hers. "I love you."

"I love you too." She smiles into a kiss, and I'm the luckiest bastard in the world.

Her hands grip my shirt, fingers fisting in the fabric as she kisses me back with a desperation that matches my own. I leave an openmouthed kiss on her neck, over her racing pulse, as she grinds herself down on me, her breath coming in quick pants as we lose ourselves in each other, breaking away in short bursts to remove clothes. But each time, we come back together, hands in hair and lips on necks, rocking against each other, pushing each other's need higher and higher.

Nic and I play a lot, but sometimes it's nice to do this. Be with each other without any games or goals or toys. Only her and me and the love between us.

With us both naked, I keep her on top of me so I can enjoy the way she moves, adore every inch of her perfect body, all smooth and soft and arching against me, begging to be touched. I cup her breasts, leaning down to take turns, sucking on each of her nipples until she's yanking at my hair and rubbing her soaking wet pussy against me.

"Come here." I help her raise up on her knees, and I hold my cock up, dragging it through her wetness once, twice before notching it at her opening. "Come take it."

She hisses as she presses down, accepting me to the hilt.

"That's my girl." I lean back and grip her hips, savoring

every moment of this. Every gasping pant and shudder. Every moan and imprint her fingernails leave in my skin. "That's it. So fucking good."

With her eyes closed, she angles herself so each circle of her hips rubs her clit against me. Sure, I love being in charge, but I love seeing my girl *taking*.

"You're so beautiful," I tell her. "So brave. So perfect."

My words spur her on, and she flutters her eyes open to meet my unblinking gaze. I don't want to miss a second of this, especially when she's so close to coming, speeding up and breathing hard.

She's hot and tight like a vise around my shaft, and it's always like this when we have vanilla sex. I'm always so close to popping off like some teenager. When there is nothing else to focus on besides how good she feels and how good it is between us, I have a hard time holding back.

But I have my good girl trained well.

She sets her forehead against mine, shivers racking her body. "Can I come?"

"Yeah. Come, baby. Come for me."

She does, convulsing around me, soaking me even more. I press my thumb against her clit, riding her into another immediate orgasm as I thrust up into her a few times until I release with my own orgasm.

She drops her head to my shoulder, and I hold her close to me, kissing her neck, her head, her hair, any part of her I can reach, until she raises up once more, blinking sleepily. "I love you."

"Carved on my heart," I respond, pressing her palm over where her name is tattooed on my chest. I always hated the idea of inking a spouse's name, knowing how often relationships can and do fall apart, but there was never a second thought where Nicole was concerned. I'd been hers from that day in Sweet

Cheeks. Hell, probably even before that—I simply never realized it.

There was no hesitation to make it permanent on my part.

"I do want your name," she says, tapping on the upper part of her left breast. "Right here."

No hesitation on her part either. "Yeah?"

She nods. "Yes, sir."

"That's what we'll put on your ass."

She rolls her head back to her shoulders, laughing, and I take advantage of her position to lick a line up to the exact place she'd just pointed to as the spot I'll tattoo her. "Tomorrow."

She meets my gaze, agreeing. "Tomorrow."

"Tonight, we celebrate."

We both love keeping my cock in her after we finish, and tonight is no different, so she stays as still as possible and reaches back for the glasses, holding them out so I can refill them.

I raise my glass to hers. "To you."

She clinks her glass to mine. "To us."

We drink down the bubbly, and then we pick up right where we left off.

With laughter and love, passion and desire.

And as we lie there, finally spent and sated, I know this is only the beginning of the book we're writing. We have so many chapters left in our happy ending.

Epilogue

Ian

Ian, Taryn, Griffin, Roman text thread:

ROMAN

Hey.

ROMAN

Can you meet me at our house tomorrow?

TARYN

I'm sorry. What??

TARYN

Who are you addressing this to?

ROMAN

All of you.

Brother, where've you been? No one's heard from you in months.

ROMAN

I know. I'm sorry. I was trying to get my shit together.

Epilogue

ROMAN

I'm sorry.

It's okay.

GRIFFIN

It's really not. You haven't talked to anyone in a year, and suddenly, you want us to come to you? No.

TARYN

I'm still confused about all of this.

TARYN

Whose house?

ROMAN

Our house. Our old house.

Mom's house?

ROMAN

Yes.

GRIFFIN

What the fuck is going on?

ROMAN

I need to see you. I need to talk to you.

ROMAN

In person.

* * *

Ian, Griffin, Taryn text thread:

GRIFFIN

What the fuck is going on?

TARYN

I have no idea.

Epilogue

> He's clearly trying to make amends.

TARYN

By meeting at our old house?

TARYN

To do what?

> We'll find out when we get there.

GRIFFIN

What the actual fuck?

* * *

Ian, Taryn, Griffin, Roman text thread:

> Rome, we'll be there.

> What time?

ROMAN

Ten?

> Okay.

* * *

Ian, Griffin, Taryn text thread:

GRIFFIN

What the actual fuck?

> We're not going to turn our backs on him.

> He needs to see us. So we're going to see him.

Epilogue

GRIFFIN

I don't like it. I don't have a good feeling about it.

Suddenly you have feelings about shit?

GRIFFIN

Shut the fuck up. I'm already pissed about all this.

You better be there tomorrow.

GRIFFIN

Of course I'm gonna be there.

GRIFFIN

Finally get to tell that little shit off in person.

Go get Andi to suck your dick and calm down. We're going to see our little brother for the first time in years. Don't pretend like you don't want to.

GRIFFIN

You're too calm about this. Has Nicole sucked your brain out of your dick?

Actually, yeah. I've got nothing left in me after this morning.

GRIFFIN

Dirty old man.

Show up tomorrow.

GRIFFIN

I will.

You too, Tar.

TARYN

Oh, now you're going to include me in the conversation after all the dick-sucking talk is over? Great. Thanks.

Epilogue

Hey, you've got a bigger dick than both of us.
Hope Dante likes it.

TARYN

He does. That man would suck anything I
asked.

GRIFFIN

Fucking stop. I can't stand either one of you.

Love you too.

* * *

Almost a year from when I texted Roman a picture of it, Griffin, Taryn, and I stand outside of our old house. Aside from the big SUV parked in the drive and the missing For Sale sign, it looks exactly the same—in desperate need of some love.

"What are we supposed to do?" Taryn asks, looking around at the quiet neighborhood. "Wait for him to show up?"

Griffin checks his watch. "It's 10:01. Where is he?"

Of course he's annoyed that it's one minute after ten o'clock and Roman hasn't appeared. Although as I stare at the front door of the house, something tells me he's already here. I ignore my brother and sister squabbling behind me to make my way up the walk and ring the doorbell.

"What are you doing?" Griffin asks at the same time Taryn says, "I'm texting him."

A moment later, the door swings open, revealing my baby brother. My heart stops, breath catches. Vaguely, I note Griffin and Taryn quieting in stunned silence.

Roman doesn't move at first, brow pinched, eyes squinted. He's nervous. My little brother, whom I haven't seen in years, is nervous I'll be mad. So, I do the only logical thing and throw myself at him, wrapping my arms around him. Once his

289

surprise wears off, he exhales harshly and grips me back, his hands digging into my spine like he doesn't want to let go.

But I feel Griffin and Taryn behind me, their trepidation palpable. When Roman and I finally let go of each other, he eyes our brother and sister, and I know their welcome will probably be a lot different.

Although before anyone can greet each other, a small head pops up beside Roman with bouncing chestnut curls and big brown eyes, staring up at us.

My brain doesn't compute. Apparently neither do Griffin's or Taryn's until Roman clears his throat. "This...is my daughter."

"What the fuck?" Griffin, Taryn, and I say at the same time.

The little girl puts on a cute little pout, her fist on her hip. "Yeah, Daddy. What the fuck?"

* * *

Bonus Epilogue

"You need to put that away," Nicole says, batting at my hand, and I can't help the smile that pulls at my lips. Always such a good girl, my wife.

Even though she's long stopped giving a fuck about what people thought about her and has become mistress of herself, she is still a rule follower. God forbid the plane takes off, and I'm on my cell phone.

"Call the air marshal," I deadpan, tilting the screen so she can see the latest picture of our grandchild.

Nicole likes to joke about me being a hot grandpa, but she's horrified by the idea of her being called Granny or any other sort of name for grandmother. Except that's what she is. A hot as fuck grandmother. It doesn't matter that she's not biologically related to my kids or the newest addition to the Stone family. She put together the baby shower, helped to decorate the nurs-ery, and she was there during the labor and birth. She is as obsessed with the baby as I am.

Just don't call her Grammy, or Nana, or Meemaw.

I voted for Kitty. Thought it had a good ring to it—in and out of the bedroom—but she promptly vetoed it and eventually decided on Coco.

Nicole takes my phone from my hands to read the text message **Have fun, Pops and Coco!** and the accompanying photo of baby Lenox with a gummy smile and hands out in a wave.

"Awe," Nic coos. "Look at that face." She makes some more schmoopy noises, admiring the little guy before the flight attendant tells her she has to put her phone away. Then she promptly tosses it in my lap, blushing red as a tomato.

Laughing, I put the phone away then take her hand in mine. She clucks her tongue at me, annoyed I got her in trouble, but I only lean over to kiss her neck. "Few more hours to paradise."

She sighs and rests her head back against her seat. Since this is our anniversary trip, and we almost never travel anywhere by plane, I sprung for first class tickets. I don't want to think about how cramped I'd be in the those other tiny seats. But up in the front, we can relax, and once we're in the air, we both order drinks, sharing earbuds to watch the same movie on the screen because we're disgusting like that.

Even after being together for a decade, I still can't get enough of her. I still want to know everything she's doing, hear every thought in her head, and it's a chore to do anything else that takes me away from her. I married Nicole not long after I proposed, in a small ceremony at the bookstore. Jay served as our officiant, while Jas and June were our best man and maid of honor, respectively. About a dozen or so people attended, our closest friends—our family, and it was exactly what we wanted.

Unfortunately managing two small businesses doesn't leave a lot of vacation time for us, so an entire week on the beach is practically unheard of. And I don't plan on waisting a moment of it.

I pluck Nicole's ear bud out and tell her, "Go to the bathroom and take your underwear off. I want it in my hand when you come back."

She tilts her head, eyes drifting between my own, and she bites into her bottom lip, still fighting her naturally shy instincts. But I see the moment she makes her decision, and I nod. "Good girl."

I stand to let her up into the aisle and smooth my hand over her hip, patting her ass in a little "Get going" gesture. When she tosses me a stark eyebrow over her shoulder, I give her my stern glower in return, and her cheeks turn my favorite pink.

I don't bother sitting back down and instead take the few minutes to stretch my limbs and check the time. We still have a little over an hour to go until we land in Jamaica, headed for an all-inclusive resort where my wife can drink margaritas and float in a lazy river all day. Exactly as I promised her.

I've barely formed the picture of her naked and wet in my mind when she makes her way back to me, her left hand fisted and held against her stomach. She waits until we're both seated again to give her panties to me. I rub the soft material a few times before stuffing them in my pocket and angling myself toward her. Not that anyone can see or hear what we're about to do, every passenger busy with some screen or book, but as much as I tease Nicole, being arrested for public indecency on a plane would be a terrible way to start this vacation.

"You ready to play?" I ask, and she darts her eyes around, nervous, so I place my hand on her thigh, squeezing lightly. "I'm not going to touch you."

"You're not?" She almost sounds sad about it, and that has me swallowing a groan.

"As soon as we're in our room, I won't be letting you out for a good long time. I'll feed you your dinner while you're handcuffed."

Her blush spreads to her throat, and I kiss her there, over her pounding pulse. Then I place my hand on her collarbone, thumb on one side of her throat, fingers on the other, and gently press her back to her seat. "Close your eyes."

She follows my direction after one more sweep of her gaze around the plane. Hoping to settle her, I lift her hand and kiss her palm, toy with the ring I inherited from my mother and gave to Nicole when I got down on one knee, before nuzzling her inner forearm tattoo. She's up to five now.

It's an honor to be the only person she's ever allowed to tattoo her, to be the one she trusts implicitly. I will work the rest of my life to show her what a treasure her love is.

"I want you to picture us on the beach," I tell her, my lips against her ear, my fingers drifting up and down her arm. "Imagine the sun setting behind us, the heat making your skin dewey, salt from the water in your hair and on your lips."

She releases a contented sound that makes my dick semi-hard.

"You're wearing that hot little black bathing suit that ties behind your neck and makes you look like a pin-up girl."

She flutters her eyes open. "I bought a new one. In red."

"I know. You're terrible at hiding things, wife." I cover her eyes with my palm so she closes them once again. "Now, you need to be quiet or we can't keep playing. Are you gonna be quiet?"

When she nods, I continue. "I like that you bought it for me, that you think about making me happy. I like when you try to please me."

Her mouth tips up, lips curving over her teeth like she doesn't want to give into how much she enjoys my praise. Deep down, Nicole has been and will always be a people pleaser. That won't change, but now she's more selective about who she choses to please.

And fuck if I don't love being her number one.

I brush my knuckles over her throat and down to her breast, purposely avoiding her nipple and skimming the side. "I can't wait to see what you look like with that bow tied between your perfect tits."

She huffs, and I bring her hand up to nip at the tip of her index finger, a reprimand. She shifts, her hips rocking ever-so-slightly, but then I suck on her finger, and she hisses, teeth buried into her bottom lip.

"You feel the sun?" I ask, pulling her back into the game. "You feel hot how it is?"

She nods.

"You're hot, too, hm? Wet all over, but not from the water. Because I told my good girl not to touch herself, and she's desperate."

She nods, squirming more.

We fooled around last night, but I didn't let her come, and when my brat went to the bathroom, I made sure to follow her so she didn't touch herself when she wasn't supposed to.

That earned me an eye roll and annoyed mumbling about how it wasn't fair, which earned *her* ten minutes on her knees as she sucked me off.

But I told her I'd make it up to her.

"I'm behind you," I go on and set my palm on her leg, squeezing her thigh, "my hands roaming all over you, your neck, your chest, and I twist your nipples, make them hard as glass and so sensitive. You feel it? Feel how they connect to the rush in your pussy?"

Her answer is a quiet sigh.

"And my girl is so needy, searching, desperate for me to

touch her lower." I drag my fingernails over her leggings, pulling that the materials, eventually plucking it between my fingers, keeping her nerve-endings on edge. I know it's working from how she's breathing through parted lips, licking them over and over. Her right hand is clenched around the armrest. She ready.

"I trace the edge of the bikini bottoms, getting closer and closer to wear you need it, until you're writhing and begging me. I love when you beg, you know that? Of course you do. You're all attitude until you can't handle it anymore, and then you'll do anything for an orgasm, won't you?"

With her eyes still closed, she inclines her head toward me, searching for my lips, but I don't give them to her. Instead, I nip at her jaw. "I pull the strings at your hips, and the fabric falls away so I can slip my fingers inside you." I suck in a purposeful breath and scrape my beard on her throat before licking the shell of her ear. "Jesus, you're wet."

She whimpers.

"You're so ready for me, aren't you? Slippery and practically vibrating, one touch to your clit, and you cry out for me. Say it."

"Ian," she says before I capture her lips, licking into her mouth like I want to her pussy. She rubs her thighs together, trapping my hand between them, a futile attempt to quell the ache I've ignited within her. I pull a hair's breadth away from her, and she pouts. "Please, Ian."

"Not yet, baby. Not yet."

She groans, chin dropping, so I remove my hand from between her thighs and take her face between my palms, keeping her still, my mouth back at her ear. "I slide one finger inside you, then another, stretching you, preparing you for the moment when I'll replace my fingers with my cock."

Her hips subtly rock in time with the rhythm of my words.

"You're moaning now, not caring who hears, who sees. All

that matters is the feeling of my fingers inside you, the promise of my cock filling you up."

She's breathing hard, turned fully into me, hands around my wrists, face screwed up tight. I don't speak for a while, letting her live in this space, teetering on the edge, testing her.

It took over a year for me to train her to come on command with only my words, and still sometimes she doesn't make it, too impatient. But I know she can do it now. She will do it.

With only my words.

"Open your eyes, Nicole."

Her eyelids flutter open, her pupils huge, and I can see the wildness there, the need for release.

"Come, baby. Come for me."

And just like that, she does, her orgasm washing over her silently, her body trembling with the force of it. I hold her, talking her through it, telling her what a good girl she is, kissing her cheek and temple and mouth.

"You did so good."

She drops her forehead to my shoulder, breathing deeply a few times, and I rub her back until she fully relaxes down from the high. She eventually tips her head up, lazy satisfaction curling her lips. "I love you."

I hum my agreement and stroke her cheek. "Love you too, Mrs. Stone."

Her smile amplifies a few megawatts as she straightens. "I don't think I'll ever get tired of hearing that." She places her hand on my chest, over where her name is inked. "I've found my home with you. I found my family."

I never thought my heart could feel like this, somehow so full and yet so light, and I don't have the words to tell her that she is everything. She is my wife, my best friend, my family, my sub, my pulse. So, I kiss her.

I tell her without words. I promise with my lips and tongue

to love her until my dying breath. And then I wrap my arm around her shoulders and hold her against my side as the pilot announces we will soon be making our descent.

One more chapter to write in our book.

Another blessing carved in stone.

What's next?

To stay up to date with all things Sophie Andrews, use the QR code on the next page to stay in touch!

Acknowledgments

This book was originally meant to be a novella until Zoe York got her hands on it and said, nope, you need to make this a full length novel because the more Ian Stone there is in the world, the better. And she was right. As always.

Thank you to Lily Bear for the amazing covers. As always, Libby and Lisa have turned my brain vomit into a pretty decent novel, which is always a miracle.

Biggest thank you to all of my readers. Thank you for your DMs and for your early reviews and for making all of this worth it. Without you, I'd literally just being writing these books and reading them out loud to myself like I used to do when I was a kid. And while that's fun, it's so much more fun to know people love these silly little books. I am forever grateful for you.

If you're seriously interested in learning more about the BDSM lifestyle, I'd recommend starting with Chief at: https://kinkyevents.co.uk/about/

And if you'd like more information about me, you can find it at https://sophieandrewsauthor.com/

About the Author

Sophie Andrews is a contemporary romance author who writes steamy books that will leave you smiling. As a millennial, she's obsessed with boybands, late 90s rom-coms, and will always be team Pacey. When she's not writing, she's most likely trying to wrangle her children or drinking red wine. Or both at the same time.

Also by Sophie Andrews

Stone Family

Under One Roof

Just This Once

Right Next Door

For The Weekend

Single Dads' Club

The Rehearsal Fling

The Nanny Tenure

The Dating Pact

The Bartender's Baby

Tangled Series

Tangled Up

Tangled Want

Tangled Hearts

Tangled Beginning

Tangled Expectations

Tangled Chances

Tangled Ambition

Stand-Alones

How to Ruin a Wedding

Love at a Funeral and Other Awkward Conversations